I0600589

# Desire & Protection

*A Slow-Burn Psychological*
*Suspense Novel*

## Heather Marsala

www.HeatherMarsala.com

*Desire & Protection*

ISBN 979-8-9991656-0-2
Cover design by Melisa Mulyono
Editor: Christopher Cervelloni, Blue Square Writers Studio


For permissions or inquiries:
www.HeatherMarsala.com

# Content & Author Note

This book contains depictions of domestic violence involving a firearm, substance use, and trauma. Reader discretion is advised.

Though this story explores violence and substance use, my intent is never to glorify harm but to honor the resilience of those who have been affected by it. If you are struggling, please know you are not alone. Resources are available at:

Domestic violence support:
*www.thehotline.org*

Mental health and substance use support:
*www.findtreament.gov*

Listen as you read

Some of these songs have been part of the story since 2016
when I began writing *Desire & Protection.*

Crafted over the years and dear to my heart, they carry
the emotional weight of the novel.

# Dedication

*For those who have lived in pieces*
*and found their way back*

# CHAPTER 1

## Deceptively the Beginning

Bedsheets creased in the boy's hands, clenched into a tight, knotted ball. The fabric trembled between his fingers as his eyes adjusted to the dark. The house shuddered as his father's voice thundered through the walls and clashed against his mother's from downstairs.

"That little shit!" Victor's shout struck the walls harder this time. "He's been hiding my gun in his vent!"

A vent cover rested on its side by the closet. *What?*

The sheets fell from the bed as he dove forward, his knees burning against the carpet. *No, no, no.* He reached into the slot and pulled out the black trash bag, weightless in his hands.

*He has it.*

Antique china rattled in the cabinet as Loretta moved through the living room in a frenzy. "Because he's afraid of you," she said. "All the struggles you've caused!"

"He won't struggle long. Wait till I put one straight through his head!"

The boy's pupils flared, eclipsing the doorway.

He stumbled toward the window. His sweaty palms slipped against the glass as he pushed at it. Splinters punctured his fingers as he grabbed the edge of the wooden window frame and pried it open. Midnight air broke across his face. If there was ever a time to escape, it was now.

The frame creaked under his weight.

"Victor, no!"

The frame's creak froze as the crash of shattering dishes swallowed his mother's cry.

*He's gonna hurt her again.*

The boy yanked himself back inside.

Thuds rattled through his body as he sprinted down into the living room. Shards from the toppled china cabinet littered the floor, and smoke curled above the smoldering cigarettes in the ashtray.

Loretta's hands shook as she blocked Victor's fists.

"Dad!" The boy lunged in front of his father. "Please stop!"

Victor sneered, anger weaving through the dry wrinkles on his face. *"You!"* The veins at his temple strained, outrage coursing through each one. "Get out of my way, Roman!"

Roman flinched, his voice cracking. "Please don't do this!"

"Get your ass back upstairs!" Victor smacked Roman's hands aside and raised the gun.

Roman didn't stand a chance. He fought with all his might to gain control of it—a blow to his jaw knocked him to the floor.

Loretta snatched Victor's arm, his rough skin trapped beneath her nails. "Keep your hands off him!"

The floor tipped beneath Roman as he touched the fresh cut on his lip, fingertips slick with warm blood.

Victor tore his arm free of Loretta, the gun juddering in his grip. "That's enough oughta you!"

"Please stop!" Roman reached out to balance himself. "I promise I won't take your gun again!"

Glass cracked under Victor's boots as he stomped toward him. "You better believe you won't. Now get out of my way!"

Roman's knees knocked against each other. "Mom, please! Stay behind me!"

"Move your worthless ass out of my way!"

Her scream rattled the cabinets. "No one's as worthless as you!"

Victor's gun clicked against its own tension, the barrel angling sharper.

"Stop—I'll do anything!" Roman blocked her with both arms as she bounced on her toes. "I can fix this!"

Her lips pressed into a strained line. "There's no fixing what your father's done!"

Roman slipped on a shard of china, slicing into his heel as he cried out and caught himself. "Please don't do this!"

Victor closed the gap between him and Roman. "Get out of my way!"

"Please!" Roman drew back, waving his palms. "I'll be better! We can be a normal family! I can—"

"Family?" Victor's sadistic laugh sent a chill down Roman's spine. "This has never been a family."

She rounded on Victor and jabbed her finger into his chest. "I should have left you a long time ago!" Her rancor twisted into something satisfied, as if she were savoring the moment. "I *never* loved you."

Victor's hand crashed into her temple. "If you feel like getting a bullet, just say so!"

"Please stop!" Roman's tears warped their faces. "Both of you! Please!"

She scowled at Victor through strands of tangled hair fallen across her face. "You should just shoot yourself since you want to pull the trigger so bad!"

"No!" Roman's lip ripped further open, his cries falling on deaf ears. "I'm begging you, please!"

Victor and Loretta shouted back and forth like the bitter enemies they'd become, their hatred for each other suffocating the room. Roman told himself everything would be okay, that they fought like this all the time. That they'd

3

forgive each other, like they always had. He knew his father had anger issues, but he would never—

The shouting ceased as a deafening crack split the room. The gun exploded.

Roman slowly lowered his arms as one of his parents collapsed.

* * *

Roman gasped as he sprang forward, damp heat clinging to his skin. His heart hammered against his ribs as he scanned the room for anything he recognized.

There wasn't much to recognize, though. Just a borrowed apartment in New York, part of his undercover assignment. The room was still, but his pulse hadn't caught up. The dream had felt familiar. Too familiar… something old.

As the alarm nagged in the background, he rubbed at the sore indentations left by the ankle bands of his gray sweatpants, wondering how many more years he'd have to survive what had already happened.

He opened the dresser drawer and tugged on a T-shirt, the fabric brushing the jagged scar above his pelvis, a mark that had become part of him a year ago. That was the start of it. The reason he left Chicago. The reason he was there. Or so he thought.

He left the run-down apartment as strangers scurried along the withered sidewalks. The sun ached to wake, casting a dim glow across the path to the promenade.

He, too, ached, determined to outrun the wreckage of his childhood.

The path ahead taunted. He took off, the soles of his sneakers scraping across the pebble-strewn pavement. His father's angry voice clawed at his mind, but with each stride and push forward, he grew faster and stronger, propelling himself toward the distant bushes. Wind swept fallen leaves ahead of him, crackling beneath his feet. The chill whipped past his ears as frigid air fought to tighten his expanding lungs, coiling around his arms. Salt sharpened the air. He matched the waves, racing them to their destination.

His burner vibrated in his pocket as he neared the bushes. He slowed and pulled it out. Two missed calls. He recognized the number, but suspicion stirred.

4

Only his handler and a few of the criminals he was infiltrating had this line. A text popped up from the same number. It was his former police chief. "Meet me at your old district tomorrow at noon. Don't be late."

* * *

The next day in Chicago, a disorderly line of hungry people wrapped around the crumbling corners of the homeless shelter, waiting their turn to check in. Among them was Aniella, a young woman who, though curious, carried a shyness she'd never admit to. Mothers rocked their crying babies, and others asked how long they'd have to wait to use the restroom.

Aniella handed out pizza slices from a nearby shop. As she worked her way up the line, she came to a woman sitting near the stoop of the entrance. Aniella offered her a slice on a paper plate.

"Chicken wang." The woman shooed Aniella away from her weathered lawn chair. "I want chicken wang. Everybody gets me pizza."

Aniella gently set the paper plate and pizza box by her chair.

Three brass bells jingled from their string when the door opened, disinfectant and coffee cutting through a stale-laundry tang that hung in the overcrowded space. A man folded a blanket into sharp corners on his cot, and a volunteer taped tomorrow's job board flyers to the wall.

Aniella approached the community kitchen, where another volunteer wiped ranch from their fingers on a stained apron.

"Can I get you anything?"

"Yes, good morning!" Aniella sat on a stool, folding her hands ever so neatly in her lap. "May I please have a cup of hot chocolate with whipped cream on top, please?"

The volunteer took in her polished demeanor as they poured the hot chocolate. "We don't have whipped cream."

A child's shoes pattered across the dull tile as the child ran up to the counter. "How much is a glass of juice?"

"Depends, Eli," the volunteer said. "We go over this every time. How much are you donating?"

Eli held out his hand, palm full of linty change. "I have seventy-five cents!"

The volunteer poured the juice. "Then it'll be seventy-five cents."

Aniella swiveled on the stool toward Eli. "Do you stay here?"

Eli stuck out his tongue, as if the effort helped him reach far enough to drop the coins on the counter. "My mom works here." He gulped his juice and wiped his mouth on his sleeve. "I was five years old, but now I'm six because my birthday was last week."

"Oh, happy belated birthday!" Aniella tucked a few stray locks behind her ear and returned her hands to her lap. "Did you get to do anything fun?"

"Well, I had to be here cause my mom works here, and she was working. I'm adopted, but she's really nice." Eli set his empty cup on the counter. "We got ice cream after, and I got to pick out a toy because my best friend was supposed to come visit me and bring one, but he never came."

"Oh, I'm so sorry to hear that. I'm sure your friend had a good reason they couldn't make it."

Eli nibbled his nail. "Well, I've never seen you here before, and I'm here almost every day."

She smiled at his curiosity, as it reminded her of her own longing for answers and connection. "That's because I just moved here." She unzipped her purse, withdrew a twenty-dollar bill, and handed it to him. "Happy birthday."

"That's a lot for juice!"

"It's not for juice," she said, laughing. "Get yourself something special for your birthday, okay?"

"Sure!" Eli wrapped his fingers tightly around the bill. "I'm gonna show my mom!" He took off running, shoes pattering across the tile once more.

"Aniella Fasquelle?" A woman across the room held open a door leading to a small, humble office.

Aniella turned, her rich brown hair swinging gracefully. "Yes, that's me!"

The woman leaned back as if to get a clearer view. Her gaze dropped to Aniella's heels, then climbed, pausing at her unruffled posture and the rare, radiant energy of self-possession. By the time they finally faced each other, a tight, polite smile had formed, but that first beat had already given her away. A flicker of startled offense Aniella recognized all too well. The kind that issued a challenge without a word. The uneasy recognition of another's light.

"You found your way to the community kitchen," the woman said, her smile loosening just enough to pass for cordial.

Aniella knew why people stared. Cheerful warmth came naturally. Even then, she didn't bristle. She simply chose not to respond. Aniella had no desire to live in a world of silent comparisons or unspoken resentment. She believed in kindness, in compassion, in rising above, and she lived as if the world she wanted already existed. It wasn't that she was naive, as people often assumed. She saw it, and she still chose the light.

Aniella smiled. "I did, yes. It's such an upgrade from the usual soup kitchens at most shelters."

"Local restaurants donate food on certain weekends." The woman motioned toward the room. "Come on in. I'll interview you in here."

* * *

At a red light, Roman let the headrest take his weight, grateful to have finally made it through the twelve-hour drive from New York to Chicago. He'd called his handler several times, but no one picked up.

He rested his wrist on the wheel, waiting as a crowd crossed the busy street. An elderly woman eased off the curb, her white curls and patterned skirt flowing in the opposite direction. Her walker's front wheel jammed in the concrete rubble. She tugged at it, but the walker slipped from her veined hands and clattered onto the asphalt. She patted down her hair, uncertain what to do.

Roman flipped on his hazards and leaped out. "Hey there." He picked up the walker and placed it in her hands.

Her focus climbed the zipper of his open bomber jacket until it met his bold, pensive face. "Well, aren't you a welcomed sight?" She took the walker, her legs wobbling forward.

Roman spotted another hole ahead. "Ma'am, steer your walker right."

She kept trucking.

He jumped in front of her. "Turn your—"

The walker rolled over his shoe.

She stopped, then peered down. "Don't tell me that was you."

"Let's keep going," he said, shaking it out.

"Kindness is rare these days," she said, oblivious to horns blaring and cars zigzagging around them.

He cupped her elbow, gentle and steady. "Let's get you off the street."

Roman ducked back into his car, killed the hazards, and revved the engine, hungry to make up for lost time.

Traffic thinned as he pushed toward the far side of the city. A radar sign flashed his speed. He ignored it. *Perks of being a cop,* he supposed. The road ahead cleared until a car nosed into his lane, its blinker ticking. He tightened his grip on the wheel as the car ahead inched left. The light stayed green. *Don't be late.* The demand from his old police chief echoed.

A Chevy nosed up behind him, horn blaring. Roman glimpsed the man's face in the rearview, the man shouting things he didn't need to hear to get the point. He tapped the wheel, already fixed on the lane in front of him. There was no time for stupid.

When the car ahead finally crept through its turn, Roman hit the gas. But the yellow light turned red, and he slammed on the brakes, stopping just before the white line. The driver behind swerved into the opposite lane and flew past, middle finger waving.

Brakes screeched—*slam.*

Metal folded like tinfoil. Glass burst like confetti. Tires snapped free, flying like graduation caps.

Roman braced himself, forearms shielding his face. A van barreled through the intersection, launching the Chevy fifty feet, until it bent around a telephone pole.

Moments lingered, with no movement from either driver.

Roman hadn't realized he was holding his breath until he released it. He unbuckled and pushed the door open, bracing for what he'd see.

He stared at the mangled metal. Stared at what was left of the Chevy. Or, more accurately, what was left of the man inside. The guy who couldn't wait. The guy who couldn't slow down. He stared a second longer at the crumpled metal. At something that used to be a man.

As paramedics rushed in, Roman headed back to his car. He checked the time. *Noon is blown.*

"Hang on a sec." An officer hitched up his duty belt as he crossed the street. "Hell of a sight."

Roman angled away from the wreck. "Yeah. Horror show."

"What happened?"

"Guy ran the red."

The officer read Roman's New York plates. "That's a long way from here. Where're you headed?"

*Someone likes to pry.* Roman paused just long enough to stay believable. "Nowhere in particular."

\* \* \*

The door chimed as Roman entered the shelter. The crowd chattered near the community kitchen as he took stock of the space.

*Where are you, little guy?*

A quick tug pulled at his jacket hem.

9

"You're late! Super late!"

Roman turned. It was Eli, arms folded and nose scrunched, a twinkle brightening his grin.

"I thought you were never coming back," Eli said, pushing his pout.

Roman knelt. "Hey, buddy. I told you I'd be back as soon as I could."

"You said you'd try not to miss my birthday! Cause those are extra special days."

Roman squeezed Eli's shoulder. "Remember what else I told you?"

Eli grunted. "That you had to go away for a while." He kicked at the tile. "But I don't like it when you do, so are you back for good now?"

"I'm not sure, buddy." Roman reached into his inner jacket pocket for the toy. "But I brought you something."

"A race car!" Eli threw his arms around Roman's neck. "You're still my best friend."

Roman returned the hug, patting his small back. "I earned the right to keep my title, huh?"

Eli's mutter was muffled by Roman's collar. "Maybe."

"Maybe?" Roman unhooked Eli's arms from around his neck. "Explain yourself, little man."

"A really nice lady gave me twenty dollars so I could buy something for my birthday because she felt bad you didn't come see me."

Roman feigned offense. "Yeah? Did you tell her the part where I always try to make it up to you?"

Eli spun shyly. "No."

Roman smirked. "Of course not."

"Well, what about you?"

"What about me?"

"Do you have money in your wallet, too?"

Roman tousled Eli's hair. "Aren't you a hustler!"

\* \* \*

Aniella slid off her beige peacoat and draped it over the back of her grandmother's ornate chair.

"How was the interview, dear?"

Teacups clinked in the kitchen, where her grandmother arranged a tray of teas.

"It went well." Aniella called from the dining room, rubbing her arms before checking the thermostat. "It's a bridge job until I find something in my field." She cranked the dial up a few degrees. "But helping means a lot to me."

"You've always been a giver." Her grandmother set the tray down. "When you were younger, you'd spot extra silverware and ask to take it to the shelter."

Aniella poured tea into her grandmother's cup. "I met the cutest boy. He was so unassuming." She smiled. "Adorably naive."

Her grandmother eased into her seat. "That sounds familiar."

Aniella paused mid-pour. "How so?"

"Like someone I used to worry about," her grandmother said fondly. "Still do."

Aniella set the kettle down. "You think I'm unassuming?"

"You said naive, too." Her grandmother dropped a sugar cube in her tea.

Aniella picked up her cup, savoring the rich aroma. "What makes you say that?"

"Well, dear, you let everyone hurt you." Her grandmother stirred her tea with a clink. "Because you still haven't learned."

Aniella brought her teacup halfway to her lips, then stopped. "I learn, Grandma."

"Okay, you learn." Her grandmother leaned in. "But you let 'em hurt you anyway."

There was truth in it, even if it wasn't meant to hurt.

Aniella went to take a sip, but the walker propped near the steps stalled her. "How'd you get all those scratches on your walker?" She lowered her teacup. "I can run errands for you. I moved in so I could help, so please let me."

"A young man walked me across the street." She rested her hand on Aniella's.

"It's something you would've done. When people are kind, I'm reminded how much of you there is in the world."

* * *

Roman took the stairs to Homicide on the third floor of the Twenty-Ninth District.

The bullpen was tighter than when he'd left six months earlier. Desks sat in neat rows, no longer in a crooked grid. The break room door was gone, and even the hallway to Evidence had been scrubbed of history.

One thing hadn't changed. His desk. The old, chipped, dusty-blue one still sat a few spots down from the admin station. It was worse than he remembered. The kind of thing that should've been junked years ago... unless someone had fought to keep it.

Roman drifted closer. A half-eaten tray of chocolate-chip cookies sat on top. Crumbs trailed to the keyboard, as if the mess had crossed no one's mind.

Then he saw him. Scott Hoffman.

Roman handed him a coffee. "Hey, Scottie."

Scott, whose once-athletic figure was giving way to processed carbs and cheap beer, reached for it with a hum. "Nice, I didn't have time to grab one this morning," he said. "How'd you know?"

Roman shrugged. "That bromance crap or whatever. I just knew."

"*Crap?* I thought we had something here!"

Roman leaned back on the desk like it still belonged to him. "So everything's changed. Except this."

Scott dabbed at his mouth with the cookie like a napkin. "Might as well keep a piece of you here."

Roman let his hand linger on the edge of the desk. "You took it over?"

"It was the only way to convince them not to trash it." Scott dunked the cookie in his coffee. "I like to sit here pretending I'm not worried you're dead."

Roman inched the cookie tray closer to Scott. "Don't be so dramatic."

"You know me, drama queen." Scott rotated the foam coffee cup, too deliberately. "So, uh… you stopped by the shelter to see the boy?"

Roman slipped his hands into his pockets. "You can say his name."

"Eli. I meant Eli." Scott fiddled with the plastic lid. "You ever gonna tell him?"

Roman's thumb pressed against his pocket seam. He watched him, then met him head-on. "Eventually."

"He's not a kid forever."

"No. But he's too young to understand."

"Well, I hope he doesn't blame you when you tell him."

"Hope not." Roman pushed up from the desk. "You don't seem surprised I'm here, and that the chief needs me."

Scott slurped, buying time.

"I'm not in the mood to follow breadcrumbs," Roman said, eyeing the trail on Scott's shirt. "Though I see you brought your own."

Scott choked out a laugh. "Cute. But I'm—"

"Viento!"

Chief of Detectives Iver Hackett blocked the short staircase outside his office. He stared Roman down, then backed inside and slammed the door, the glass pane rattling.

Roman rubbed the back of his neck. "Guess I'm gonna find out."

He took the stairs two at a time and closed the door behind him.

Iver paced behind his desk. "You're late."

*Called out for being late. Not as endearing when it isn't Eli.*

"I thought you said two." Roman shifted his weight, humor landing dry. "I texted you about the accident."

"Why'd you wait for paramedics if they were already dead?"

The elderly woman, the near-miss, and stopping to see Eli had all stacked up.

"Seemed like the decent thing to do."

Iver stopped, his broad frame obstructing the window behind him. "Do you know why you're here?"

"You mean why this is the first time someone besides my handler's reached out mid-op? Or why I drove twelve hours without a heads-up? Yeah. I'd like to know."

Iver pointed at the chair. "Sit."

Roman sat.

"Your handler's been taken off the case," Iver said.

"And the reason for that?"

"None that I'm at liberty to discuss." Iver lowered the blinds, and the room became cloaked in seclusion. "I'll be taking over the rest of the case."

"My old chief taking over a case outside his jurisdiction." Roman folded his arms. "That raises a hell of a lot more questions."

"A case I got you assigned to in the first place." Iver wedged into his chair. "The king gets favors when he needs them."

"And why would you need such favors?"

"I'd prefer you answered some questions." Iver leaned back, weighing down the chair. "How have things been? Has it been tough?" A tremor ran through his lower lid. "Even if it were, you wouldn't tell me anyway, would you?"

Roman tracked the tremor. "Things are better."

"I've thought of you often," Iver said. "Was hoping transferring you and giving you this case was the right move."

"It's given me something else to focus on."

Iver nodded, drawing out the pause. "Good. Good."

*How long are you going to stall?* "It's been six months. I'm being pulled, or you need an extension."

Iver linked his fingers. "I'm not pulling you out."

Roman felt the pull. Suspicion, strain, something harder to name.

"Intelligence wants to listen in," Iver said. "To see if it's worth keeping you under. Especially since there's been a change of hands."

Roman leaned forward. "Listen in? I'm not wearing a wire. No bug. Nothing."

"The devices are undetectable."

14

"I've been sold that lie before." Roman's hand grazed above his pelvis. "Have the scar to prove it."

"No one could have predicted that," Iver said, clicking his pen several times. "It'll be concealed inside a watch. No one will know."

"Except I don't wear a watch when I'm under." Roman didn't blink. "But I guess that slipped your mind."

Iver stood, brushing past the unspoken accusation. "We'll figure something out."

"You don't make it sound like I have a choice."

Iver opened the blinds. "Do I need to remind you what I risked to protect you last year?" He tucked his oversized shirt further into his pants. "I'll need a few favors from you now. First, get a psych slip. Hoffman's been tackling paperwork since he still doesn't have a partner, so in the meantime just help him with whatever shit he's got going on."

\* \* \*

Roman returned to the bullpen. *Something's off.*

Scott lifted the last cookie from the tray. "What was that about?"

"Old misfiled case," Roman said, heading to the dusty-blue desk. He nudged the mouse to wake the screen.

"Why would the chief wanna talk to you about that in person?"

"You know how he is." Roman typed his old password. It failed. He nudged the keyboard aside. "We got a big day or what?"

Scott squinted, then took a sip of his cooled coffee. "Yuck." He tossed the cup in the trash.

"You wanna get out of here?" Roman asked. "Take your unmarked?" He squared the stack of paperwork, a messy heap. "No way I'm digging through all that."

\* \* \*

15

Scott turned down a side street and cranked the volume. "Holy cannoli! It's been forever since I've heard this!" He wiggled like a kid just released for recess, singing the 'Bad Boys' theme song.

"Oh, man." Roman leaned against the window. "I'm rethinking this relationship."

"Come on!"

"Don't know the lyrics."

"Yes, you do. Come on, Rome!" Scott gave the wheel a playful swerve.

Roman shot out a hand to brace the dash. "All right, all right..." He straightened, clocking a group of men roughing up a teen near the alley wall. The joke died. "Did you see that?"

Scott eased onto the curb. "Looks like some bad boys. Let's go ask them what they're gonna do when we—"

"Really, Scott?"

They swung their doors open and stepped into the afternoon grit. They knew this block and its run-down bodega, corroded fence, and the alley behind it that never stayed quiet.

A man leveled a gun toward a teenager against the brick wall.

Roman drew his firearm. "Drop it!"

The men bolted, launching Roman and Scott into pursuit. As they neared the end of the alley, someone tossed the gun to the teen. Unexpected.

The men scrambled over the fence. One snagged on the wires, thrashing.

Scott grabbed the belt of the writhing perp. "I got him, Ro, go!"

Roman shoved his gun into his waistband, vaulted a wooden crate, and cleared the fence. He landed hard, shoes skidding as he pushed back into a sprint. The men scattered, but Roman stayed locked on the teen gripping the gun.

Roman caught up, grabbed the teen's collar, and took him to the ground. "Why you running?"

"I don't know!"

"You don't know?" Roman asked. "Hands on your head. I'm not gonna ask you again. Why you running?"

The teen put his hands behind his head. "Cause I don't know you!"

"You got something to run from?"

"No."

"Help me understand, then." Roman's gaze swept the ground. "Where's the gun?"

"What gun?"

"Get up." Roman hauled him upright and cuffed him. "What's your name?"

The teen mumbled, too faint to catch.

"Can't hear you."

"Craig! It's Craig!"

Scott popped up alongside Roman. "Look what I found." He held out the gun like it was both evidence and a trophy. "He must've tossed it when you were jumping the fence."

"Look at that." Roman scoffed. "He found the hot potato everyone's been passing."

"Not mine," Craig said. "I've got nothing to hide."

"Then empty pockets won't scare you." Roman turned him.

"You don't have the right to go through my pockets!"

"Got anything sharp I should know about?" Roman patted him down, checked for sharp objects, then pulled out a small bag of pale-yellow powder. He flicked the bag. "This doesn't look like 'nothing,' does it?"

"Never seen that before."

"Keep lying." Roman passed the bag to Scott. "Take off your shoes."

Craig yanked his shoulder. "What I gotta take my shoes off for?"

"Do it."

Craig raised his cuffed hands. "How? I'm—"

Roman tightened his grip on Craig's collar just enough to get his attention. "Kick them off with your feet."

The shoes thudded to the ground.

Roman tapped Craig's leg. "Bend your knee. Bring your foot back." He brushed the sole, reached into the sock, and fished out another bag. "Think you're slick?"

Craig spat on the sidewalk, not far from Roman's feet. "*¡Púdrete!*"

"Watch your mouth," Roman said. "And your spit." He steered him toward the unmarked car.

"Hey!" Craig craned his neck. "What about my shoes?"

Roman slowed for half a step. "We'll take care of it." He continued walking. "Where's the other guy?"

Scott beamed like it was his proudest moment in months. "He's in the back memorizing 'Bad Boys' so he can sing with us on the way back in."

\* \* \*

Detective Simone Doyle, good for favors, raised a box toward the observation glass, where Craig slouched on the other side. "Hey, where are his shoes?"

"He wasn't wearing any when we found him," Roman said.

Scott shot him a look, but Roman kept his face flat.

Simone handed Roman the box. "So that's what this was for," he said.

Roman took the box. "Thanks, Doyle."

The door clicked shut behind Simone.

"I wanna give this kid a break," Roman said. "I don't want him to end up without a future. But we gotta wake him up first."

"Don't you think you were already hard on him?" Scott asked.

"Not enough to make it stick."

Scott smoothed the edge of his sleeve. "Maybe just... don't teach him the way you were taught."

"Better he answer to me than to someone who won't give a damn if he ends up in a river."

Scott paused. "What do you have in mind?"

Roman slid the box across the table.

Craig opened it, revealing a fresh pair of sneakers. "Damn." He ran a finger along the stitching, trying not to look impressed. He lifted his cuffed wrists. "Guess I'd put 'em on... if I could."

"We'll help you with that later." Roman eased onto the edge of the table. "Carrying a gun without a license is a serious crime."

"Told you. I never had one."

"Saw you with it in the alley," Scott said. "You tossed it during the chase."

Craig struggled with the shoes. "Like I said, I never had it."

"I did some digging," Roman said, standing. "Word is, you're into racketeering."

"Whoa, slow down. Never even been a part of that." Craig forced a foot into the shoe. "You lost your mind."

"That's a clever crime," Scott said. "Don't you think, Roman?"

Roman shrugged. "Sure. If it wasn't a crime that could land you twenty years of worrying about the showers."

"What?" Craig sent the box skidding across the floor. "I'm not involved in racketeering!"

Scott snorted. "Just like you don't know where the gun came from."

"And just like you don't know how drugs ended up in your socks and pockets," Roman said.

Craig's gaze pinged between them. Their expressions didn't budge.

"Hope your fingerprints aren't all over that gun," Roman said. "Wonder how many crimes it's tied to."

"Screw you both." Craig's cuffs clinked against the table. "This really gonna go down like this?"

"Maybe not," Roman said. "Tell us who your drug supplier is."

"I ain't saying shit!"

The table took the hit, the crack landing like a dare. "Cause you're not a *rat, right?*"

Craig sat taller. "That's right!"

"Fine." Roman dragged his hand from the table. "Maybe your buddy next door feels like talking."

Scott trailed Roman to the door.

"Wait, wait! You giving him a deal?"

Roman held. "Think he's gonna run his mouth?"

Craig hesitated. "What kinda deal?"

"You're staring down a Class B felony," Roman said. "You want out of that? You gotta stay clean."

Scott rested his hand on the doorknob. "And feed us intel when we ask."

"Be a snitch?" Craig's pitch spiked. "I'll be dead!"

Scott loosened his grip on the knob. "We can make this disappear, or you can serve a long stretch. Your call."

"People believe the first thing they hear," Roman said. "Doesn't matter if it's true."

Craig struck his thigh. "This shit ain't right!"

Roman leaned in, dropping his tone. "I'm offering you a deal. But if you don't *want* one."

"No! No…" Craig's head dipped. He rocked in place, fists tight in his lap. "I want one. I'll take the deal."

Roman dragged out a chair and sat across from him. "Talk."

# CHAPTER 2

## Divarication

Aniella slid open the mirrored closet doors. A pastel pink blouse with cascading ruffles sparked a thrill. She paired it with a beige pencil skirt, high-waisted and flattering to her hourglass figure. She strapped on matching heels, then added glittering studs and a bracelet that hugged her dainty wrist. Though she wore little makeup, she never left the house without a wisp of mascara and a swipe of translucent lip balm. Last, she spritzed on her perfume, an enchanting swirl of iced blackberry and vanilla musk that melted into the warmth of her skin.

Outside, she hailed a taxi, rifling through her purse for her balm.

The taxi slowed at the curb, its wipers squeaking against the drizzle. Aniella grabbed the handle, slick with morning rain.

She scooted across the cracked leather seat, ignoring the musty smell as she unzipped the inner pocket of her purse.

"Good morning!" she said, gliding the balm over her lips. "How's your day going so far?"

The driver met her reflection in the rearview mirror. "Where to?"

She gave the address and settled in, quiet with wonder as the city blurred past.

\* \* \*

Scattered files covered the chipped, newly reclaimed desk, a reminder of how quickly things got out of order. Roman stacked them into neat piles, while Scott gnawed on an oatmeal cookie and flipped through the local newspaper.

"Glad I can help with all this paperwork," Roman said. "How's the sports section?"

Scott spoke through a mouthful. "Haven't read it yet."

"Mm-hm." Roman stacked another pile. "You didn't tell me why you weren't surprised to see me back."

Scott turned a page. "You know what I can't shake?"

"The crumbs off your shirt?"

Scott peered down, his chin folding. He shook his shirt, crumbs falling to the floor.

"No one wants a rat invasion," Roman said.

Scott grabbed the dustpan beside his desk. "Speaking of rats, how's Craig doing as your CI?"

"Nice try." *Press him.* "Try again."

"Well, uh…" Scott swept the crumbs into the dustpan. "I overheard the captain from his office."

Homicide's captain, Ethan Polinski, had grown suspicious of Roman's absences, which had started after last year's undercover stabbing. The tension was hard to ignore. Several months later, Hackett leveraged his connections for a transfer to New York's Sensitive Operations and Undercover Unit. The approval came faster than most recovering detectives get and left both the captain and Roman relieved.

"There's no way you overheard from there," Roman said.

"The walls aren't as thick as you think." Scott slid the dustpan back into place. "And no offense, but I've heard him yelling at you from there before."

Roman shuffled loose papers into a folder. *Set the trap.* "You're saying he was yelling about that?"

"Well, I don't know what to tell you." Scott tugged his ear, a nervous tic. He cringed. "Oh, shit." He grabbed the paper and buried his face behind it like it could save him.

Roman slapped the folder down and crossed to Scott's desk. "Give it up, Scottie."

"Don't 'Scottie' me." Scott draped the paper over his head like a curtain.

"Come on, Mr. Loose Lips." Roman ducked and peered beneath the curtain of newsprint, a smile flickering. "What do you know?"

"I hate when you call me that!"

Roman snatched the paper away. "What is it?" he asked, crumpling it and dropping it into the trash.

Scott reached for the paper. "I was just about to read the sports article!"

"You don't overhear confidential info by accident." Roman ran the possibilities, but none fit. "The only way is if…" He stiffened. "You're getting involved in the case."

Scott clapped his hands. "Welp, before you flip out—"

"You agreed to it?"

"Well, they kinda talked me into it. But I'll always help a friend."

"Help? If anxiety had a name, you'd own it."

"I mean, that's true. But I wasn't supposed to tell you, so don't go to his office."

"I'm not going to his office."

Scott's shoulders dropped. "Phew, that's a relief." He fished the crumpled paper out of the trash. When he lifted his head from the bin, the room had gone still. Roman was gone.

* * *

"Am I in la-la land?" Roman asked, the door hanging open behind him.

Ethan's grip tightened on the handset. "Let me call you back." He hung up,

23

stood, and buttoned his navy pinstriped suit, a size too tight for his lanky frame. "You must be. You think you can just barge in here?"

"Not on my case."

Ethan angled toward the open doorway, where Scott sat in the bullpen. "Doesn't change what's done just because you squeezed Hoffman like a source with a hot tip."

"If you bring in someone they're not expecting—"

"Then we'll see if they trust you," Ethan said. "Because if they don't—"

"They trust me. But this could make them second-guess and cost me everything."

Ethan scratched at his sideburn. "Or you gain an extension."

"Not under these circumstances."

"Then we'll pull you from the case."

Six months of control. Six months of necessary distraction. Now it was all unraveling. The harder Roman worked the angles, the faster the facts slipped away.

"I'd take my chances if I were you," Ethan said, brushing dandruff off his lapel. "Otherwise, you just wasted half a year."

\* \* \*

The buzzer stuttered as Aniella tapped the doorbell. The chain slid and the deadbolt clicked.

"Hey, girl, don't mind the mess." Fern held the doorway wide. "I wasn't expecting company, so the place is a dump."

Aniella moved inside, rubbing her numb hands together. She sidestepped a drift of mail. "You told me to stop by this morning." She couldn't find a surface to set her purse down on that wasn't already covered in dust.

Fern plopped onto the lumpy mattress on the floor. "How's the new job?"

*Maybe she forgot.* "It's my first day."

"Where'd you apply again?" Fern dragged purple eyeliner across her lid in the cracked mirror propped against the wall.

"The homeless shelter by my grandmother's house."

"God, I can't believe I forgot that." Fern licked her finger and smudged the liner into her lash line. "I knew they'd hire you because you're pretty, but come on." She licked again. "You could do better."

Aniella's purse still hovered over the cluttered end table. *Better?* "Thanks, Fern."

"Just saying." Fern sprang up and crossed the room, staleness wafting across Aniella. "By the way, George saw the picture of us I posted on Insta. He's dying to meet you, so I set you two up."

\* \* \*

The psychiatrist's office. The most dreaded room in the precinct. Walls bright enough to blind anyone who endured a full session. In a failed attempt to make the space feel safe, an oddly shaped rug stretched beneath the coffee table. The psychiatrist's chair, trimmed in gold, sat there tone-deaf and untouched by the world's burdens. Across from it sat another chair, its sagging cushion and frayed fabric telling an opposite story.

"Hey, Doctor Shrub," Roman said, breezing in.

The light found Judy's glasses as she looked up. "Detective. Good to see you."

Roman sank into the threadbare chair. "How's the husband?"

"Still has selective hearing, but otherwise he's good." She ran her hand along the velvet armrest. "How've you been the past six months?"

Roman knew the play. "Can't complain."

She waited, pen idle on the side table. Roman recognized the silence for what it was. Another subtle psychological nudge.

"I assume it doesn't get easier," she said.

"What's that?"

"Undercover." Judy picked up the pen. "You keep checking in to make sure you're still pretending. That you're fooling everyone else and not yourself." She flipped to a fresh page. "It takes a toll. And now? You're back to desk work while waiting to return to a life that isn't yours. How does that feel?"

"I've heard I compartmentalize well."

"I'd guess it's a skill that could save your life in dangerous situations."

He nodded.

Judy scribbled in her notepad. "What's it been like? Devoting so much time to this?" Her pen kept moving.

He leaned in just enough to play the part. "Leaky ceilings. Mold at hazardous levels in the bathroom. It's been a struggle."

"Wit will keep you sane." She grinned. "Any lingering thoughts that bother you?"

"You find your purpose in life, and that's it. You accept what comes with it. Same for you. Does it ever wear you down? Hearing people's problems all day, when most won't even listen?" He paused. "I'd guess your answer is yeah, it's hard. But worth it, for the tiny hope you might change a few lives."

Her expression shifted.

*Landed.*

"That's one way to get me to see your perspective," she said, more guarded now. "Do you have any fears about continuing this process?"

"If you're asking if I'm worn down, I'm fine. Is it demanding? No doubt." *Careful.* "But does that tiny hope of changing a few lives drive me to get up every morning?" He let the moment linger. "Absolutely."

She peered at him over her glasses.

*That's her limit. She knows it.*

"Okay," she said, the notepad's cover concealing what she'd written. A journal slid across the table, its spine whispering against the wood. "That's for you. If you ever feel like jotting anything down."

Roman glanced at it but didn't touch it.

"I'll sign your slip."

\* \* \*

Rows of lockers lined the New York City's Twenty-Second Precinct locker room, each marked with an officer's nameplate. Cracked tiles riddled the floor, and stains marked the stalls and sinks.

Scott fastened the department-issued watch around his wrist, already wired to the cover team. "This is pretty decent."

Roman rummaged through his locker. "Yup."

"Thanks for letting me pick the code word," Scott said, fiddling with the watch hands.

*Don't yank your ear. Keep your hands steady.* Saying these out loud to Scott would only make it worse.

"Had to make sure it'd be something you'd remember," Roman said, pulling his gym bag from the locker.

Scott peeled off a paper towel and wiped sweat from his forehead. "I'm trying to match names to faces," he said. "Wes, Kirk, Julian…"

Roman stuffed gear into his bag. "Don't worry about Julian. He won't be there."

He'd picked a time when Julian would be out, knowing Scott wouldn't pass if Julian showed.

"Can't believe I'm doing this," Scott said. "Must've been an accident or something."

"An accident?" Roman pulled on a worn hoodie. "Or poor judgment?"

Scott twiddled with the clasp again, as if testing whether Roman was joking.

"What?" Roman asked. "Accidents happen."

"You know, sarcasm's one of your best traits."

Roman almost grinned. "And here I thought it was being an asshole."

"Yeah, well, you qualify for that too." Scott pitched his words like a bad infomercial. "Act now and you can be all of the above for just three easy payments of $9.99."

\* \* \*

In a vacant body shop, Wes wiped oil off a socket wrench and set it on the toolbox. Kirk sat in a car with the door open, tangled in speaker wires.

Wes approached, giving Scott a cynical once-over. "Who's this?"

"Just a buddy," Roman said. "That cool with you?"

"No worries," Wes said. "We're not talking business with him here, though."

"I would've run that by you first." Roman shrugged. "He's just tagging along."

"Class act." Wes struck Roman's arm with an oiled cloth. "Too bad you were made for the streets."

"I was made for the streets too, you know," Scott said, a thin laugh slipping out. "I, uh, I know a lot of stuff. Real rough out there."

Wes sized him up. "Who's this again?"

"I'm a friend of Julian," Scott said.

Roman stepped in. "Wrong Julian. He means the stereo kid by the bridge."

"A friend?" Kirk popped his head out of the car. "How good a friend?"

*Going ugly.*

"You know, we're cool with each other." Scott tugged his left ear. "It's no big deal."

"No big deal?" Kirk chuckled as he approached, but the laugh wasn't friendly. "Since you know so much, you know Roman cracked two of Julian's fingers a few months ago, right? So any friend of Julian's wouldn't be a friend of Roman."

"Cracked fingers?" Scott asked.

"Now *that* Julian's fingers were on my throat," Roman said. "Quick math."

Scott pinched both ears. "You guys are friends with both Roman and Julian... right?"

*Not your friend. Stop saying friend.*

"We're business partners," Wes said.

*Walk it back.* "We're good now."

"Not a chance," Wes said. "That son of a bitch doesn't have a forgiving bone in his body."

*Keep him on me.* "He didn't mention our deal?"

Kirk and Wes shared a quick exchange. "What deal?"

"Shit, I guess he didn't," Roman said. "Never mind, then."

Wes sized Scott up again. "Last I heard, Julian wanted blood. Tell me when things were patched up."

"We came to an agreement, more or less," Roman said. "Word is he needed a couple of favors. Only ones I could handle."

"You're handy, Roman," Kirk said. "But that seems like a stretch."

"You don't trust me?" Roman asked.

"I trust you." Wes reached for his phone. "I don't trust *him*. Gonna get the real story."

"Use mine." Roman held out his phone, screen on the dialer. He angled toward Scott. "Grab a few waters from the bodega. Two minutes."

Scott clapped his hands. "Crumbs!"

Wes jerked up from his phone. "What's up with this guy?"

"He's been on some weird shit lately," Roman said, digging his fingers hard into Scott's shoulder. "I'm gonna drop him off and swing back later—"

"It's my thing when people can't agree! You know, because it's, uh, a crumby situation!"

*Boom.*

The front entrance blew inward.

"Down! Down! Everybody down!"

The cover team stormed in with rifles up, boots trampling the shop as commands cracked throughout the room.

A table overturned. Roman spun on instinct and dropped. Hands behind his head. Cuffs snapped shut on his wrists. Scott hit the ground beside him, pale as drywall, cuffs clinking against his watch. The criminals lay flat, rifles aimed at their backs.

The entire takedown lasted under twenty seconds.

Across the street, in the surveillance van, Iver tore off his headset. "Bring Viento in now!" He tossed it against the console, a panel light blinking out on impact.

\* \* \*

The air shifted as the hinges gave, and Iver filled the interrogation room doorway, fury pinned on Roman.

"You broke someone's fingers?"

Roman stilled. "Ah, jeez."

"Did your handler sign off on this?"

"Sign off on self-defense? You want the full story?" Roman stood. "What was I supposed to say? 'Hold up while I call my handler' while getting choked out?"

Iver closed the gap until the table bit into Roman's hip. "No, smartass!" Rage broke across him.

*Too familiar.*

Roman steadied, then drew back.

"Maybe reread the undercover guidelines," Iver said. "Since you don't get how serious this is."

"Every guideline's been broken since last week. And I get how big a deal it is to someone behind a desk. But my life depended on a split-second choice."

"That's great. So now we can't take this to the DA. They'll want Hoffman's bug, and once it confirms you broke protocol, it's over."

"You've buried worse than this."

Iver planted his hands on his hips and shook his head. "Again. Conduct, Roman."

Roman kept still.

"And you said you didn't want to talk about last year," Iver said.

"I need to see this through. We can't let them off. If I don't get that extension, I'll have wasted months for nothing."

"I wouldn't care if you wasted years," Iver said. "Time's cheaper than your life." He spat Roman's line back at him. "Quick math."

"Are you kidding me right now?"

"You'll make do with your firearm possession." Iver's lower lid ticked. "Before you broke protocol. Or fingers."

There it was. *Same tell as Chicago.* The vent hummed above them, pushing heat against Roman's back.

"This is what you wanted all along, wasn't it?" Roman asked.

"Pardon me?"

"You handpicked the case, wired Hoffman, steered the rules. This wasn't a setup?"

Crimson edged Iver's collar. "You're walking a fine line, Viento."

"You've got something going on. If I'm part of it, say it."

"It's over. And if you don't want me airing out what got you sent here in the first place, back off. From me and the case." Iver's hand cut toward Roman, finger rigid. "You're flying back to Chicago with me."

He left without another word.

The blinds rattled in the draft Iver left behind. Roman shoved the chair back, the legs screeching against the tile. Papers on the table fluttered once, then rested. He set the chair upright and sat, jaw tight, the hollow tick of the wall clock dragging him back to every second he'd fought to outrun.

*Six months. Six brutal months.*

Scott knocked on the doorframe. "I screwed up, Ro. I don't know why they picked me."

Roman slumped forward and pressed his hands to his mouth. "They wanted you to fumble it."

"What? What makes you say that?"

"Haven't figured it out yet." Roman's words came muffled. "But it doesn't matter. They bagged the case."

"I can't imagine..." Scott shuffled in. "Uh... this is bad timing, but... you're like family. So it's not personal, but I..."

Roman let his hands fall to his thighs. "What is it?"

"I'm glad you're back, but I asked if they could pair me with someone else."

Roman fixed on a scuff he'd left in the floor.

"I just see the risks you take, and—"

Roman raised his head. "I get it."

* * *

Chicago.

Roman drove his knuckles into the heavy bag, each swing winding him tighter.

The smack of leather rose to meet him, the chain above straining in protest.

Control had always meant survival, but it wasn't control anymore. It was memory and anger colliding under his skin. Each hit dragged ghosts from Chicago—the hospital's white glare, the blade's unforgiving strike, the echo of a childhood that never let go and Iver's promise that the transfer would save him from an inevitable spiral. The ceiling mount quivered under the weight of it, metal creaking with each pull. He drove the bag harder, chasing a reason he still didn't have. The bag swung on its chain, each strike shuddering through his bones.

*Time.* Pound. *Effort.* Pound. *Sacrifice.* Pound.

He left for a distraction. But it was ending in nothing.

Pound, pound, pound.

At last, his arms gave out. Roman hooked the bag and held it until the swing died.

His phone lit up on the bench nearby. Eli's adoptive mother, Igna, was calling. With no coverage for her overnight shift, Eli had curled up on a cot at the shelter, half guest, half fixture in the place.

* * *

The usual daytime bustle of the shelter had quieted. Fluorescent lights flickered over the linoleum. With curfew in place, the few remaining workers moved through the hushed space, the scent of disinfectant still hanging in the air.

"You came!" Eli's shoes tapped across the floor as he ran up to Roman and hugged his leg.

"Hey, buddy." Roman knelt to meet him. "What's going on?"

Eli's nose ran, lids low, and he clutched his toy race car against his shirt. "I had a bad dream."

Roman rubbed Eli's arm. "I'm sorry to hear that, bud. Can you tell me about it?"

"It was so scary. I woke up screaming."

Roman wiped a tear off Eli's chin. "What made it scary, bud?"

"A really loud gun went off. It shot... it shot my daddy." Eli clutched his toy tighter. "He stopped moving."

The truth fell out of Eli's mouth like a marble slipping off a table, innocent and unstoppable. Blotches marked his cheeks. Tears slicked his skin. The toy's wheels chattered in his hold. He had no clue what vault he'd just opened.

Roman's fist knotted in his jacket. He let go as if that could keep him from unraveling.

"Is that why he's not here?" Eli asked. "Why can't I remember him? I have a daddy, right?"

Roman cupped a hand over his mouth, then reached for Eli. "Let's go one question at a time." He rubbed along the boy's knuckles. "Can we do that?"

"Did my daddy die?" Eli tipped his face, waiting.

Roman fought the urge to break away. He stayed with him. "Yes."

"How come I don't remember him?"

"You were four. At that age, it's hard to remember."

"Is that why I'm adopted?" Eli stirred in place. "Where's my real mom? Did something bad happen to her, too?"

"She's fine."

Eli twisted his fingers together. "Where is she?"

Roman took his hands again. "I'm not sure. But she loved you. Enough to place you with your adoptive mom, because she could take better care of you."

"Why couldn't she take care of me?"

"Because some people can't handle as much responsibility as others." Roman gave his hands a gentle tug. "But it wasn't your fault, I promise."

"I don't want to have bad dreams." Eli wiped his face. "Do you have bad dreams?"

"I think everyone has them."

"What about my daddy? Is what happened to him in my dream real?"

A flash of steel. The blade slicing above his pelvis. The memory locked in.

The words crowded Roman's throat but stayed there. He nodded.

"How do you know?" Eli asked.

*Be honest.*

"Because I was there."

"You knew my daddy?"

"Do you remember what I do for work?"

"You have to go away a lot and you protect people."

"That's right. And that night, I was protecting you."

"But I don't remember you from anywhere but here." Eli spun the wheels on the toy. "I thought I met you here."

Back then, Roman was nothing like himself. "You were hiding in a closet," he said. "Do you remember that?"

"No, I don't remember." Tears welled again and his small chin quivered.

"It's okay, buddy."

"You were protecting my daddy, too?"

Roman's lips parted. He wanted to say he'd tried, but the words wouldn't come. "Let's get you tucked back into bed."

He tickled Eli's ribs until a reluctant squeal cut through the heaviness.

"Safe now," he said quietly, settling Eli beneath the blanket.

Eli's fingers slackened around the toy car, his small body sinking into the cot as peace returned where fear had been.

Roman retraced his steps past the cots and into the community kitchen, replaying their exchange, each pass splitting a little deeper. He'd thought he'd be clear when the time came. Now, that certainty wavered. Eli wasn't ready. And neither was he.

A woman shouted as her purse clattered to the floor, its contents skidding across the tile. A man hunched over a loaf of stolen bread, clutching it as he tore for the exit. He elbowed past volunteers and barreled into Roman.

Roman took the hit on his shoulder. The thief bolted out and the chimes on the door rattled behind him.

The woman crouched, gathering her things in a rush. Roman dug under a chair for a lint roller and a tube of lip balm. They knelt side by side, hands brushing in tandem. When he passed her the items, his hand lingered.

He was trained to notice everything. Scan scenes in seconds. Hear lies in an echo. Catch the flick of movement before someone reached for a weapon. Breaking people down came by instinct. He tracked patterns, risks, and the things most people missed. But she didn't read as a threat. Nothing in her raised his guard. Disarming.

*Since when did beauty matter?* Softer than anything that had cut through in years.

Lashes, wispy. Glossy hair framed her features in precise lines, worn without effort. Olive skin carried a warmth. Her lips were defined, a subdued mauve.

He'd been staring too long.

"I'm so sorry." She brushed a few strands forward as if to hide the flush at her cheeks. "I can't believe I dropped my purse."

Trying to recover, she tucked a receipt back inside.

"It's all right," he said, quieter than he meant.

She slowly looked up, meeting him fully. Her stare held, and he knew what she saw—silver-green tempered by gray, a ring of brown holding steady as if refusing to give. Beneath grief too old to name, beneath restraint so practiced it passed for control, something restless still lived there. What she wouldn't see was clearer still. Whatever the hue, that surface had long stopped giving anything away. Yet she stayed with him, as if something in him already gave her reason.

Her expression was unguarded. He'd seen depth in damaged people before. This wasn't that. He'd lived in lies, cover stories, half-truths and volatility.

Openness usually masked performance or manipulation. But not here. No flirtation, no pretense. Just… honesty. The one thing the world had never given him.

His hand stayed raised, lip balm and lint roller hovering. At last, her grip found them.

Her lashes fluttered. "Thank you."

They stood. Her neck bent back as he towered over her. A gravity in him anchored her there.

Roman cleared his throat. "Did we get everything?"

"Uh…" The receipt slipped out again, and she caught it, tucking it back inside. "I think so." Aniella pivoted, gripping her purse straps as she rushed for the exit. "Thank you!"

The door chimes rattled on her way out.

"No problem."

He tried to shake off the encounter, but the clarity of what he'd recognized in her lingered. Too clean, too real. Maybe that was why she'd left so suddenly. He could have stayed and learned her face forever. But for the first time, he'd felt seen—and that, more than anything, could have driven her away.

# CHAPTER 3

## Fate Finds You

Short-tempered arguments snapped through the bullpen. Footsteps thudded past. Phones chirped from every corner.

In the morning haze, Roman slipped into the chief's office, unnoticed.

"You wanted to see me?" he asked, the latch clicking behind him.

Iver cut the intercom. The light died. "Have you registered Craig as a CI yet?"

*How the hell does he know about Craig?* "Not yet."

"Don't."

"Don't?"

Iver drifted toward the plaques lining the wall, tributes to his own legacy. "I've given a lot to this department and this city. But I haven't been perfect." The plaques dulled in the pause. "You were right. I didn't want your extension approved."

The intercom sat dark, its little red eye gone cold.

"I know you sabotaged the case," Roman said. "Why?"

"You were circling the drain before I gave you that case. About to tank your career. I covered for you. New York was supposed to steady you."

Roman settled into one heel. "Why, Chief?"

The brass names gleamed like proof.

"You were getting too close."

"To what?"

"To people I can't afford to lose."

The moment locked.

"You've known them the whole time," Roman said, finally breaking it. "That's why you pushed for my transfer."

Iver's silence was a confession.

"You didn't assign me to that case to save me," Roman said. "You planted me in it."

"I needed someone I trusted on the inside."

"And when I was close..."

"I took over." Iver squared a crooked plaque until it sat true, as if it had been obvious all along. "Then sabotaged it."

"So I should be grateful?" Roman asked, the question landing like a file snapping shut. "You used my rock bottom as a cover to make me your errand boy."

"I protected you. I sacrificed—"

"You protected your payout."

"I took a risk on you," Iver said, the bullpen's rhythm underscoring him. "Now you return the favor. Julian's crew is relocating to Chicago and I need distance. They still don't know you're a detective."

The case dangled as a lifeline. Now it mocked him. Six months under, gutted to nothing. Used, then dragged back into the same dirt.

"Weren't they charged with felony firearm possession?" Roman asked.

"The courts are overloaded with more heinous crimes at the moment."

Too easy for "The King" to get favors. The shuffle outside swelled, like the building itself had chosen a side.

Roman nodded once, lips tight. "Julian's not gonna forget about his fingers."

"Then find a way to make him forget."

Roman gave a dry laugh. "You want me to shake his hand and run his money?"

The bullpen dimmed back to a distant rhythm, the office boxed tight around them.

"I want you to introduce Julian's crew to Craig. Keep the money moving. If it goes south, Craig takes the heat," Iver said.

"He's nineteen."

"He agreed to be a CI. And you? You're the best liar I've got. People believe you. Use it." Iver checked the intercom. Still dark. "I'm not asking you to kill anyone. It's cash. Petty cash."

"What if he won't do it?"

"I watched you interrogate him. You wrung him out. Do it again."

Roman gave it flat, unreadable. "Suppose I walk."

Iver switched the intercom back on. "You won't."

\* \* \*

"Why aren't you registering me?" Craig asked, pacing in short bursts up and down the alley. "Isn't that like insurance? So you can't screw me over later?"

Roman leaned his back into the brick. "I wouldn't do that."

"So I can trust you now? We got a system?"

"Yeah, we got a system." Roman pushed off the brick. "You keep your ear to the ground, your nose in everyone's business, your line of sight clear, and your mouth shut. That's the system."

Craig kicked at scraps of trash curling off the curb. "Any perks in that?"

"You're asking if you can break the law again and get away with it."

Craig waved his finger. "You know, the way you word things sometimes…"

"I'll be in touch." Roman turned away. "In the meantime, don't break the law."

\* \* \*

No one at the check-in counter, Roman set the box of donated food at his feet.

A service bell sat on the counter. As a kid, he'd liked ringing those. Few happy memories, but maybe that's why he couldn't resist now. He lifted his finger, hovered over the bell, then tapped it. The room stayed empty for a beat, until movement flickered down the hall. The worker was already coming toward him. He recognized her instantly, but she reached the counter before he could speak.

"I'm so sorry, I had to step away." Her posture straightened. "Hey, you're the guy who helped me pick up my things."

"Yeah. How are you?"

"I'm great." Her smile stretched. "How about you?"

"Haven't chased any more runaway lip balms, but I can't complain."

She laughed, the sound catching faintly on the walls before fading into the hollow lobby.

Roman cleared his throat, noting her badge. "Didn't know you worked here."

"Oh yes! Aniella." She brushed a finger over her name. "Ahn-yella."

Her careful pronunciation almost made him smile. He didn't need the help, but it lingered anyway.

"I'm Italian," he said. "I can say it."

She held out her hand. "Nice to meet you."

He took it with a brief shake. "Roman. Likewise."

"We wear badges so the kids know our name. It makes them more comfortable." She adjusted it with a small, proud smile. "Like they already know us a little."

He couldn't remember the last time kindness came off that genuine, and it left a strange echo.

Silence pooled. She shifted the donations form as if noise could fill whatever was lingering between them.

"I'm normally not at the desk," she said. "I'm covering someone's lunch."

"What do you do here?"

"I'm a Crisis Intervention Advocate! I help them find housing, build resumes, practice interviews, and anything else they might need."

Purpose bled through every word. Too much to fake. Still, something in him braced. Instinct, habit, who knew.

"When did you move here?" he asked.

"How'd you know I wasn't from here?" A hand met her hip. "Do I not have that Chicago grease?"

He let out a low laugh, caught off guard by her playfulness. "No, nothing like that. Just a hunch."

"Oh wow, good hunch!" She twisted her bracelet around her wrist. "I moved here a few months ago. What about you? Are you new to the city?"

"Been here a while. You just start here then?"

Her smile held, though her focus narrowed. She'd caught the dodge, and he could tell.

"Yes. My first day was actually when you helped me," she said. "It was a long day, but rewarding."

Roman lifted the box. "I'm dropping this off."

"Oh, that's fabulous!" She rifled through the counter clutter. "I apologize. I'm still collecting my bearings around here."

"It's usually under the keyboard," he said.

She lifted the keyboard, the paper sliding free. "Oh my goodness. Thank you." A quick laugh. "Do you drop off donations often?" Her fingers brushed his hand as she took the box from him.

He caught himself liking their rhythm. So much that he forgot her question. "Do you have a number?" he asked. *What the hell am I doing?*

"Oh." Her hand swept across the counter until a pen holder toppled. "Here, I found it!"

She handed him a card, which only displayed the shelter's address and phone number. He could read most people before they spoke. This one? Nothing. Either she was naive, or politely telling him to back off.

Roman leaned on the counter. "I meant your number. For dinner. If you're not interested—"

"That sounds great!" She grabbed a napkin from under a clipboard and tore it in half, scribbling her number quickly. "Here," she said. "This is mine."

He didn't know why she tore the napkin in half, but for some reason, that small quirk got to him. "How's Friday?"

* * *

Ethan checked his watch as Roman threaded through the bullpen. "Where have you been?"

Roman dropped into his chair. "Had to run an errand."

Flecks dusted Ethan's dark suit as he scratched. "How long does it take to run an errand?"

"I'll use personal time."

"Start showing up presentable." Ethan nudged his chin toward Roman's jeans and the bomber jacket over a T-shirt. "Slacks and a button-down tomorrow."

"Sure."

Ethan slid a signed document across Roman's desk. "Welcome back to the district, then."

Roman took the paper.

"Hackett approved my request to put you on desk duty until further notice," Ethan said.

*Benched?*

Roman skimmed straight to the bottom line. Iver's signature.

"You need time to reintegrate after working undercover. Get reacclimated to the internal flow." Ethan pulled at his suit coat. "Being on-site should also cut down on those unexplained whereabouts you rack up."

The page indented as Roman lowered it. Iver hadn't mentioned this. The downtime would help, though. The past few months had chewed him up. But he doubted it was the break it seemed.

Nothing in this district ever was.

# CHAPTER 4

## Unanswered

Aniella's bedroom was usually hotel-neat. Tonight, it could've passed for ground zero after a getting-ready grenade. Open makeup bags, shoes abandoned in the corner, two rejected dresses slung over her vanity chair.

Fern leaned into the mirrored closet doors, layering on mascara. "I don't know anyone else who takes two hours to get ready."

Behind the restroom door, Aniella combed through the glossy fall of her hair. "You try getting ready for someone this intriguing. Insatiably good-looking doesn't help."

Fern pointed her mascara wand toward the doorway. "No man's worth two hours." She jammed the wand back into the tube, reconsidering. "Maybe an hour and a half." She applied another coat. "He's already seen you barefaced and still asked you out, so relax."

The restroom door slowly opened, and Aniella drifted into the bedroom.

Fern nearly dropped her mascara wand. "I mean, damn. Worth the two hours after all."

Aniella smoothed a hand over the black lace cinching her waist. "It's not too inviting?"

* * *

The napkin with Aniella's number lay spread under Roman's hand. He folded one corner, then flattened it. Ink seeped through the cheap fiber, but the digits still read. He pulled his chair in and lifted the handset. He keyed three digits, then paused.

*Shouldn't call.*

He keyed the rest.

A finger pressed the hook switch, killing the line. Tyler Grave stood there, sleeves rolled, wearing that trouble-baiting smirk like armor . He'd had it in for Roman since day one, maybe because Roman never took the bait. Lately, he'd been pushing harder to see if the man would ever flinch.

Roman left his finger on the switch. "You need something?"

"I know you're not interested, but I need your help with a suspect." Tyler released the switch. "Can't crack this guy and we're coming up on forty-eight."

The dial tone hummed back. *Good.*

"Run the evidence again." Roman set the handset down. "Shake for new witnesses."

"Here's the thing." Tyler perched on the desk edge, invading space. "We've got plenty, but the DA's calling it circumstantial. Says not to come back without a confession."

Roman rocked back in his chair. "I'm on desk duty, remember?"

"I won't tell anyone."

"They'll have it on camera that I went into an interrogation room."

"Full of excuses tonight, aren't you?" Tyler's heel knocked the chair frame. "Ask forgiveness, not permission."

Forty-eight hours.

Aniella's number.

Roman flipped the napkin over. The relief that followed surprised him. He wouldn't have gone. Not tonight. Maybe not ever.

* * *

"Hold up," Fern said, the flash sparking from her phone. "This dress needs proof."

Aniella tucked her hair behind her ear.

"Don't be shy." Fern angled her phone for another shot. "Give me the cover-girl smile."

"I'm just… anxious."

"Girl, don't be. He's going to die when he sees you in this and he'll be the one sweating." Fern's phone keys popped under her nails. "And one of these is going straight to George."

* * *

The interview room wasn't much. Gray cinder blocks, a table bolted to the floor, a chair too hard for comfort. The suspect sat accused of murdering a bodega owner who'd tried to defend his shop.

Roman came in, easy, and dropped into the opposite chair. "You wanna snack or something?"

The suspect adjusted his hoodie drawstring. "What you got?"

"I only had a ten for the vending machine." Roman sorted through the options he'd brought. "I grabbed cookies, Twizzlers, and M&M's."

"You can keep the Twizzlers."

Roman feigned enthusiasm. "You don't mind?"

"Do your thing."

Roman ripped open the Twizzlers, the wrapper crackling sharp in the small room. They chewed in silence.

The suspect drummed the table, restless. "So, uh, what are you? Like another detective?"

"Yeah," Roman said, the slouch in his posture making him appear less intimidating. "But my boss hates my guts."

The suspect slid the empty cookie wrapper aside. "Oh shit."

"I'm the office paper pusher right now. My punishment."

"Rough." The suspect tore at the candy wrapper. "What's he hate you for?"

"That's the unfair part. I have no idea."

"Man, I know all about that."

Roman let it hang, then leaned in, a trace of interest. "Yeah? What's that mean to you?"

"Fake ass people doing unfair shit."

Roman rested back, just enough. "Tell me about it."

* * *

Fern scrolled on her phone, unimpressed. "So? What time was he even picking you up? Text him and ask him where he is."

Aniella's dress felt heavier now, the black lace cinch turning from flattery to humiliation. "He never gave me his number. He just has mine."

Fern stopped scrolling. "Wait—he's had your number for a week, never called, never texted—and you still got ready?" Her remarks were barbed. "How'd you even know what time? You just guessed?"

*What was I thinking?* The way that silver-green hue had lingered, she'd been certain, in that moment, it meant something. Enough to spend hours tonight believing it still could.

Her toes curled. "He said Friday. He's the one who asked for my number. Why ask if he didn't mean it?"

Fern tossed her phone onto the comforter. "Oh my God, wake up. He didn't even play you—you played yourself."

Color climbed Aniella's cheeks. Her reflection glared from the mirrored closet doors. It offered no mercy, throwing her naivety back at her.

"You thought he'd magically show up today?" Fern asked, still biting. "Even when he hadn't checked in all week?"

46

Aniella turned from the mirror, fast, unwilling to face what stared back. *Grandma's right. Maybe I do let everyone hurt me. Maybe I don't learn.*

* * *

For hours, the suspect ranted about how unfair his life had been, winding the story back to the bodega.

The suspect knotted his hoodie strings. "Why you listening this long?"

Roman twisted the bottle cap until the seal broke. "You lost your temper." He gave a slow shrug. "It happens. What matters is intention. Intention can be everything." He spun the bottle cap once on the table, then stilled it. "I know a few DAs. I can frame this as heat of the moment, not murder. That gives you a shot at help instead."

"Why would you do that for me?"

"A jury won't see the version of you I've seen. And there's a bitter family looking for justice. They'll likely go hard for you to get life without parole. But if you own up and show remorse, it'll go a long way." Roman eased back. "You want a chance at a life after this, don't you? A deal with a DA beats a jury that can throw away the key."

Wheels turned. "You got video of me doing this?"

"We do."

They didn't.

"…And you're sure it was me?"

"Best move is to take accountability. We've got tape. Witnesses. Enough to bury you. Show how sorry you are, even if you gotta put it on a little. That's what gets you a deal." Roman spun the bottle cap again, this time pressing it flat as if sealing the deal himself. "There's no walking clean. You've just got to be smart about the rest."

The suspect tightened his hoodie strings. "I see what you're saying."

"Frankly, you seem like a decent guy who made a mistake. I'd love to help you out."

It landed flat as if it were fact, not persuasion.

The suspect reached out his fist to Roman. "I appreciate you looking out for me, man."

Exhaustion dragged at Roman as he left the interrogation room. Playing the trustworthy friend was a mask he'd worn often, and it had earned him the confession.

The bullpen had gone still. A room built for noise left hollow by the hour. Only Simone lingered, pulling his jacket from the coat rack.

"That must've been hell," Simone said.

"It was." Roman worked a grain of sugar grit from his molars. "I hate Twizzlers."

Simone laughed, zipping up. "Thanks for taking one for the team. Those DAs can shove it now."

Roman scanned the empty bullpen. "Where's Grave?"

"He took off hours ago." Simone slipped out into the hall, the faint chime of the elevator following. "Saw the number on your desk. Sorry for messing with your plans."

The doors slid shut behind him.

Roman checked the digital clock at 1 a.m., right beside the napkin with Aniella's number, the edges worn thin.

He picked it up and studied the digits.

His pocket or the bin.

The pocket meant chasing the spark. Yielding to the unknown, to the way she'd unsettled his grip on control. The bin meant discipline, the distance he'd survived on.

# CHAPTER 5

## Buried Identities

Scott dug his nails into the football laces. "Go wide!"

"I'm as wide as I can get," Tyler said, hands up. "Pass it."

Tyler caught the ball and tucked it away just as Ethan crossed to their desks. "Hey, Captain. How's your morning going?"

"Where's Viento?"

Scott took Tyler's cue. "The, uh, coffee in the break room isn't that solid, and he was here till late last night."

"I know our coffee's garbage," Ethan said. "Tell him to see me when he gets back."

"Yes, Captain," they said in unison.

The football still rocked on the short filing cabinet beside Tyler's desk.

"You have too much time on your hands if you're standing around passing a football," Ethan said. "Get to work."

\* \* \*

The cafe bustled as the owner handed Roman a tray of coffee. "You're all set."
Roman reached for his wallet.

"Don't worry about it." The owner stuffed a wad of napkins between the coffee cups. "I'm sure you'll spend your share soon enough now that you're back around."

"You don't have to do that."

"Nonsense." The owner shuffled through the crowd toward the kitchen. "Tell the boys I said hi."

"Thanks. Will do," Roman said, backing away.

Roman pivoted toward the entrance and clipped a passerby. Lids hissed, napkins slid, and he leveled the tray before anything tipped out.

"Oh my goodness, I'm so sorry!"

He knew that soft-spoken lilt from anywhere.

"Aniella?"

She lowered her cupped hand from her mouth. "I didn't mean to bump into you like that. Can I help?"

Roman studied her kindness, her rosy cheeks, then checked his shirt. "I don't think anything spilled," he said, no longer caring about the coffee.

"Oh, that's good." Aniella moved aside for passing patrons, offering sweet smiles as they went by. "I'm so sorry."

*Is she clueless about how cute she is?* "It's nothing."

His phone chirped.

She twiddled the small charm on her necklace, attention settling on the napkins. "I'm glad your coffee survived."

"Not on a coffee run yourself?" he asked.

"I'm actually here to see if the cafe would donate nightly leftovers to the shelter."

The layers of selflessness kept piling.

"You're ambitious," he said. "Good for you."

"I'm normally so comfortable talking to people," she said, pressing her cheeks, "but I'm a little nervous about asking for free food."

He balanced the tray. "I know the owner if you want an introduction."

His phone chirped again.

"High demand?" she asked.

"Probably just my caffeine-addicted coworkers waiting on their fix."

Aniella let the charm on her necklace drop. "Is that why you couldn't call?"

*Not always shy.*

"I couldn't make the numbers out."

* * *

Ethan skimmed Roman's casual clothes, disapproval plain. "Two things."

Roman set his coffee on Ethan's desk. "Sure."

"Your whereabouts last night." Ethan paused. "And Craig."

*Mr. Loose Lips.*

Ethan cut in. "Roman."

"Interview ran long. And Craig's more valuable as a CI than a stat. I'm moving him that way."

"Not in my system you aren't." Ethan bent the corner of a folder. "There's no agreement, no control number, no initial debrief. By now, there should've been something logged."

"All respect, Captain, I don't want to be here any more than you want me to be. But I'm not gonna have my every move babysat."

"You're on paper duty. You shouldn't *be* moving. And you don't run free-range assets out of my house. Charge him or register him. Those are the lanes."

"Give me twenty-four. I'll bring you everything then."

"Twelve."

"Eighteen."

"I won't have my detectives negotiating my orders." Ethan flung a point at the door, his dandruff floating aimlessly in the office light. "Now get out of my office!"

\* \* \*

Aniella burst into Fern's apartment. "Oh my literal goodness!"

"Whoa." Fern came around the corner, shower cap on. "I know I said you don't have to knock, but for God's sake, at least do it."

Aniella clutched her purse to her chest, panic spilling out. "You'll never guess who I just ran into." She went to set her purse down, but nothing was free. "He didn't even try to make it up to me."

"You're spiraling."

"I saw Roman at a cafe. He didn't bring it up—I had to. And he didn't even try to make up for it." Aniella faced Fern. "He didn't even ask for another date. It was like it never happened."

"What a jackass." Fern swiped her phone open. "So will you finally let me set you up with George? He's *actually* interested."

\* \* \*

Roman nursed his drink at the bar, its low light throwing gold across the counter.

Scott draped his jacket over the seat beside him. "Long day?"

"You could say that."

The bartender polished a glass. "What'll it be?"

"Beer on tap," Scott said. He drew Roman's glass a few inches across the bar, the base dragging condensation along the wood.

"It's club soda," Roman said.

"Of course." Scott set a lime wedge on the coaster. "I heard some yelling earlier. What was up with you and the captain?"

Roman drew the glass back to him, trailing the same path of condensation. "They're forcing me back into the department."

"Did he give you a reason?"

"Didn't get into it." Roman took a sip of his soda.

Scott pushed the lime down the neck of his beer bottle. "Maybe this is good. You're back in homicide, and I don't have to worry about you as much."

The muted sports highlights flickered across the bottles.

"Yeah."

Scott tossed cash on the counter. "Do me a favor."

Next thing, Roman was at the pool table, soda on the edge as he racked the balls.

"Hey, remember that girl you saw a few times right before you left for New York?" Scott asked, chalking the cue.

"Yeah. Why?"

"Think I spotted her lookalike."

Roman smirked, lining up the pool cue to break. "Then you should've yelled 'Duck!'"

"Well, then…" Scott pointed his pool cue at the woman standing behind Roman. "Duck."

Roman turned, and before he could react, the woman seized his face and kissed him.

He caught her wrists and pulled them down. "What the hell are you doing?"

"Kissing you, dummy. Don't be such a jerk." She tore free. "Where have you been? Too busy to pick up the phone?"

Roman leaned close. "I'm not interested. That's it."

She snatched his drink and splashed it in his face. "Screw you then, asshole!" She stormed off.

Roman took the drench, soda pouring down his face. "Just when I thought this night couldn't get better."

Scott laughed, glancing around. "Sorry. No napkins."

Roman wiped his face with his shirt.

A loud thud of one man shoving another made them turn.

"No, don't do anything." Roman raised a hand in protest. "If it escalates, we'll deal with it."

A waitress stumbled, crashing down with a tray of cocktail glasses.

Scott rested his stick against the wall. "Escalated enough?"

* * *

Iver halted mid-stair when Roman and Scott entered the district with the men from the bar.

"Viento."

Roman's expression flattened.

"I'll take care of them," Scott said.

Roman released the drunk into Scott's hold.

He advanced on Iver, shadowed in a dark corner. "Hey, Chief."

"You been avoiding me?"

"No. I just needed a minute."

"Did you think it through? The opportunities, the extra cash?"

Roman checked the hall. "Yeah, I did."

"And?"

Roman measured the distance, the stairwell shadows stretching behind Iver. "I think I can help with it."

"I need your hundred percent."

"You have it, like always." Roman hesitated, taking in the corridor. "Polinski's on me about dress code. What am I supposed to do when I meet the crew, change like I'm Superman?"

"That's the least of your worries. Tread light."

"I'll be careful."

Iver reached into his pocket. "Here's your ID."

Roman took the ID. It matched the one he'd carried during his six-month operation.

"I pulled that quietly," Iver said. "Keep it buried."

Roman pictured the floor vent where he'd once stashed his father's gun. "I know a place."

54

# CHAPTER 6

## Things Left Unsaid

The low rumble of an outdated refrigerator filled the department's break room. Roman stood at the rusty sink, tugging at the tie that came with the captain's strict dress code. The counter beside the sink held a coffeemaker and a microwave, both inundated with coffee grounds. A long folding table stood at the room's center, surrounded by mismatched chairs. Along the far wall, vending machines embezzled more change than they gave in snacks, beside a bulletin board no one bothered to read.

"Where's Viento?" Ethan's accusatory tone from the bullpen stilled the detectives in their routines.

Still tugging at his tie, Roman leaned into the doorway. "Right here."

"You're off the desk." Ethan held out a slip.

Roman came into the bullpen. "What about the mountain of important files you said I had?"

"Now's not the time to be a smart ass." Ethan grimly scouted the room. "We've got a homicide. A minor. All hands on deck." He held the note against Roman's chest. "You're taking lead on it."

* * *

Yellow tape sealed off the area several yards from the brick apartment complex. Cameras flashed as forensic investigators collected evidence, while patrolmen kept reporters and stunned neighbors at bay.

Roman, Tyler, and Scott ducked under the tape, passing blood-streaked grass and a lone unlaced sneaker.

They approached a patrolman standing guard, a tarp stretched over a small body.

"What we got?" Tyler asked.

"Not sure, but something brutal," the patrolman said. "It was hectic when we got here, just trying to prevent neighbors from getting too close to this side of the building."

Roman lifted the tarp, revealing shredded muscle and dark clots seeping through torn flesh along the child's head, neck, and arms.

Tyler bent back. "Holy shit."

Scott cupped his mouth, gagging dry as he turned away. "Wasn't ready for that."

Roman knelt, the tarp reflection silvering his face as he studied the body.

A forensic tech snapped more photos. "Lacerations to the neck, multiple stab wounds in the right shoulder, chest, and left side of the head."

*Personal.* Roman lowered the tarp and stood. *This isn't where it happened.* He scanned the area. *Not enough blood on the ground.*

A bedraggled woman barreled toward them, breaking past patrolmen who tried to hold her back.

She stumbled into Roman's arms, nearly toppling. "Please! Find who did this! My poor boy!"

Roman caught and steadied her. "Who would do this?" He tried to meet her shifting face.

She sagged, clutching his shirt. "Please, detective, find who did this!"

Roman clasped her hand as her grip tightened. "Does he have enemies? Family he's argued with lately?"

The woman wailed, collapsing into the dirt, her body bowing with grief. "Why my son? My baby!"

Patrolmen hovered, waiting for Roman's signal to remove her.

"Get her some water and a blanket before you take her in," Roman said.

Once they led the woman away, Roman turned to see Scott hunched over, heaving up bile.

A forensic tech adjusted their camera strap. "He eat something bad last night?"

Tyler scraped his boot through the grass, the edge of a grin forming. "Probably dunked too many cookies in his whiskey."

Scott retch into the grass.

"Get it together, Hoffman," Roman said. "We've got work to do."

The woman's cry still carried from the patrol car, thin against the sirens.

* * *

"You've seen the offices at your disposal." Chase, from Human Resources, led two recruits into the bullpen. He read down a list of names in his folder. "Our on-site psychologist, Judy Shrub, isn't available right now, but you'll meet her soon. It's a unique opportunity to have her on-site."

The tour's tidy rhythm fractured when the bullpen doors burst open—two detectives hauled in a suspect, the hum dropping to a heavy silence. Another detective trailed behind, bile stains crusted across his shirt.

Chase slapped his binder closed. "Detectives."

Roman stopped mid-stride, hand dragging down his tie to flatten it. A breath passed before he spoke. "I'll be in, Grave. Give me a second."

Tyler hauled the suspect toward the interrogation room without looking back.

Chase guided the recruits forward, binder lifted in a half-salute toward Roman. "Good to have you back safely, Detective Viento." The binder flashed against the glass. "Meet our newest recruits, Brett O'Neil and Aniella Fasquelle. O'Neil, Fasquelle, meet Undercover Specialist and Homicide Detective Roman Viento."

Roman forced a grin. "Nice to meet you."

*Why is he introducing himself as if we've never met?*

Chase's mouth kept moving, but his words faded.

*A detective. His enigmatic demeanor makes more sense now. But why act like a stranger? He's a good liar.*

Unwilling to confront him in front of everyone, she took his outstretched hand. "It's nice to meet you as well."

Chase flipped a page in his binder. "O'Neil will be Hoffman's new partner. Fasquelle will serve as the Administrative Aid while she works toward her Intelligence Analyst title." He shut the binder. "I heard you're on the desk, Viento, so you'll have plenty of time to train them. They'll report to you for their first few weeks."

Roman's grin faltered. "I'm not on the desk anymore." He pointed toward the interrogation hallway. "And I gotta get in there." He started through the bullpen, the corridor narrowing around him before he disappeared inside.

Chase dropped his folder into his briefcase. "O'Neil, if you'd like, you can observe from the viewing room."

Aniella anchored her purse against her side. "May I please as well?"

\* \* \*

An overhead bulb cast a tired cone of light across the interrogation table.

Roman pulled the suspect's chair closer, locking its front legs beneath the table lip. "You're changing your story again."

The suspect crossed his arms tight. "I'm telling you facts."

"No," Roman said, boxing him in. "You're throwing shit at the wall to see what sticks."

"Enough bullshit," Tyler said. "Let's go over your whereabouts again."

"I don't know why where I was has anything to do with what happened to him."

Roman spread the photos across the table, one after another. "First you swore you hadn't been near his apartment. Then you said maybe you had but couldn't remember why. Now you're giving a ballpark time and reason you were there. If you're being honest, why does your story keep changing?"

"It's not changing. I'm remembering details." He angled away. "I can't help you with your case."

"You mean your nephew?" Roman asked. "Interesting way to describe something that personal."

The suspect's cuff seams strained under his tug. "You two want to piss back and forth while my nephew's killer is out there?"

Tyler and Roman stepped into the observation room, the tension following them in.

"This asshole." Tyler adjusted the blinds to half-view. "Where's Hoffman?"

"The anxious blond guy?" Aniella asked, eagerness spilling through. "With the stains on his—"

"He went home to shower and change," Brett said.

Tyler and Roman exchanged a look, a silent verdict between them.

"We gotta play his game," Roman said. "Get in his head."

"We can't go in there playing a different tune after that."

"We can. Let him sit a while."

"And if he asks for a lawyer in the meantime?"

"If I may?" Aniella's calm threaded through the heat, unshaken. "I might be able to get through to him."

Beads along the curtain rattled as Tyler pulled them down a notch. "To do what?" His challenge rode the noise. "What could you do?"

The current shifted, Roman tracking only her.

She brushed the charm at her collarbone. "A different approach might help."

Roman locked onto the brightness she exuded. Too sweet for a room like this, but unsettlingly steady.

"A *feeling?*" Tyler asked, the line thinning. "I don't know who you are, but we would never just let you walk right in there—"

"Go." Roman nodded at the interrogation room door. "Get in there." If she could soften him after Eli, maybe she'd have the same effect on the suspect.

The beads rattled again in Tyler's grip. "Are you crazy?"

"Give it your best shot," Roman said. "But go now."

The suspect's stare stalled, confusion clouding the room as Aniella entered. "Are you a lawyer?"

She sat across from him. "I'm sorry you had to deal with those guys." The ruffles on her blouse swayed as she settled in.

He checked her out openly. "Talk about inflated egos."

"And the fact they weren't respectful to you. At all."

The change in tone landed loud. His guard loosened, though his arms stayed clamped to his chest.

Aniella fluffed the ruffles at her collar. Roman tracked the movement. Was she steadying herself or drawing him out?

The suspect's gaze dropped lower.

"You like my blouse?" she asked, innocent enough to pass for small talk.

From the other side of the glass, Roman caught the way her movement held his attention. He couldn't tell if it was deliberate or just her unguarded grace. Either way, the suspect was loosening.

"I'm actually looking at your charm," the suspect said. "That's nice."

She rubbed the pendant, warmth in every word. "Oh, thank you! My grandma gave it to me. Wanna see it?" She rose, the charm picking up the table's glare as she drifted in, an unspoken cue flickering toward the glass.

"Yeah, let me take a look at that." His fingers twitched toward her, sleeve riding high.

Raw, jagged scratches marred his wrist. Confirmation of a struggle he'd hidden—until now.

Roman replayed the interrogation in his mind. His own focus fixed on breaking the man down while the suspect kept his arms locked to his chest. From the observation glass, Aniella must've seen what they'd missed.

The door jolted open and Roman and Tyler surged in. "Get out!"

Adrenaline spiked through Aniella as Roman's grip seized the suspect, wrenching him back into the chair. The thud rattled the table, the air turning cold in its wake.

Roman's command cut harder than the slam. "Not another move."

\* \* \*

Aniella didn't stay for the rest of the interview. From Roman's vantage, she poured herself into taming the chaotic administrative station, stacking rouge papers, lining up supplies, and finally arranging pale pink roses until every stem obeyed.

The bullpen stretched hollow as the hours of questioning dragged on. Finally, a confession was logged and a DNA swab from the suspect's wrists taken.

Roman and Tyler came down the hallway into the bullpen. Roman brushed past Tyler and went straight into the break room without sparing Aniella a look. Ethan followed him in.

Roman clenched a disposable cup between his teeth while filling another coffee on the counter.

"You let the not even an hour old administrative aid go into an interrogation room to question a suspect?"

Roman didn't need to look to know who it was. "I was right behind her," he said, his voice muffled by the cup wedged between his teeth.

"I don't know what shit they let you get away with in New York, but I've been running a tight ship since you've been gone, and you sure as hell won't be breaking anymore rules around here." Ethan moved in on Roman. "You risked the wrong case, not to mention the liability I'd have on my hands if something went sideways."

Roman noted Ethan's lack of control as he pulled the cup from his mouth.

"She got him warmed up to a confession. Is it that bad?"

Ethan's chin pinched. "Okay, *smartass*. Here's *this*, then. You're back on the bench. Got a problem with that?"

Roman bit the cup back and murmured between his teeth as he poured more coffee. "No, I love being a fuckin' yo-yo."

Ethan snatched the cup from Roman's mouth. "What did you just say?"

Their gaze fixed on one another.

"I understand," Roman said, a broken piece of styrofoam clinging to his lip. "Won't happen again."

With the break room open, Aniella had already seen Ethan jabbing at Roman mid-reprimand.

Moments later, Roman stepped into the bullpen and slowed at the admin desk, where Aniella was still perfecting the roses. She fussed, then fussed again, as if symmetry could hide whatever she was feeling.

"You okay?" he asked.

"Yes, thank you." Her tone stayed bright, but the strain threaded faintly beneath. "I hope I didn't cause trouble for you."

"It's nothing." Roman shifted toward the open break room, then pulled back to her. "What you did was sharp. What made you try that angle?"

She perched the vase of roses on the wall shelf. "When you and Detective Grave were interrogating him, I noticed he seemed concerned with keeping his arms to himself. More focused on that than on answering you. Even when you pressed him, he wouldn't budge. People don't normally hold that kind of posture unless they're hiding something."

"Hmm." Roman weighed that, the detail slotting into place. "Impressive."

"Thank you."

Hurt contained, not erased.

Her thanks lingered between them, but before Roman could reply, Scott called from the hall.

"Ro, you coming?" His fresh shirt hung loose, as if he'd rushed to change.

\* \* \*

Scott lingered at the records-room blinds, peeking through the slats. "What exactly do you need me to do?"

"Keep a lookout." Roman balanced a laptop on a dented filing cabinet shoved into the corner, the screen casting a glow. "Quietly."

"Sure, sure." Scott hovered. "What's, uh… what's the laptop for?"

"Don't ask."

Scott let out a thin laugh. "I think you should at least tell me something."

The keys clinked under Roman's steady rhythm.

"You gotta swear we won't get caught."

"We won't get caught." Roman handed him a key. "Top drawer, behind you. There's a kit inside."

Scott unlocked the drawer and drew out a black zippered case. He eased the zippers. On top lay a laminated sheet labeled: "Access Prohibited Unless Warranted by Authorized Personnel."

"I doubt we're authorized personnel."

Scott sifted through the case containing a tangle of cords, a tech box, a USB AirCard, and a cell phone. He flipped the sheet: Access and review of recorded evidence collected for Case Precinct0704-12.

"Rome, what the hell are you up to?"

"Just keep an eye out."

Scott handed him the case, then moved back to the window and parted the slates for another look.

Roman inserted the USB AirCard into the laptop. "It'll be quick."

Scott wiped his palms down his shirt, damp streaks darkening the fabric. "Man, I just changed this shirt."

"Relax."

"You don't know how anxiety works." Scott jerked from the slats. "Doyle's coming!"

Roman's focus stayed on the screen. "He never comes in here."

Scott dipped a slat, peeking through. "… Right."

Roman closed the laptop and held it out. "Can you keep this for me?"

"Isn't there dangerous stuff you shouldn't even have?"

"If this gets into the wrong hands, you'll wish it were only dangerous."

\* \* \*

The bullpen sagged with exhaustion, the day's weight draining them all.

Roman and Scott entered, their steps carrying a hush.

*Where have they been? Has Roman been calming him down?*

The two seemed close.

Brett leafed through the onboarding handbook. Tyler idled his mouse back and forth across the pad, the cursor aimed nowhere. The bullpen still functioned around them, but the atmosphere made her hesitate.

"The boy's mother called to thank everyone," she said. "She appreciates how quickly you solved her son's murder and all the work you put in."

The quiet stretched.

Roman sifted through paperwork, command always there. Easy one beat, steel the next.

*Is he reckless? Or did he have faith in me? He let me be alone with the suspect. Should I feel validated or unprotected?*

She liked getting to know people, to understand them. With him, it felt foolish. She kept watching. *He has tragedies to juggle, Aniella, not small talk. But is it today burdening him, or a whole history stacked on his back? And why pretend he didn't know who I was?*

"… Yes?" Roman stilled, brow hitching like he'd felt her questions.

*A dare I'd never win, as if he were saying,* guess all you want. You'll never see anything I don't show you.

She tucked the last box of staples into a drawer. "Do you not like to share much with people?"

He stayed still, hand deep in a box of files, faintly amused. "You ask a lot of questions."

*I only asked one.* "You seem difficult to get an answer out of."

"You noticed, huh?"

"I'm a curious person."

He rummaged through the files, mouth ticking like he'd already moved on. "I hadn't noticed."

He seemed untouchable. Yet maybe his humanity was still there, waiting to be found.

"If we're going to work together," she said, "we should probably know more."

"What makes you think I don't?"

She tilted her head, matching his dryness. "Because you just met me today, remember?"

He took her in, then pushed the box aside. "I know plenty. You're curious. You collect people." He set it on the floor and sat. "But I'm not your project."

Heat tinged her cheeks, the giveaway that always unraveled her courage. She sank into her seat, defeated.

*So much for the guy who helped me pick up my things. The one who donated food. The one who asked for my number. So much for thinking he had humanity. What a jerk.*

She let the sting settle, then realized it wasn't worth keeping.

*I was just trying to be nice. It's choosing kindness, even when it's pushed back. Other people's moods? That isn't about me.*

She gathered herself, then stepped to his desk and tried a small smile. "Only if you ask nicely."

Roman secured two files together with a paperclip. "About what?"

"About not trying to get to know you."

The paperclip snapped shut again, sharper this time. "I didn't ask nicely?"

His sarcasm needled under her composure, and she wished she hadn't approached him again.

She steadied. "Requests usually come with some courtesy. Maybe try saying 'please.'"

"Do it," he said, something locking behind his face. There and gone. "I'll thank you after."

The bullpen seemed to shift. A shadow under control. He showed nothing, yet something still slipped.

Iver stepped into view and Roman stood.

"If you'll excuse me."

Polite. Too polite.

Roman disappeared into Iver's office and the blinds slid shut.

*A lot of private conversations go on in this place.*

\* \* \*

"Let Polinski keep you benched." Iver reached into a dish and cracked a nut shell open. "He thinks he's punishing you."

Roman stopped beside the filing cabinets. "A heads up would've been nice."

"You're good on your feet. Don't act like you need one."

"Polinski's got me babysitting rookies. How's this supposed to work?"

"That's his leash." Iver chewed, then flicked the shells in the bin. "Juggle both. He'll throw a tantrum if I let you off the hook." He circled the desk. "But it works for us. Tell Polinski you've got to grab a few things from your locker in New York. I've got a job for you."

Iver dropped another shell into the bin, the crack lasting as long as the pause. "I need this flawless."

Roman grabbed for the handle. "You got it."

"Your life was confidential when you were undercover. Now it stays that way. Every piece of it."

# CHAPTER 7

## The Silent Mask

Rain slicked the gravel outside an abandoned warehouse as Kirk hauled the final freight box from the truck. Overhead, clouds churned, heavy and low.

The warehouse by the water had once been a graveyard for wrecked eighteen-wheelers. Seagulls, filthy from the muddy shore, circled as the only company now.

Wes waited at the warped doorway, the wood swollen from years of damp. "Kirk. We're all waiting."

Inside, concrete pillars broke through stacks of freight boxes, cluttering the open space.

Kirk levered open a crate packed with guns. "Everything's here."

"And the semi-automatics?" Wes asked. "When will they be ready to ship back to New York?"

"Couple weeks," Roman said, prying open another crate. "All on schedule."

"Nice," Wes said. "We gotta get the handguns into the briefcases."

A gull's cry knifed through the warehouse. Rain pressed harder through the ceiling cracks, insistent. Someone was here.

Julian stepped in, braces binding two fingers, his stare fixed on Roman.

Air rasped through Roman's teeth, the taste of rust and bitterness clinging to it. "Hey, business partner. Long time."

"Really? I thought it hadn't been soon enough."

Wes snapped a briefcase open, the latches filling the gap. "Good. Then we're all partners again. Iver said everything funnels through Roman now. He wants distance."

Julian stepped closer, water dripping from his jacket. "Since when did you become the middleman? I didn't even know you knew Iver."

Wes cut in. "That raid you missed? Roman made his one phone call to Iver, and the charges disappeared. Whole reason we're standing here."

Kirk loaded handguns into a briefcase. "If Roman wasn't worth something, Iver wouldn't make him the bridge now."

The silence that followed wasn't agreement, just acceptance. Julian needed Roman, whether he liked it or not.

Julian held out a folded note. "Guess we'll see if he stays useful. Bring a briefcase."

Wes nudged a spent shell with the side of his boot, sending it skittering across the concrete. "You act like he broke your fingers in your sleep. Your hands were around his throat, remember? What'd you expect the man to do?"

Roman reached for one of the cases, the metal clasps clicking shut. He hadn't taken the note.

The note snagged against the braces binding Julian's broken fingers. "Go ahead." His words carried a false ease. "I'll play nice."

\* \* \*

Aniella's heels clicked as she approached the admin station. "Good afternoon, everyone!" She set fresh roses in the vase, their sweet nectar rising, then pressed play on her voicemail.

"Morning, Fasquelle." Scott swept crumbs off the desk. "Grave. Captain wants you on Simone's double homicide."

Tyler smacked the mouse against the pad. "Again? This is the third case on top of my own. Where the hell is Viento?" He snatched his raincoat. "Anyone know where he went?"

Aniella kept half her ear on the exchange, tending to a petal that strayed.

"Uh, Italy, I think."

"He's on vacation?" Tyler asked.

"Yeah, well, not for work. Since he's reintegrating, they let him visit family—his mom." Scott crammed another bite of cookie in. "He's visiting her."

Cookie mush clung between Scott's teeth as he mumbled through a mouthful. Aniella lingered, entertained despite the tension.

"Must be nice getting vacation," Tyler said.

"Not too nice." Scott's words were barely clear. "His mother's sick."

"Aw, now I feel like a jerk," Tyler said.

"Yeah, it's unfortunate."

"I'm being sarcastic, Hoffman. Everyone gets sick. Am I supposed to call off every time life comes up?"

Tyler stormed past Simone in the hallway.

"He's having a day," Simone said, dragging his chair out. "Who ruffled him?"

Scott spat the mush of cookie into a napkin. "Not sure," he said. "I'm grabbing coffee. Want some?"

"I've already chugged four cups of that shit today," Simone said. "I'll overdose on caffeine if I have any more."

A rainbow arched across the windowpane, streaking color against the bullpen's gray. Aniella imagined basking in it, free for a moment.

"I can grab your coffee, Scott," she said. "That way you don't have to stop what you're doing."

"Well, I'm just eating cookies at the moment, but thanks. I take mine with two creams and a sugar."

She grabbed her purse. "Two creams and a sugar coming up!"

\* \* \*

Roman spotted movement across the street. Bright, quick, impossible to miss. Aniella, purse swinging, half-skipping down the block like the morning belonged to her.

She called out before he could turn away.

"Hey! How are you?"

Roman pivoted, his grin delayed. "Hey…"

"I thought you were in Italy." Her purse strap slipped down her shoulder, and she nudged it higher.

Roman bent closer as if he hadn't heard her, then stopped himself and straightened. "I just got back."

Her smile stayed guileless, but he knew better. If she was playing harmless, he'd seen that act before.

"Oh, welcome back!" She looped a strand of hair around her finger. "I was just grabbing coffee for Scott. Want to come?"

The strand coiled tighter, knotting in circles.

"Another time." He walked on.

She tucked her hair back and trailed after him. "If you didn't mind, tell me why you…"

His attention skimmed past her, tracking the street. "I don't have time for this, Fasquelle."

"I'll just take a second," she said lightly. "I've been so curious. I should've asked before, but—"

Roman halted and squared her, his height casting a shadow over her petite frame. "It's not a good time."

For a moment, everything stilled. Her lashes gave the faintest beat, as though the world had skipped.

Roman stepped back, then turned.

She quickened her pace to match his strides. "Is it because you know what I'm going to ask?"

"No. I've got somewhere to be." His voice frayed in the traffic's din.

"I would just like a quick explanation. If you could, please just tell me why."

He reached the driver's side of a car, the hinge groaning as it opened. "I don't have time."

She met him on the passenger side. "It'll just take a second." She blinked. "Please?"

His thumb struck sharp against the roof's metal. "Can't right now."

"That's okay!" She yanked the passenger handle and ducked inside. "We can talk in the car."

His expression pinched, then went flat. "Are you kidding?" He braced the frame. "I thought you were shy."

She shut the door with a snap. "Only when I get in my head."

"Then get back in your head."

She froze, then stretched the seatbelt until it clicked across her. "Too late."

"Not to be rude, but I need you to get out."

"Oh, now you're concerned about being rude?" She folded her arms. "Don't start now."

"This isn't my car, and I'm not supposed to have anyone in it." He took a beat, temper held. "Now get out."

"Maybe if you asked nicely."

His thumb struck against the metal again. He tugged out his phone, checking the time. He scanned the street once more. Pressure mounting, he dropped into the driver's seat and started the engine.

She went quiet, as if unsure what came next.

Roman geared it into drive and zagged through traffic, checking the rearview mirror.

She cleared her throat. "So... you were saying you just got back from Italy?"

"Yeah." He checked the mirror again as he merged onto the highway. "But that's not what you wanted to talk about, right?"

"No, I…" She clutched her seatbelt tighter as the speedometer needle chittered. "How fast are we going?"

His hold locked on the wheel.

"Where are we going?" she asked.

"We? We're not going anywhere. I'm dropping you off at the nearest gas station."

"You'd literally drop a woman off at a gas station by herself in the middle of nowhere?"

"We're not in the middle of nowhere."

"It is for me." Her tone went brittle. "I'm not from here." She angled to the window, posture locked into a poised stillness.

The silence grew dense. He let her carry it, waiting for her to break. She didn't. Every second stretched, his discomfort grinding deeper.

His hold cinched tighter on the wheel. "We, uh. We have to get this car back to the friend I borrowed it from."

"It's okay, you can just drop me off. I'll be fine."

The wheel went rigid under his grip. "That was out of line," he said. "I apologize."

By the time he finally took the exit, the sun had fallen, the road steering them toward a deserted town.

Roman eased the car onto the dirt road and let it idle. "They don't like guests. You'll be safe here. I'll be back."

Aniella's purse strap slid higher on her shoulder as she climbed out. A porch light glowed faintly ahead. Roman shifted the car into gear and drove off.

Gravel scattered under the tires when he returned. She stood exactly where he'd left her, as if she were rooted there.

Roman pulled over and pushed the passenger side open.

She drew back. "*This* is yours?"

"No." He gave a quick chuckle. "My engine light came on, so he took it to the shop." He nudged the frame wider. "Come on, we're taking this one."

She hesitated, then climbed in as though the truck might soil her. Wind rippled through her hair as she shut the door, a strand trapped in the seam.

Roman glanced toward her. "Did your hair just get stuck in the door?"

"Yes." She freed the strand. "I've been meaning to cut it, but I can't part ways." Her nose wrinkled. "Why does it smell like...?"

"Raw meat?"

"Ew, that's exactly it. It's disgusting."

"So you're a toughie, huh?"

She flipped her hair over her shoulder. "What's that supposed to mean?"

"'Ew, meat,'" he mocked, jamming the truck into reverse.

Her laugh burst quick, unguarded.

Roman grabbed the wrapped packet beside him. "Owner runs a meat shack downtown, uses this truck for runs. He gave me ground beef." He held it out. "Want it?"

"That's the strangest gift I've ever heard of."

"Suit yourself." He set it back.

Relief steadied him. The packet wasn't beef at all. It was an unregistered handgun tied to a job he couldn't let anyone trace.

They headed back down the dirt road.

Aniella twisted her bracelet. "Was that his briefcase, too?"

"What's that?"

"There was a briefcase tucked underneath the back right seat when we were on our way up here."

Roman arched a brow. "Hm."

"I'm excruciatingly observant," she said with a slight shrug. "It's kind of a curse."

"Then it must've been his too. The car, the briefcase, everything in it. Makes sense, doesn't it? It's his car."

Aniella studied him, searching. Roman kept to the road ahead.

"You wanna talk about it?" he asked.

She inched away from the grimy armrest. "About what?"

"Why I pretended not to know you."

She rested an elbow on the armrest. "You knew that's what I wanted to ask you?"

"Excruciatingly observant." The corner of his mouth edged up. "Kind of a curse."

She leaned off the sticky fabric. "All jokes aside, I'd like to know."

"If anyone found out we knew each other, even a little, they'd have assumed you got the job through me. You'd have been marked before you started. I didn't want that for you." His delivery was even, the lie steady on his tongue.

"Why didn't you just tell me that?" she asked.

"You went along with it." He lifted a shoulder, casual on purpose. "You never brought it up. If you wanted to know, you'd have asked sooner."

The sour air carried her irritation, close enough to catch. He let the quiet stand. Distance always brought him control.

He reached for the radio dial. The speakers spilled rapid Spanish lyrics.

"Can you understand Spanish?" she asked.

"I get by."

"What are they singing about?"

The lyrics translated easily. Clothes on the floor, limbs tangled, sex.

The seat creaked under his movement. "Something about…" Heat surged, foreign and unwelcome, unfamiliar in a way he couldn't recall, before he shut it down. "Actually, my Spanish is rusty."

He snapped the radio off.

The sun was gone, hours pulled out from under them since leaving the city.

"Since you seem more suited to a café than a gas stations, where should I drop you off?" he asked.

"I was supposed to spend the night at my friend's house." She keyed Fern's address into her phone and slid it onto the console. "So, what's it like being a detective?"

"What's it like? I don't know."

"Have you ever regretted becoming a detective?"

"No." He watched the highway narrow ahead, streetlights thinning to fields. "But I respect how difficult it can be."

She shifted slightly, her bracelet chiming. "What do you mean?"

"Friends and family don't get how much it changes the way you think."

"Like what?" She adjusted the charms.

"For one, it's easy to get suspicious over little things."

"Is that the worst of it? Being suspicious?"

"There are other habits the job drills into you. They don't translate well outside it."

"Habits like what?" she asked, letting the charms fall.

"Like never doing the same thing too often. You don't want anyone to know your patterns."

"Doesn't that stop people from getting to know you?"

"Yeah." The dashboard glow cut across his face. "It does."

"Isn't that a bad thing?"

"In my line of work, it's a good thing."

"You already told me I ask a lot of questions, so what's another?"

Roman eased the truck a lane over, engine ticking. "Sure. What is it?"

"What's the hardest part of undercover at first that you've mastered now?"

He adjusted the vent, the rush of heat filling a brief pause. "Getting inside people's heads. You don't go in to shift their mindset, you go in to learn theirs. Instinct says reject it, but the job makes you adapt. Over time, you end up collecting people's random pieces, and it changes you, whether you want it to or not."

She let herself rest into the seat, her voice softening. "Then I'm glad you mastered it, though it sounds like a lesson no one should have to learn."

\* \* \*

75

Roman pulled into Fern's driveway. "GPS says we're here," he said.

She didn't respond.

He leaned toward the passenger side. "Aniella."

Her head had tipped back, the dash glow spreading across her features. Even asleep she looked angelic, like beauty belonged to her.

He nudged her shoulder. "Aniella."

Nails tapped against the glass of the passenger window. Fern waved at Roman from the outside and pulled the door wide. Aniella jolted forward, steadying on the seat before her feet found the gravel.

"Oh, wow." Aniella blinked hard, a crease from keep marked across her cheek. "How long was I asleep?"

"I told you, you've been working too much!" Fern's grin flicked toward Roman. "And you are?"

"I work with Sleepy Head," he said.

"Oh no, don't let that turn into my nickname at work."

"It's our secret," he said.

"Thank you for the ride." Her words softened into a smile. "Good night, Roman."

"Night."

Roman waited until Aniella got into Fern's apartment safely, then rolled the truck down the street. He pulled out his phone and called Scott.

Scott answered, already stammering. "Hey, I really tried not to be Mr. Loose Lips, but I know that's probably why you're calling."

"I ran into Fasquelle from across the diner. Why did she think I was in Italy?"

"You were near the diner? I told Tyler you were away. She must've overheard me. I'm sorry, that was the best I could come up with on a whim."

"You didn't have to come up with anything. Hackett told Polinski I was in New York. I didn't know where she'd heard Italy from, so I went along with it. It's another lie I have to keep up with."

"Grave was giving me a hard time and I freaked out, I'm sorry. I don't know why I made up Italy."

Roman held the phone tighter. "You gotta keep your nerves in check."

"You know I never have bad intentions, Ro."

"It's not about intentions. You're the only one I trust, and I'm risking a lot to keep this under wraps. If anyone gets curious, it goes bad fast. People only know what you tell them, so from now on, don't tell them anything."

Fern's lit window flickered in the side mirror, Aniella somewhere inside.

"She's observant. Be careful what you say around her."

# CHAPTER 8

## Close Enough

The phone trilled across Aniella's desk, slicing through the bullpen's daily shuffle.

She lifted the receiver with practiced cheer. "Thank you for calling major crimes Twenty-Ninth District Homicide department. How may I direct your call?"

"Thank you so much for calling." Tyler layered on the sweetness until it cloyed, a caricature of her cheer.

Simone nearly sprayed coffee across his paperwork. "Be nice," he said, choking down a laugh.

Aniella switched the receiver to her other ear. "I can't understand you. May I put you on a brief hold?" She cupped her free ear against the distraction. "Sir? I'm going to place you on a brief hold. One moment, please." She pressed the button and turned toward the detectives. Both were suddenly riveted by their computer screens, lips sealed tight. "Do either of you speak Spanish?"

"Phew." Tyler tapped the mouse like it owed him money. "I thought you put them on hold to yell at us."

"Have Roman take it," Simone said.

"His Spanish is a little rusty," she said. "Can one of you take it?"

Tyler swiveled toward her, a laugh riding out. "Where'd you hear that?"

"From him," she said.

"Don't know why he would've told you that." Tyler laughed again, turning back to his screen. "He can take the call."

The hold light flashed on, seconds stacking while the caller waited.

"So if he's the only one that can take it, where is he?"

"Break room," Tyler said, dry. "Unless he's in Italy again."

Aniella patched the call to Roman's line and walked to the break room, where he poured coffee into a chipped mug.

"I transferred a call to your desk," she said. "They're on hold."

Roman looked up from the pour. "I'll be right there." Her stance in the doorway held steady. "What's with the look?"

"Nothing."

Roman returned to his desk, coffee in hand, and picked up the line. "Detective Viento."

"Hola, soy Craig. Sé que se supone que no debo llamar a la comisaría, pero no prude comunicarme con usted en su celular y necesito reunirme con usted."

Roman paused, attention drifting toward Aniella's steady stare.

Her stare held, reading more than he meant to show.

He shielded the mouthpiece and angled slightly aside. "Where?"

"Mmhm." Aniella flipped open her admin binder.

Roman hung up. Before he could speak, Ethan stepped into the bullpen.

"Fasquelle?"

"Yes, Captain?"

"Burglary's buried in calls on the second floor. Their admin's out. Can you cover?"

She flicked Roman a glance as she stood. He offered a half grin she didn't return.

"Certainly."

* * *

Craig scuffed his sneakers against the pavement, brand-new but already worn in. "Didn't you tell me not to break the law?"

A couple hurried by the alley's edge, their umbrella tilting to block the view.

"If I tell you not to, you don't," Roman said. "If I tell you to break it, you do."

Craig ground his shoe through a puddle, sludge rippling out. "You said hit you up if I heard anything worth a damn. You also said be ready when you call. I figured that went both ways." Water dripped from the fire escape above, marking seconds. "I've been hanging near Kirk, but Wes ain't warming up. You told me not to push, so I didn't."

A metal sign shuddered on its chain above the dumpsters, the wind swinging between them.

"Get to it, Craig."

"Been keeping my ear to the ground, like you said. Julian's talking, a lot, saying it's weird you went dark after Iver pulled everyone out. Kirk don't push it, but Julian? He wasn't buying the ghost move. Think you should iron it over with them."

A loose scrap drifted down the alley.

"… Thanks, Craig."

Craig held his hand out flat. "That worth anything? Could be lifesaving."

Roman gave a slow nod, stepping closer. "You're either running old gossip, or he's testing you. I'm leaning stale." He stayed flat. "Life-saving Craig? If it was, you showed up too late."

A crumpled bag skated across the puddle, tracing swirls before sinking.

"Not my fault you take forever to respond," Craig said.

"So keeping you out of jail is an opportunity you wanna shit on?"

A weak gust slipped through the alley.

"You right, you right."

Roman clocked Craig's clothes. Same as last time. "You staying clean?"

A loose drip from the gutter seemed to stall mid-fall.

"What?"

"Answer the question."

"I'm straight."

Roman peeled out a few bills and held them out. "Get clothes. Or whatever you need."

Craig grabbed the bills, but Roman's grip wouldn't release them.

"I need you predictable, Craig," Roman said, the bills drawn firm between them. "If I can't predict you, I can't trust you. And if I can't trust you, you're no good to me." He let the warning sit. "Don't pull this shit again."

\* \* \*

The detectives crowded around Simone's monitor as the footage advanced frame by frame.

"Here's where he goes inside," Simone said.

"That him?" Roman asked.

Simone inched closer to the screen. "Yep. Purple cap."

"First mistake." Roman gave a single shake. "Fashion's a crime too."

The suspect drew a gun and fired at the clerk.

Brett covered his face in his sleeve, dodging the image.

Simone snagged Brett's arm. "Watch, O'Neil."

"I don't know how you watch that on repeat," Brett said.

"Not all of us can," Simone said. "That's why Hoffman's missing the fun."

"You miss things that matter to the victim's family," Roman said. "Think of it that way."

"There's nothing to miss," Brett said. "He whips a gun and pops off."

"And after the clerk dropped?" Roman asked. "Or did you check out?"

Brett stalled. "I'm not sure... I stopped watching."

Simone reversed the clip, the replay flickering as the shooter vaulted the counter.

"He's about to scoop the register," Brett said.

"No," Simone said. "Stay with it."

The shooter nudged the clerk with his foot, bent to check for life, then left without touching the till.

"That's the angle you'd use," Roman said, spine straightening. "Without this, interrogation's guesswork. Roll it back but slow it down."

Simone adjusted the playback, the motion slowing until each frame crawled.

"Freeze it." Roman tapped the monitor at a single frame.

"What am I missing?" Brett asked.

"The hesitation," Roman said. "The way he holds the gun, the stance before the shot. He almost pulls back."

The screen's footage spilled across Brett's notes. "It's quick. Blink and you miss it."

"That's why you don't blink," Roman said.

The chair's casters rolled an inch as Simone cut the feed.

"That's enough training today." Simone slid his notes to Brett. "Hope this helps."

"Thanks," Brett said, taking the notes.

Simone stepped out, leaving Roman and Brett in the bullpen.

"I'll take advantage of your time," Brett said. "How do you spot lies so easy?"

"Learn to trust your gut."

Brett clicked a pen, then braced over his pad, expecting more.

The cursor on Simone's empty workstation flashed once as Roman spoke. "It's not really something you can write down. It happens with time and experience."

Brett shrugged. "Anything could help though. How's time and experience taught you how to do it?" The pen held tight in Brett's grip.

Roman took in the bullpen glass, debating if it was worth the effort. "You don't always need facts to know someone's lying. You just need to present evidence well enough to make them admit it. The pause trap is a good one."

"What's the pause trap?"

"People hate silence," Roman said. "Stay quiet after they finish, and they'll fill it. It's usually something incriminating."

"That's good to know." Brett scrawled notes, but the pen jammed mid-line.

Roman slid a spare his way. "Try jumping around the timeline. A suspect rehearses in order. Break that, and their story starts to tangle."

"Definitely going to give that a try," Brett said, ink staining his palm. "What else should I know?"

Roman rested against the desk. "Ever heard of ERC?"

Brett stared blankly, pen frozen over the pad.

"Extract, read, control," Roman said. "Extract information, read them, and control the conversation."

"I like that." Brett's pen sped up. "What's it look like?"

Roman crossed one shoe over the other. "Hyper-awareness. Read fear, anticipation. Any crack they give away."

"How's that?"

"Set the base. Talk casual, like you're pals. Sports, cars, whatever keeps them talking."

The quiet stretched. Then the desk shook under a sharp impact, the sound clean, deliberate.

Brett's pen fell from his grip. "Shit!"

"Why'd you jump?"

"Cause you scared me."

"You perceived a threat. So if we're talking baseball or cars, and suddenly I ask where you were last night at eleven, you react. Any hitch shows you felt the hit. Why? Because I'm digging at what you want to protect."

Brett underlined the phrase three times, the notepad nearly tearing. "That's genius."

Roman's heel brushed the tile once, a rhythm of approval. "It's effective."

* * *

The elevator opened on its chime. Roman caught Aniella stepping out, back from Burglary for her purse.

The bullpen sat hollow, phones asleep, copier idle. She slowed at the corner where a lone lamp pooled light across her station.

Roman stayed at his desk, head pressed into his palm as if the weight belonged there. Papers sprawled across an open file. The pen turned slow between his fingers, rhythm without thought.

The chair gave a tired creak, then stilled.

She lingered at the lamp's edge, her voice small against the hum. "Do you need help with anything?"

Roman's pen stilled mid-spin. The space between them held, unfamiliar in its ease.

"I'm good," he said.

"Okay." She hitched the strap higher on her shoulder. "Have a good night."

The chair gave another complaint as he stood. "You heading out?" He noted what wasn't there. No keys in her hand, no ring clipped to her bag. "How are you getting home?"

"Oh, I take a taxi or an Uber."

"You wait outside in the dark?"

"Not a far cry from a random gas station."

He let it pass. "You're still at the shelter?"

She folded in on herself. "Do you disapprove of that too?"

"It's admirable," he said. "What you do." Roman closed the file on his desk. "I just finished up. I'll take you home."

"Oh, no. It's probably out of your way. I don't want to be a bother."

The thin fabric on her shoulder wouldn't keep out the cold.

"It's not a bother," he said. "Wait here."

He crossed to the break room and returned with a thick mustard sweater. "Here."

She took it, her hold faltering as citrus notes clung to the knit.

"… I can grab another if you don't like it," he said.

"It's fine." Too quick, betraying the stall.

Roman adjusted his footing. "What is it?"

"It's nothing."

"Nothing?" The clock ticked through his patience. "You're making it louder by avoiding it."

She turned aside, then back. "Why are you so curious? It's not a case."

"I can't help it. The more you dodge, the more I want to hear what it was."

She paused. "I'm not dodging. It's just… this doesn't seem like your style, that's all."

"Not my style." He echoed it, flat.

"I didn't mean the sweater not being your style, I…"

He let her last beat fade. "Then what did you mean?"

"It just doesn't smell like…" The sweater bunched under her grip.

Roman pieced it. "You thought it was mine." He leaned back on the desk edge, grounding his weight. "But the cologne's different. You knew it wasn't."

She went still, as if he had pressed somewhere private.

"That was it," he said, more statement than question.

The copier's indicator light blinked red, imitating her embarrassment. "You, uh… usually rustic. Or aquatic." She couldn't keep till, even in place. "Something like that."

Pressure gathered at his mouth, held tight.

"What?" she asked.

The pressure broke wider despite him. "I think it's interesting you know my scent."

"It's not that I know your scent, *per se*. I just never…"

"It's Hoffman's," he said, rescuing her from having to finish. "He keeps a spare in the break room."

She scrunched the knit. "That makes sense."

The room itself seemed to reset. Nothing aligned the same.

"What about what you're wearing?" he asked.

She lagged half a second before she answered. "Blackberry vanilla mix," she said, the words tripping.

"It suits you."

Her cheeks warmed again. "Thank you. I wear it every day."

He allowed the line a softer landing. "I know."

The clock ticked sharp, each beat too loud for the hollow room.

She drew back a fraction. "Can I ask you something?"

He left the space open.

"Why did you never call?"

The tension thinned, the clock's second hand breaking the stillness. "A case ran long."

"You could have texted."

"You're right. I could've." The desk shifted faintly under his movement, the motion closing the height between them.

She drew back another step. "There's another question. If I don't ask now, I never will."

He was steady. "Go ahead."

"I thought your Spanish was rusty."

A rare laugh broke loose until he smothered it with a cough. "Ah, ha."

"Why lie about something as simple as speaking another language?"

"The song wasn't workplace material." His focus stayed where it should.

She readied a word.

The floor seemed to draw them closer.

"Your turn to share something," he said.

The copier's standby light pulsed across him as he stepped once, twice. She backed until her spine met Tyler's desk.

Roman waited, time thinning through every flicker of her hesitation. No push, no save. Her hand searched for balance, skimming until a stapler slid off and clattered to the tile.

He widened back half a pace. "Sorry."

She steadied against the desk, while he forced the want down, letting it harden into something unnamed. The moment sat between them, fragile and unfinished.

Roman checked the hall. "Come on. I'll take you home."

* * *

He tossed his keys on the entryway table and switched on a light. Numbness hit, same as always, the moment he crossed his threshold. Nights brought the same routine, bad dreams if he slept at all. He cracked the window. The wet street crept in with the rain. He yanked his tie loose, left it hanging, and buried his hands in his pockets. His focus tracked past the city lights, reaching for nothing. The job left him scraped raw, demand after demand.

And now Aniella, complication on top of complication. Worse than the hours were the lies. He hated every one of them. Rain distorted his reflection in the glass, splitting it apart in streaks. He shut the window. Hunger gnawed at his gut, but he was too tired to answer it. He shuffled to the bedroom and let his body drop on the bed.

*Get up. Change. Shoes off. Lights.*

He gave himself the order but stayed flat, staring at the ceiling until exhaustion forced him under.

* * *

"No—" The word tore out of him in the dark.

A gun lifted.

His mother's scream.

Blood flooding the floor.

A bang.

The mattress bucked beneath Roman, the dark tearing open. Sweat slicked his skin, pulse hammered his ribs.

It took him a moment to remember where he was, to separate the past from the present.

His bedroom.

His bed.

Four walls that weren't closing in.

He dragged a trembling hand down his face, the chill from the window cutting through the night.

"Not again."

The room held still, fractured only by a car alarm down the street.

But the silence didn't offer comfort. It pressed in on him.

His nightmares had been dull for weeks, hushed whispers of old wounds.

But tonight was different.

The past clawed its way out of the grave, pulling him under.

The dream had returned with teeth.

And he knew why.

Aniella.

# CHAPTER 9

## Missed Chances

The bubbler gurgled, water hiccupping as Roman filled a plastic cup from the tarnished fountain spout.

"Good afternoon!" Aniella said, cheer brightening the corridor.

Her entrance and greetings always lifted the department's usual drag, brief but undeniable.

Her heels marked a brisk rhythm along the tile as she entered the break room. "Good afternoon, Roman."

He sipped from the cup. "Afternoon."

"Thank you again for taking me home last night."

He drank, the water standing in for an answer.

Aniella fed coins into the vending machine. "I'm trying to save my appetite for lunch, but the craving for chips won't go away."

She tapped the display button. Again. Again. The machine didn't budge.

Roman stepped in. "Takes a few kicks." He rocked the machine until the bag dropped free.

"Oh, you're a lifesaver. Thank you." She drifted toward the drink machine, pace light, almost playful. "Can you stay a second in case this one robs me too?"

*Now.* Roman lifted a cup from the break table and held it out.

She paused over the cup. "For me?" Steam curled from the lid's opening, sugary and heavy. "You… you got me hot chocolate?" Coins chimed across the table as she set them down and took the drink.

"I've never seen you with coffee," he said, hoping he'd guessed right.

Her pause made it clear she hadn't expected him to notice something so small.

"That's it." Tyler's shout cut across from the bullpen. "Who let a raccoon loose on my desk? And where's my stapler?"

… The stapler.

Aniella etched grooves into the cup with her nail.

… Last night.

Roman tipped his cup until the ripples settled.

The memory was there, unsaid.

"I, um…" Her hesitancy pulled them back into the break room. "I've…"

He held. *What does she want to tell me?*

Her nails clicked against the glowing red digits on the display. "I've been trying to eat healthier… but it's hard. Especially when Scott keeps bringing cookies."

*That wasn't it.* "You want me to arrest him?"

"Ha, no. I… um…"

He lowered his cup. "Everything okay?"

She gathered the coins one at a time into her palm. "Yes! Absolutely."

The overcompensation rang clear.

"You sure?"

"Yes, thank you." She brushed past him, the hot chocolate raised between them as if it might ward off whatever lingered between them. "I have to use the ladies' room."

In the bullpen, a bouquet dominated Aniella's station. The roses she usually kept perched on her cubby were small and polite. These were different. Bold, planted dead center, with a note jutting out.

He sat, checked voicemail, skimmed email. But the colors blared, hollering. He glanced toward the hallway that led to the ladies' room, then back at the bouquet. The note dared him.

He took a pen from his desk and moved closer.

*Sympathy card? Birthday note? Congratulations?*

Aniella returned, one last click of her heel before she halted at her desk. "Did you need something?"

"Returning a pen." He set it down.

She eyed the holder crammed with pens on his desk, an unspoken question hanging.

*Ding.*

The elevator slid open, and a young man strode out with a ready smile, heading straight for Aniella.

"George." Aniella's hand brushed the vase, almost involuntarily. "I thought you were meeting me downstairs." She checked the clock. "You're early."

"They sent me up," George said, giving Roman a wordless nod. "I hope that's okay."

Aniella twisted around. "I just have to grab my purse." She pulled it from the cubby, then scanned the bullpen, as if hoping for someone other than Roman.

But the bullpen was empty.

At last she turned his way. "I'm taking an early lunch."

Roman lifted his gaze, flat. "Enjoy your lunch."

Aniella and George crossed back to the elevator, their steps fading, leaving Roman with the bouquet and hot chocolate.

George pressed the first-floor button. "I can sense when another man's interested," he said. "I'd hate to go after someone whose heart's already taken."

"Oh no. You don't need to worry. We're just coworkers. Strictly platonic."

George pressed the first-floor button again, as if to seal her answer. "I'll take your word for it."

"Yes, please do." She stepped inside as the elevator chimed open. "Thank you for the flowers."

* * *

Cardboard boxes stamped with detergent logos lay split open, filled with anything but detergent. Rust-ringed mop buckets sagged in a corner, sloshing dirty water.

Kirk swiped the tablet, the screen uploading. "DOB matches. Recovery email's clean. We move?"

Wes flipped a laundry basket upside down, its plastic ribs bowing as he leaned into it. "We move."

Kirk shoved the tablet at Roman. "You're the one who can sell it. Talk like you were born on that account."

Roman scanned the cold numbers. "Yeah, they'll believe I'm them." He dialed. "Here we go."

The line clicked alive.

"I'll need to verify your identity first," the call-center woman said.

He slid into the role instantly, voice smooth, professional, believable. Account number. Date of birth. Routing. Checking. He delivered them like he'd rehearsed a hundred times, though none of them had. The confirmations kept her typing.

"Mother's maiden name?" the woman asked.

That wasn't on the tablet.

The room held stiff, waiting for Roman to cover the gap. He stalled, the beat buying them seconds. "I'll spell it out for you."

Craig ripped through the cluttered shelves for anything to write on. A box of dryer sheets sat across the room, out of Roman's reach. He snapped once, sharp. Kirk lunged and grabbed it. Wes dropped, arm wedged into a crack between crates, stretching for a lost marker. Kirk hurled the box across the room, dryer sheets fanning as it flew into Wes's reach. Wes tore one free and scribbled furiously, ink smudging.

Roman gave it like a drumbeat. "A. L. V. A…"

The woman on the other end typed without a question.

Kirk smacked Wes's chest, a muted whoop masked by the whine of the spin cycle.

They pressed on with email, recovery address, security code. Roman guided her like traffic through an intersection, turning the free fall into a clean landing.

Click. Call ended.

Wes whistled low. "That's why you're on the phone."

"That could've killed us," Kirk said.

The spin cycle droned, shaking the walls, as if the machines had swallowed their secret whole.

* * *

The radiator clanged in the shelter's common room, the place barely holding itself together.

Eli hunched at the edge of a cot, knees drawn up, one hand hanging open where the little car used to rest.

Roman crouched in front of him. "Hey, buddy."

"They took my car. The red one you gave me, the one with the spinning wheels. I told them it was mine but they said it wasn't and ran off with it." Eli's knees gave. "They were laughing, too."

Roman brought Eli's feet together with a gentle clap. "Don't worry. I'll get you another one."

Eli shook his head. "But it won't be the same because that's the one you gave me for my birthday. And you said birthdays are extra special, so that makes it different."

Roman watched him for a moment. "Remember what I taught you?"

"You tell me a lot of things."

The cot squeaked under Roman's weight as he sat beside him. "You make choices so the world can't. You choose what hurts. You choose when."

Eli bit down, testing the edge of his tongue. "Ow!"

Roman nudged Eli's shoulder. "It doesn't have to be your tongue. You can choose anything to be your distraction."

"What's yours? You have to have at least one. You're like way older than me."

"Don't have one." Roman chuckled. "But do what feels right for you."

Eli unwound the twist of his shirt hem. "So I can choose anything?"

"That's right. Anything."

"What did my daddy choose to do? Will you tell me more about him?"

Roman's hand closed around the cold metal post. "Ah, I don't know that, buddy."

"You said you knew him. What did he do?"

Roman leaned on the pole. His thumb found the metal and ticked. He stood abruptly, the cot groaning. "Listen, I'm glad that helped. Keep your head up. If those kids bother you again, tell your mom."

Eli's shoulders slumped as Roman pulled away, the space between them widening. "But you're the only one who can tell me about him."

The cot sagged in Roman's absence.

* * *

Simone stood by the office printer, scrolling through glossy real estate listings while it stuttered awake.

Since Roman's return, Aniella hadn't said more than a handful of words.

She stayed anchored at her desk, refreshing the same screen each time it loaded. She played with the volume buttons on the phone, though no message had come in.

He knew the weight behind his own silence. Eli. Asking about his father. The question had knotted Roman's mind all afternoon.

The office carried on, but Roman clocked the shift in Aniella's tempo, and the small wasted movements that betrayed her calm.

Ethan entered the bullpen. "Just the two I needed." He waved a file toward the doorway. "In my office."

Aniella's smile thinned. If last night's fiasco at Tyler's workstation had made it to surveillance, she'd be bracing. Being summoned together meant something.

Ethan slapped the file onto a steel cabinet. "Hackett has you on local work in the city, hm?"

The memo looked routine. Casino surveillance, low priority, but Roman knew better. Iver had been inventing busywork for weeks, keeping his name clear while the real work moved underground.

"Good old Chief," Roman said. "Can't stand to see me wasted on paperwork."

Ethan opened the folder across his desk. "Says here there's a new hotel opening. The chief wants you to scan the scene, see if local dealers try a meet and greet." His delivery lost polish. "Push their product as hello."

Roman knew the setup. A push to keep tabs. "Yeah, good call." He angled his focus down, dry. "Got a problem with that?"

Ethan's stance reset, a hint of satisfaction in it. "Not at all." He motioned toward Aniella. "Cause she'll be your cover."

Roman's attention rose from the file. "She's admin staff."

"Well I just signed off on the team list and added Fasquelle for intelligence training. She's been on track while she covers admin work."

"An assignment?" Aniella asked, bright as ever. "That's excellent. I didn't expect one so soon." The sound skimmed above everyone's mood.

Too much, too fast. Working for Iver on the side, now tethered to Aniella.

"Lot of changes since I've been back," Roman said. "But I don't need a cover. It's a one-man job."

Aniella shifted closer to the cabinet, eagerness catching. "What will I be doing?"

"I disagree," Ethan said. "No company? A man alone at a casino opening sticks out." His focus paused on her blazer. "She fits the setting. As your partner, you'll blend in."

Aniella blinked, still bright. "It's not dangerous, is it?"

"It's a simple intel job," Ethan said. "Roman's trained. You'll be fine."

"At least give her realistic expectations," Roman said.

"These are real," Ethan said. "Especially under your standards of safety. Wrong?"

Roman let doubt play across his delivery. "For an operation like this?"

Aniella's posture found the concern. "An operation like what?"

"He's trying to scare you off," Ethan said, opening a drawer to set the folder in like the act alone kept him from saying something worse. "The file barely touched my desk. It's *that* safe."

"I'm not trying to deter her," Roman said. "I want her clear on what she is. Not a field partner. You're using her to save budget, right? And if she were killing it in admin, you wouldn't hand her off to be babysat by me."

Ethan shoved the drawer closed, the thud shivering through the foundation. "Aren't you the one who needs the babysitter, Viento?"

"May I be dismissed?" Roman asked.

Ethan spoke through his teeth. "*Please.*"

The office din rushed back around them.

Aniella clutched the folder to her chest, her stride quick across the tile.

She turned on him near the cabinets, brightness gone. "Are you acting like a jerk because I had lunch with George?"

"That's not narcissistic at all, Fasquelle. To assume everything's about you."

She gasped, folder pressed close.

He kept walking.

Whatever story she built from this, his reasons were different.

Roman pushed through the district doors, phone tight against his ear.

Iver picked up. "Talk to me."

"You have to deal with Polinski," Roman said. "He just slapped Fasquelle's name on the casino cover you filed for my weekend with Wes."

"Roman, slow down. What are you talking about?"

"Exactly what I said. Polinski's sending her to get her feet wet since it looks like an intel gig."

"What the—" He broke off with a curse. "Can you postpone Wes?"

"I can try to stall once, but if he keeps attaching her, I'm done. They'll spot a pattern."

Traffic streaked past, the rush of cars echoing how fast he could get burned.

"Relax, she's just a secretary. You can handle her. She won't have a clue."

Iver sounded confident, but all Roman tasted was doubt.

"So I hit this casino opening and what?" Roman asked. "Pretend it's real? Waste of time."

"Be smarter than her. Or scare her out of it."

Aniella asked questions. She noticed things. She was curious. The traits that made her harmless in the bullpen could make her dangerous under the casino facade.

"If I can't push Wes, how the hell am I supposed to be in two places at once?"

"Figure it out."

The line went dead.

Roman lowered the phone, its weight dragging in his palm. The traffic thinned. The trap was clear now. Ethan's leash was tightening, link by link.

# CHAPTER 10

## No Alibi

The chandelier blazed above, a constellation of cut glass throwing prismatic light across the high-rise lobby. Polished marble stretched in all directions, every surface aching to impress. Bellmen wheeled brass carts past them with white gloves, wheels whispering over the floor.

"So beautiful." Aniella tilted her face upward, the words slipping out faint, almost private.

Roman kept his shoulders squared, luggage at his side as if the surrounding shine didn't register.

The clerk slid two keycards across the counter. "Connecting queens, nineteenth floor."

Roman took the cards. "Thanks."

*Connecting rooms?* The captain made it clear. Yet Roman wasn't protesting. *Aren't we supposed to pose as a couple?*

Roman shifted in beside her, luggage handles snapping open. "Stop gawking at everything. You'll draw attention." He extended the handles, the wheels gliding over the marble as he escorted them toward the elevator.

* * *

Roman dropped his suitcase at the foot of the bed. The zipper rasped open as the weight fell slack.

Aniella flung the curtain wide, the city spilling in. "Can I be excited now?"

Roman set the remote on the dresser without turning on the TV. "Knock yourself out."

She worked the curtain wider. "I wish I could explore the hotel before the ribbon-cutting."

"Boring, yeah, but you wanted the job."

The curtain rings rattled along the rod. "Do you think we'll catch dealers trying to push their product?"

"Stay alert. Nothing more."

"Right. No talking, no mingling." The words ran ahead of her, but curiosity broke through anyway. "But what if we do see something suspicious?"

"We note it in the report." He shook out a shirt, squared the seams, and laid it flat.

*Another shirt? For what?*

"I'm gonna nap for the long night ahead," he said. "Can you keep the excitement on volume two?"

"Only if you ask nicely."

The lid of his suitcase snapped shut. "Could you do that for me?" he asked. "Volume two?"

Her playfulness thinned to nothing.

"I know you don't want me here, but can't you show some courteousness?"

The zipper pulls clinked along their track. "Never mind, be as loud as you want." He slipped through the connecting room, the lock signaling a kind of space she hadn't known he needed.

* * *

Slot machines clamored and roulette wheels spun, the racket weaving through a haze of cigar smoke.

Beyond the Craps table, a short man in a plum suit built chip towers, the felt freckled with damp circles where sweat had lived too long.

Roman and Aniella claimed seats at the crowded bar, the lacquered counter tacky with spilled mixers. Behind them, bottles rose in backlit rows.

"What are you ordering?" she asked.

"Gin and tonic."

Her attention snagged on the untouched coaster he'd dragged close. "You don't strike me as a gin and tonic guy."

"I'm not."

"Oh." Sequins on her dress spattered flecks across the counter. "Then why are you ordering one?"

"On a job, you do everything differently. Won't drink it anyway."

Martini glasses dangled overhead, their rims flashing a neon glare along the steel rail.

"Well, I like fruity drinks," she said.

"Then get something bitter. Or sour."

The bartender swept by with a table tray, order slips feathering the edge, and didn't stop.

Aniella lowered her voice. "I know we're supposed to keep a lookout for supervisors drifting in and out of the pit, but… where is the pit?"

"Behind the specialty games."

Aniella angled toward the back wall. "That guy near the service door behind the slots on the left side looks kind of suspicious."

Roman let the scene pass across him without hurry. "No. Not our problem."

"What makes you say that?"

"Experience."

"Well, I've been passing my courses and trainings, and from an intel standpoint, his pattern is messy. I can tell by the way he keeps looking around."

The man slipped through a side door.

"You don't need to use tonight to try and prove yourself or your training."

Her coaster started a slow spin.

"Don't get bold," Roman said.

She pushed off her stool and broke from the bar.

"Aniella—" Roman cut through the crowd, but she'd already vanished through the same door, the metal swinging shut behind her.

*Shit.*

Roman drove into the door—the handle stopped hard. He racked the panel. "Open up."

The latch gave half an inch.

"Who are you?" the voice inside asked.

"My date. Sequin dress. She came through here."

A shadow marked the corridor. "That way."

Roman pushed down the hall, checking each doorway on both sides as he went. A scream cracked the hall. He broke into a run.

"Aniella—where are you?"

At the hall's end, he found Aniella with a broad man in a tailored jacket, a gun resting like a centerpiece between them on a table.

Roman let his posture read relaxed. "You good?" he asked her.

"She's fine." The question sliced clean toward Roman. "Any reason she's snooping?"

"You'll have to excuse her." Roman edged between Aniella and the gun. "She's a little inclined to curiosity."

Aniella sequins scratched the table, their glitter out of step with the back room's grit. "I just wanted to know what was back here."

Roman extended a hand for Aniella and drew her close. "That's enough excitement for us tonight," he said, setting a path with his shoulder to guide her out. "If you'll excuse us."

"If that's what you want."

Roman took the outside of the corridor, giving her the wall.

"The way he said that was weird," she said.

Roman kept the pace brisk. "Not now."

* * *

Roman slammed the hotel door, his tie already half-undone as he ripped it free. "What the hell were you thinking?"

Aniella startled as Roman stormed past, the keycard sleeves sliding along the table. "I'm sorry, I had a hunch!"

He yanked the lamp chain so sharply the shade wobbled. "A hunch? You can't act on hunches."

"You act on hunches."

The ice-bucket lid jittered on its tray.

"Because I have over a decade of knowing when to act on one." The top button of his shirt gave with a snap.

"Didn't you see the gun?"

"Of course he has a gun!" Roman tore off his jacket and flung it to the carpet. "He's security!"

Aniella backed toward the bed, sequins shivering with each step. "Please stop yelling at me!"

Roman's fury fractured, Victor's echo still pounding in his skull. The same walls, the same words. *Stop, Dad. Stop.* Aniella's plea collided with it, and for a moment he saw himself small again, gripping the sheets like a rope.

Remorse split through him, but her face stayed hidden behind her hands, missing it.

"… Just get some rest."

He retreated through the connecting room, the latch catching behind him.

* * *

Aniella lay rigid under the comforter, heat trapped around her feet. She counted, then gave up and padded to the sink. The water tasted like a reminder of why she gave up drinking from the tap.

Back in bed, sleep stayed out of reach. *The man with the gun. He didn't look like security.*

Through the thin wall, something slid along a hanger, a soft scrape, then a bite of a zipper. A drawer rolled shut.

Earlier that day, Roman had laid a fresh shirt flat like it mattered.

Her phone vibrated on the nightstand. It was Fern, and she answered in a hurry.

"Fern, did you read my texts about what happened tonight? Sorry they were so long."

"I did, that's why I'm calling." Fern came in hard. "I'm a real one, so I'm not gonna sugarcoat it because I'm a good friend. This was your screw-up. You blew it."

"Wait, what?"

"The first real chance and you wrecked it. You should quit. You're in over your head."

The words punched through the speaker. Tears hit before Aniella found an answer. She ended the call, staring at the screen before setting the phone back on the nightstand.

She pulled the blanket from the foot of the bed and wrapped up, then curled on the hotel sofa by the window. It took her weight as she pressed her face into the cushion.

The adjoining door opened a thin seam between rooms.

Roman's steps stopped just inside. "Everything okay?"

She wiped her cheeks in a rush. "I'm fine. Why did you come in here?"

"I heard you." He stood there in a dark shirt, the suit gone. "Want to talk about it?"

"I feel weird talking to you." She loosened the blanket enough to see him. "You yelled at me. I feel like a failure." She drew the blanket tighter. "I just messed up so much tonight."

"Tonight was reckless. You had no idea what was behind that door." The space between his words eased. "I raised my voice." He sat at the far end of the sofa. "I'm not proud of how I handled it."

The blanket rested between them, a barrier that still held her warmth.

"I'm sorry," he said.

The apology hung there, quiet and unadorned. Roman didn't say words like that. A man like him only used them when he meant them, and that was enough.

"Is that why you were upset?" he asked.

She thought of Fern and her callous call-out. "Tonight was a lot. The guy with the gun, the yelling, all of it. And then the one friend I've made here told me I needed a reality check, that I'm too weak for this job—"

"Hold on." The subtle gleam of the moonlight barely slipped through the curtain, silvering the end of the sofa and his tone with it. "You landed in a new state to care for your grandmother, started a new job, and keep showing up when you feel like the odd one out." He lowered the hump made from the blanket. "That's not weakness."

Seen. Just as she had been when they'd first met at the shelter. The blanket loosened in her hands. "You really think I can do this?"

"Yeah." He leaned back a fraction. "You clocked my shirt earlier. You called your observation a curse. It's a skill."

*He noticed I noticed his shirt? How? And why does he want me to know he knows?*

"I stepped out, then came back." He motioned to the adjoining door. "Do you feel safe in here?"

The question dragged her back to the casino. Gun on the table. The man's line. The way he said it.

"Not really," she said at last.

He folded the blanket down as he stood. "Do you want the connecting door left open?"

"I'd appreciate that."

He crossed to the door.

"What's the captain going to say?"

"Don't worry." He faced her. "We don't tell him about this."

\* \* \*

The blinds cut the view into stripes, bullpen on one side, Ethan's desk on the other. He stood anchored between them, one hand on the casebook, the other on a hotel folio.

"You can't book two rooms," Ethan said, talking lines of policy that read like rules more than advice. His bark carried across the windowed wall. "If anyone checks, it reads wrong. You were on as a couple. No cots. Nothing that draws attention."

Out in the bullpen, a staple pinged off Simone's neck.

"What the hell, O'Neil?" Simone scanned his station for the missing staple.

"How come she gets stints with Viento? We started the same day. She's a secretary."

"She went for analyst training," Simone said, lifting the bent piece from the carpet. "He needed a cover. You want to play the boyfriend next time?"

Brett snorted. "Still feels like bullshit."

Simone flicked the staple back at him. "File that under 'personal growth.'"

The office door opened, and Roman stepped into the bullpen.

"How are your eardrums?" Simone asked. "Caught most of that from here."

Roman handed Simone a printout. "Captain says you two are up. Homicide downtown."

As he dropped into his station, Brett and Simone grabbed coats and moved out.

The elevator chimed. Aniella came in mid-conversation with Tyler, a humble bouquet of pale pink roses in butcher paper, dark at the stems. Last week's bouquet slumped brown in the vase at her cubby.

Tyler pulled a tennis ball from his drawer, then propped his boots on the desk and crossed his ankles. "How could you possibly know that?"

Aniella peeled the crinkled film from the fresh bouquet. "I'm a good guesser."

"You're a little too sure of yourself," Tyler said.

She set the roses into the vase and shook out the paper. "Or maybe I pay attention."

"It's just luck." Tyler tossed the ball and caught it against his palm, then tossed again.

Scott walked in from the hall with a coffee carrier. "What are you two bickering about?"

"Whether Fasquelle's as good a guesser as she claims," Tyler said.

"Ready?" Scott asked. "You never need it at home, but you never leave without it."

"A keychain," Aniella said.

Scott's mouth fell open. "Okay, that was quick."

"Pick something harder," she said.

Tyler rolled the ball in his hands. "She says she can read people. Personal stuff."

Scott lifted his brows. "Interesting."

"Read Viento," Tyler said. "If you can peg him, you're not lucky."

Roman kept his attention on his monitor. "Leave me out of it."

"What's the problem, Fasquelle?" Tyler stilled the ball. "Intimidated?"

"About what?" she asked.

"Tell us something about Viento. Only from what you observe."

"Don't drag me into this," Roman said, keys ticking at his keyboard.

"If she has a gift, who are we to not give her a fair chance at proving it?" Tyler asked. "Then we can find out if they hired her for more than being pretty."

"Are you joking?" she asked.

"What?" Tyler asked. "Never had a pretty girl in the office before."

"Will you stop speaking to me like I'm supposed to be a stupid girl who doesn't know anything?"

"You used to be sweet when you started working here—"

"Cut the shit," Roman said.

"Now we have your attention," Tyler said.

"I think your disbelief is what's pissing her off, Grave," Scott said.

Tyler set the tennis ball on the desk. "Then let her prove it."

"Humor him for a minute, Rome," Scott said. "So we can shut him up."

Roman gave a reluctant swivel to face them. "Fine. Go."

Aniella rolled her shoulders and let her focus settle. Roman read as a blank board, which meant the tells were smaller and elsewhere.

"You keep your life sealed off," she said. "You like it that way. You're close to very few people. The ones who make your circle, you guard hard."

Tyler groaned. "Everyone knows that."

She kept going. "You run on habits. You phrase orders as statements instead of requests." She lifted a finger toward his station without touching it. "When you want something done, you name the outcome. You skip softeners."

A crease formed at the bridge of Tyler's nose. "You mean he's bossy."

"I mean he's precise." She paused, weighing whether to push. The bullpen thinned at the edges. "It isn't the job that made you private. I think you're good at the job because you'd already mastered being evasive."

Roman didn't move, but the tennis ball in Tyler's hand slowed.

"You know your pain more than your insecurities," she said. "You keep yourself busy enough that you don't have to ask what you want beyond the next case. If you ever let yourself want more, you might not know where to start."

Tyler laughed. "That's—"

"Quiet." Roman's voice cut like command already respected.

Aniella held the line. "You come from a rough background. Something out of your control happened early. It taught you to hide in plain sight. You feel like an only child to me, but that didn't necessarily make you the focus in your parents' life."

Scott shifted his coffee carrier to his other hand. "Maybe stop there."

She hesitated, marking the air as if to pin the thought. "One more," she said, softer now. "Small. You steer around certain words. When you need something, you skip the courtesies."

Roman's monitor display timed out and went dark. "Coffee." He aligned the edge of a folder with his keyboard, capped his pen, and stood.

The room stayed silent as he left.

Tyler slumped back in his chair, smirking. "I have a feeling that wasn't small."

# CHAPTER 11

## Fault Lines

Forklifts chirped somewhere in the rafters. Plastic wrap rasped as Kirk cinched a pallet, the clear film tight around boxes of designer watch cases. Wes weighed a velvet roll of bracelets and snapped rubber bands over stacks of cash, bills squared against a metal ruler.

"Park on his block," Wes said. "See if he comes or goes."

Roman stood at a scarred table that wobbled on a missing foot. A neighborhood printout lay under a box cutter.

Wes penciled a route around the cul-de-sac and marked a circle where a tree blocked the street off from the porch cameras.

"Any reason I should know of?" Roman asked, reading a text on his screen.

"He lifted from me." Wes tucked the cash back into a bakery bag. "If he comes or goes, you ping me." He plucked a hex nut from the crate and knocked it off the table. "You hear me, Roman?"

"Yeah." Roman slid the phone into his pocket. "Sit on the house. Tree blocks the house cam."

"Anything important?" Wes asked.

"You'll get a ping if I see anything." Roman folded the neighborhood printout. "I'll catch up later."

Roman left the warehouse. Two blocks away, he ducked into a corner deli, ordered a sub, and sat where the front window gave him a view of the street. He ate slow, kept to the window for Wes's car that never rolled by, then crumpled the wrapper and tossed it.

* * *

The duty roster board hung on the wall, an incident-report face sheet pinned under a red magnet.

"I sent that text over an hour ago," Ethan said.

Roman nudged a loose pushpin deeper into the board, the small correction standing in for everything he couldn't fix outright. "Reception must've been bad."

"Where have you been?"

"Following up on an old lead."

On the legal pad, another incident-report face sheet waited. The RD was stamped in blue, with location and time filled. "You're lead on a homicide."

"I'm already on a job."

"Not one I assigned."

"The chief has me on something."

"And I'm hearing about this now?"

"It's small. Surveillance only. That's why I didn't loop you in."

"Great." Ethan slid the face sheet into the wire tray. "Take Fasquelle. She needs field time."

Roman held the line by the BOLO wall, flyers layered beneath thumbtacks. "Not smart. I need quiet cover, not a shadow."

"If it's as minor as you claim, she can handle a notepad. Surveillance is right in her lane."

"Small for me might be dangerous for her."

"But it was acceptable to leave her alone with a murder suspect."

"I'd just come off six months under. I was detached when I made that call."

A phone rang twice in the bullpen and cut off.

"I'm thinking more real-world now," Roman said.

Ethan reached for the case log and wrote a time in the margin. "I don't care how carefully you think now. You'll do as ordered."

The building's HVAC ticked in the vent.

"Brief me first thing in the morning. And Viento." Ethan shifted the magnet one slot over. "Lose the dead zones. When I text, you answer."

*　*　*

Cooling metal ticked under the hood. Two porches down, the target house held steady inside Aniella's line of sight.

The wrapper crackled as Roman bit into the hot dog. "Day good?"

"I worked a shift at the shelter before this." She settled the orange juice into the holder. "My favorite little boy's leaving though. Kind of sad."

Radio hiss filled the car. He let it run.

"The poor boy's been struggling. His mom's adoptive. She works there, so I see him a lot." She kept the house in view. "I'll miss him."

His bite stalled, mustard beading at the edge. "Where to?"

"They're moving to Atlanta. She wants to be near her sister."

The dashboard clock changed digits in silence.

"When?" he asked.

"I'm not sure. But why not a station unmarked? We're fine in a regular car?"

"Crews spot the usual models. This one blends."

She traced a finger through the condensation on her cup, smearing it clear. "How long do we have to sit here?"

He ate. "Until something changes."

"Then what?"

"Then we wait for instructions." The wrapper crumpled in his grip.

"They don't tell us much. It'd be nice to know what's going on." Her seatbelt creaked at another small tilt. "Wanna hear a random fact?"

"More random than asking if I want a random fact, entirely randomly?"

"Thank you for being entirely sarcastic, entirely all the time."

He smirked, as if he'd taken it as a complement. "Pleasure."

"Anyway." She twined the straw's paper tail tight. "I can do a weird trick with orange juice."

The wrapper went quiet. "You can do what?"

"I'm hungry."

"We're just gonna forget about the juice thing?"

"Yup. I'm starving."

"You're odd." He wiped his chin with the napkin. "Have a dog then."

"I eat real food."

He stuffed the trash into the bag. "I've got a random fact too." He leaned across her lap and popped the glove compartment. A brush, paste, and a travel rinse bottle waited inside. "I brush after every meal." He snapped off the dome light and cracked the door.

"I knew you were undercover," she said, laughing. "But not an undercover diva."

"Takes a second."

He swished from the bottle and spat to the curb. The door closed softly.

"So this guy we're watching. What do we do if he comes out?" she asked.

"He won't."

"For someone with all that experience, it shocks me you don't have a plan."

The house stayed dark. Driveway empty. Curb clear.

"I have a plan," he said. "He doesn't show."

"Okay, but what if someone warned him? What if he's smart enough to park his car down the block? What if he's in the house with all the lights off?"

"You watch a lot of TV, Fasquelle?" He stowed the toothpaste and brush back into the glove compartment. "Not likely."

"Shouldn't we have a plan in case he does show?"

"What's the matter? Not quick on the spot?"

"I just prefer to be prepared. Besides, last time I acted on the spot you got angry at me."

"Fair point. Give me one. Hit me with a plan."

"Would we duck?"

"No. Too obvious. We'd get caught mid-duck."

"There's something else." She worried the lid, turning it back and forth until it gave a faint squeak. "If I upset you in the bullpen, I'm sorry."

"Nothing to be sorry for." He stayed angled to the house, the place still his anchor. "You were wrong."

A tall outline shifted across the porch. Too casual to be a stranger, too late for a neighbor.

"Don't look," he said. "He's heading this way."

"That's not funny."

"Serious."

"What do we do?"

He slid a folded map from the console onto her lap. "Read."

"Oh my God, what if he sees us?"

"Keep still, you'll burn us."

The man drifted toward their side of the street, his stride unhurried. The kind that tested if anyone inside a car would flinch.

"This is why we should've had a plan!" A thin fog feathered the window. "What if he already noticed us?"

"Aniella. Easy."

She angled back toward the street. "Oh my God, this is gonna be like the casino—"

Roman's forearm bridged her window, elbow locking above her shoulder and cutting off the street's angle. His wrist line screened her mouth from the curb. The seat took his weight, pressing against her hip.

Her cup shifted in the holder. "What are you doing?"

"Cover." He leaned in until the console shadow swallowed the map's border. "Follow." His mouth brushed the edge of her cheek. Not a kiss, but close enough that the window's reflection might believe it.

The streetlamp stitched a pale stripe up his sleeve. *Cover. Not a kiss.* Yet his scent deepened between them, and the faint mint from his rinse cooled as it drifted across her lips. Her fingers wrapped around the map's edge, not sure she could keep it steady on her knees. She turned her face a fraction, her cheek grazing the scruff on his jaw. The movement barely counted, but it met him halfway.

He didn't shift back. The arm braced above her shoulder stayed fixed—an unspoken order not to move. His free hand found the console edge, anchoring his frame closer, sealing their corner from view.

He did it again, slower, tracing the shape of her cheek before settling there, his frame closing her off from the world. Her skin tingled where the last touch had been.

She found the rough edge of his jaw and mirrored his touch. His turn. Her turn. They timed it without words, each waiting for the other to move, careful never to meet at the same moment. A quiet rhythm neither could name.

His scruff grazed her cheek and stalled, then drew lower. A pause, a break, a risk—then his mouth touched the corner of hers, hesitant, unplanned, lethal in its restraint. The belt rasped. She held still, but the strap crept higher along her shoulder. The haze on the window had started from earlier nerves. She held to that mercy, hoping it wouldn't read as him, but the fog on the glass kept thickening.

"He's at our fifteen."

Her breath came uneven. "How do you know?"

"Because I'm paying attention to him, not you."

She stayed still, pretending not to feel the sting, but the map trembled once more before sliding from her knees to the floor.

The man crossed the block's far side, his shadow dragging long under the streetlamp, stretching toward their bumper.

Roman used the headrest angle to confirm the street was clear. The seat sprang free from under her as he pulled his weight back. The fog on the windows clung, too thick. Too stubborn.

The silence held, heavy as the stalled engine. Her hands locked tight around the belt strap until her knuckles blanched.

She pushed her voice into the air. "That plan was… um…"

Roman dropped the car into gear, the jolt louder than his words. "Don't ever make me do that again."

* * *

Igna bent over the donation box, lifting out a mitten without its pair. The yarn slumped, strands rubbed bare from too many washes. She turned it once, then set it aside on the counter. A stuffed rabbit followed, its ear bent the wrong way.

"If you weren't around, I knew it was because you were on a case," she said. "But lately, you barely see him. And I can't entrust him to someone who isn't consistent."

Roman picked up the rabbit she'd dropped with the mittens and set it on the other pile. The ear tipped sideways, refusing to straighten. "I've been meaning to come around more often."

"He doesn't know who you really are."

Roman pressed the rabbit's ear flat. It sprang back crooked. "No. But—"

"Do you think that's fair? To Eli?"

"He's already been moved too many times. It's bad enough he spends every day around users." Roman hooked the box edge closer. "Taking him to Atlanta will crush him."

Igna rolled two socks together. "My plan was to bring him, but with my sister drowning in seven of her own kids and her health failing, I don't have a choice. I've started the readoption process."

"I don't want him jumping from home to home, or landing in the wrong one."

"That's the process. And it isn't kind."

Roman set the box lid back in place, his thumb pressed firm along the corner as if weight alone could keep the rest contained. "What if I adopt him?"

"You've never raised a child. You work long hours. Eli's been upset when you promised visits you couldn't keep. Kids need a lot of attention." She tugged a third sock free, realized it didn't match, then balled it anyway. "I like you, Roman, but I just don't see it being possible."

* * *

Aniella detoured to the copy-room instead of the bullpen, her chair already angled toward HR's corridor, back to him. The pencil sharpener jammed, grinding air. "Stupid thing." She rattled the casing and shook out the shavings.

She rerouted past Records rather than cross his lane. He cleared the duty log to blank space.

All morning, their routes kept missing. Her prints ran late, his calls dragged long.

He set his coffee down without a sound, kept one hand in his pocket, and stuck to roster times instead of questions.

*How am I gonna get rid of her?*

Chatter carried over them, leaving a hard lane of stiffness between their desks.

Their print jobs collided. Mouse clicks overlapped, the copier's whir grinding hotter as both queues spooled.

The machine blew heat into the small space. They reached the tray together. The printer crawled, spitting pages slower than it ever had. Warm toner gave off its metallic tang. He stayed on his side of the partition, waiting for her to pull her stack first.

*Temperature check.* "Is that current?"

She stacked the papers tight, edge to edge. "Yup."

*Cold. Tread lightly.* "I wasn't asking to make small talk."

"No, thank you." She snagged the paper from the tray. "Oh, and by the way, I'm never working with you again."

"That's too bad."

She tapped the stack to square it. "You enjoy being a jerk."

"Do I?" He rolled a pen cap between his teeth, his tone curved with quiet satisfaction at her irritation.

He trailed her aisle, close enough for the scent of fresh ink on her papers to carry back.

She took a sip of her hot chocolate. His palms pressed into her desk surface, his frame leaning over, closing the space. Her mug lowered, and he was already there.

"You acted like it was my fault," she said. "But I didn't ask you to do that."

He kept it low. "Can I explain?"

"Explain what? That you're the one who kissed my cheek and made me feel like an idiot? Then had the audacity to say I made you do it?"

Roman scanned the bullpen. No one watching. "Listen, I didn't like it either. But there was no other way. Once again, you left me to cover us, to get out of a mess you caused."

"So if that was Scott all nervous, you would've kissed him?"

"I just hope I didn't put you in a bad spot." He turned the stapler in his grip. "You know, to have an uncomfortable talk with bouquet guy."

"Bouquet guy?" She pushed her chair back an inch, incredulous. "I'm not seeing him. So you didn't make me a cheater, if that's what you're concerned about."

"How did last night go?" Ethan leaned too close over Aniella's desk, a scatter of dandruff flaking toward her mug.

Roman straightened. "We've agreed it's not a fit. She didn't do so great."

"That's why it's called training," Ethan said. "Not sure why you expected her performance to be acceptable when she's only joined you twice." He pressed a file flat against Roman's shirt. "I asked the chief to run your cases by me, and this came in this morning." He pressed it once more. "Guess who you're taking with you?" He pivoted away, dandruff dusting his collar as he went.

* * *

The assignment reached her inbox that afternoon. Roman listed as lead. She knew he didn't want anything to do with her, or at least, that's how it felt. By the time they'd reached the hotel, the silence between them had settled like a fog. Lucky for him, the long shifts and the extra hours at the shelter finally caught up to her, and she didn't even make it to the surveillance.

The lock beeped. A rush of casino noise slipped in, then vanished as the door shut. Aniella stirred on the floor, the carpet's coarse weave pressed against her temple. The long shifts had finally collapsed her. She blinked at the ceiling fan, then at the sudden weight beneath her—Roman's arms sliding under her and lifting.

Her forehead brushed the faint starch of his dress shirt.

"Hey." His collar hung open, the low light rendering him unreadable. "You were really planning to sleep on the floor?" His voice was quiet, like it wasn't meant for anyone but her.

She gave a drowsy half-smile. "Captain said no cots."

He set her on the bed and tugged the sheets over her.

Pipes clanged in the restroom, water running. Through the cracked door she glimpsed him in the mirror, rubbing a towel through his wet hair. He came out in jeans and a plain shirt. Too casual for the casino floor. He tossed the towel in a basket, then reached for his wallet.

"You've been in there a while," she said.

"Not too long."

His phone lit. He answered fast, voice clipped. "Be there." He hung up and slipped the cell deep into his pocket.

Her head swam. She pressed her palms to her face. She'd never felt this tired. "I need to change into my dress."

He leaned over the bed, one arm pulling the cover higher to her chin. "Just rest."

"Not help at all?"

"Think of it as a night off. No makeup marathon."

She almost laughed. "An hour and a half. Minimum."

He didn't answer, just put on a jacket. The dull scrape of metal at his back made her glance. He slid the gun beneath his belt, then slid something small into his pocket.

"Why are you bringing that?" she asked.

"They'll be cutting corners at the checkpoints. I'll get through."

"You sure?"

He gave her a look that ended the question.

Something in her coiled. Too casual a shirt. Too quick on the phone. Something he wasn't saying. She wanted to press, but her body betrayed her as she slipped back into the sheets. The last thing she saw was him swipe the room key.

# CHAPTER 12

## Desire

Roman dribbled low, the ball thudding between his legs as Scott circled.

"You think you're taking this one?" Roman asked.

Scott lunged and missed. "I'll get it!"

"Not today." Roman faked left, cut right, and launched for the dunk. The rim rattled on his descent. "That's game." He thumped his collarbone.

"Nice move."

"Wasn't that great," a new voice cut in.

Roman turned. Two men crossed from the far end of the court, a ball under one arm. They moved like trouble.

The taller one cocked his chin. "You boys claim this side?"

Roman kept his tone even. "Just a couple of guys enjoying a game."

Scott lifted his ball. "Court's open if you wanna run it."

The second one bounced the ball once, sharp. "We don't share." He snapped it down again, this time thudding near Scott's stance. "Keep your space, rookie."

"Hey, back off." Scott tried to pass as steady. "This doesn't need to turn into anything."

The man stepped closer, sneakers scraping the court. "Or what?"

Roman closed the angle. "Or you'll have a problem."

A shove jarred Roman's shoulders. He staggered a step, then found his footing. The noise swelled. Scott shouted, the strangers baiting him, two more drifting in. Three men pressed into Scott.

An idea struck Roman. Quick. Practical.

*I know how to get rid of her.*

His fist came up clean and fast, cracking into the man's jaw.

\* \* \*

Roman and Scott stepped through the district's front doors, the sweat from the court scrubbed away, both now in pressed shirts and ties.

They barely cleared the corner toward the stairwell when a shout cracked through the lobby.

"That's him, the guy I'm filing a report on!"

One of the strangers from the basketball court jabbed a finger straight at Roman, his lip swollen purple.

Ethan's shoes scraped the tiles as he spun from the reception desk. "That can't be him." The authority held, though the words dragged. "That's one of my detectives."

"He's a cop?"

Two more pushed through the glass doors behind him, faces marked with bruises and split mouths.

Ethan shifted, his attention cutting from their bruises to Roman's still-creased collar. His ears burned red. "Upstairs. Now."

\* \* \*

Roman sat steady across from Ethan, buttoned up, tie knot neat. "Sounds like a big accusation, Captain," he said.

"Bullshit," Ethan said, his tone sharp. "You expect me to believe you didn't earn those marks?" Dandruff flaked from his shoulder as he shook his head. "When you fit the description?" His stare locked on the bruise along Roman's jaw. "You should be suspended. Strutting around like some animal. I ought to take your badge right now."

*Like clockwork.* Suspension would buy him space to move. Freedom from having to account for his whereabouts. Aniella would be safe, off his tail.

Those men had already seen him walk through the district doors, and they'd watched him vanish with a captain at his side. If that spread, his cover wouldn't mean safety. It would mean a coffin.

\* \* \*

The screen door swung shut as another group piled into Scott's annual karaoke party. Music spilled from the living room, the bass rattling the floorboards. Scott stood on a dining chair, rocking it side to side.

"Would you get down already?" Tyler said.

"I'm checking the legs," Scott said. "The table's going in the living room for beer pong."

Aniella slipped into the seat beside Simone, across from Roman. Her phone lit in her palm. *Are you on your way yet?* The text to Fern had sat opened for nearly two hours. She clicked the screen dark and tucked it away.

Scott now fought with a knot in the karaoke cord.

*Roman? Suspended?* Even losing control seemed deliberate on him. Strategic. He would never break like that, and anyone who thought he did wasn't paying attention.

Aniella leaned over the armrest. "I heard you like to brawl."

He lifted his head. "Me?"

"Something about a basketball court. Are you okay?"

Roman glanced at Scott, still wrestling with the cord. "Loose Lips."

"You could at least try to have fun."

Around them, their coworkers loosened, Tyler half-dancing, Simone laughing.

"Even Grave's moving," she said.

Roman stood. "Knock yourself out." He brushed past her and stepped outside as the screen door creaked behind him.

Her smile thinned, but she followed.

Tyler wobbled over, legs jerking to the beat. "Don't worry about him. He's sulking about his suspension." He slung an arm around her. "You can hang with me."

Aniella peeled his arm away and slipped out after Roman.

"Roman, wait." She jogged down the steps and onto the lawn.

He stopped and turned. "Why?"

His bluntness froze her. It sounded more like a challenge than a question. Still, the night surrounded her.

"Would you mind if I get a ride home?"

"I walked." There was no confusing the boundary.

She kept quiet, the quick end to his words leaving her off balance.

After a few paces, his stride changed. He slowed until he was beside her, as if deciding not to leave her standing there alone. "What's your plan? Fern?"

"She was supposed to meet me here, then we were going to her place." Aniella tugged her phone from her pocket, the unanswered texts glowing back. "But she's not answering."

"Ah. Can't leave five-two out alone to get mugged. Everyone knows better."

He guided her forward, hands buried in his pockets. The quiet sidewalk stretched, holding their unspoken thoughts.

The promenade smelled faintly of river and fryer grease, the city lights limning the water in restless rows.

Aniella walked beside Roman. The shadows seemed to favor him, gathering in the hollows of his cheeks. The streetlight caught the muted silver rim of his iris, and she hoped he wouldn't notice her watching.

They traded jokes with ease. Aniella felt a looseness between them she hadn't before. He seemed less the careful reserve she knew at work and more the man who could finally relax. Even his stiffness seemed lighter tonight.

"I feel safer walking with you," she said. It was true. "Than alone."

He didn't answer right away. When he did, the reply was almost lost to the dark.

"Good."

She wanted to ask what he was thinking, but his hands stayed buried in his pockets. He moved carefully, measured like someone pausing before a misstep.

They walked on.

"So do undercover guys usually come from out of town?" she asked.

"It's cheaper to use local bodies. Less overhead. Saves the bureau money."

"Isn't that more dangerous? Wouldn't you risk someone recognizing you?"

"No one's ever recognized me. If someone did, I'd play it off. Off-duty, drunk uncle, whatever fits."

"You'd pretend to be a dirty cop?" she asked, surprised.

He gave a short laugh. "I'd make it messy enough they wouldn't want to keep pushing."

She watched him, unsure if he was joking. The answer felt practiced, sharpened into a tool. It landed strange, part craft and part warning.

"Manipulate them," she said slowly.

He focused on the lights ahead. "People trade silence when their own skin's at stake."

She realized she was listening to the way he thought, strategic and precise, and somewhere between the laugh and explanation she felt a prickle of something complicated, safety braided with calculation.

Aniella reached the porch steps with Roman close behind. She slid her key into the lock, twisted once, then again. Nothing. "Oh, crap." She stared at the brass knob. "I forgot. My grandmother's been paranoid with all the break-ins lately, so she had the locks changed."

Roman leaned against the post, shadows crossing his jaw. "And you didn't get a spare?"

"I told her I'd be at Fern's tonight. I was going to grab a key tomorrow before work." Aniella pulled the key free. "Her hearing's terrible. There's no way she'd hear the house phone this late."

"Yeah." The words came flat, even. "If she's already nervous, waking her up would do more harm than good."

Aniella pulled her phone and hit call. The screen lit Fern's name. It rang. And rang.

Roman watched her. "Who are you calling?"

"Fern."

He exhaled through his nose, as if he'd expected as much. When the line went dead, Aniella checked the screen. No answer. No text.

Roman motioned with a tilt of his head. "Come on."

"Where?"

"My place." He said it as if it were obvious.

Aniella blinked at him. "Oh, goodness, no. I couldn't."

"Where else can you stay?"

"Well, I…" She hesitated, searching for an excuse. "I could book a hotel."

He gave a low chuckle. "That's ridiculous, paying to stay somewhere for the night." He started down the walk, hands sinking back into his jacket. "We've bunked before. I'll take the couch."

It was too easy, too matter of fact. Turning it down felt stranger than agreeing. Aniella hesitated, phone still warm in her hand. "You really don't mind?"

He didn't look back, only flicked his chin toward the sidewalk. "It's not far."

The night tugged at her heels, but she followed. His back moved steadily ahead, bomber collar dark against the streetlights. By the time she reached the stone path to his place, his keys were already out, metal ringing softly in his palm.

Roman unlocked the door and pushed it open. "After you."

Aniella dipped into a small bow as she crossed the threshold. "Such a gentleman."

"Yeah." His grin was slight. "Thanks for noticing."

His cologne trailed after her as she slipped past. He switched on a lamp, keys clinking against the entry table. The light revealed a bare, orderly space. No photographs. No books. No knickknacks. Nothing personal.

Aniella toed her shoes off anyway. "Shoes at the door?"

Roman entered behind her. "Up to you."

She drifted toward the living room. It was clean and full of empty corners, the kind of place that didn't look lived in.

Then she noticed it.

A single frame on the shelf. She lifted it, fingertips smudging the glass.

"This must mean a lot to you," she said. "It's the only one you have."

He said nothing, attention fixed on the picture.

A younger Roman stared back from the frame, hand firm on a boy's arm. His face was different, still burdened but almost unrecognizable.

Aniella tilted it toward the lamp. "You look different. And him…" She froze. "Is this Eli?"

A nearby lamp flicked on. "Yeah."

She turned toward him. "You know Eli?"

"I said yeah."

The truth hit hard. He'd denied it before, treating the boy like a stranger. Now it dropped without disguise.

"How?" The word stuck in her throat, but she forced it through. "From the shelter?"

He straightened an already perfect stack of mail on the table. "You could say that."

Her fingers traced the frame, glass dusty under her touch. "So many details, Roman. I can't keep up."

"All right," he said, as if it were done. "You need a change of clothes or something?"

She wasn't ready to put the frame back. She wanted answers. Her fingers stayed wrapped along the edges, as if the truth might surface if she held on longer.

He crossed the short space between them, every step deliberate. Roman took the frame from her hands and set it facedown on the shelf. The sound of wood meeting glass came sharp and final. His focus stayed fixed on the shelf, control drawn in the line of his shoulders. She expected him to scold her, or to explain, but neither came.

The only thing keeping the moment from feeling invasive was the small mercy of him not facing her.

Then he turned.

What had felt bearable a second ago snapped tight, charged with something that stole the air from the room.

Her hands stayed open as if still holding the frame. He started to speak, then stopped, as if warring with himself.

The room suspended, tension drawn tight as wire. His nearness crowded every thought she tried to keep straight. He shouldn't be this close. He knew it, she knew it.

But that almost-kiss in the car left the memory of his cheek against hers, electric and unfinished, charged with everything they hadn't allowed to happen.

He moved closer, the distance shrinking until it was only him. His presence filled the space, crowding every thought she tried to hold steady. His gaze stalled at her mouth, then climbed back, slow and reluctant, like he already knew what crossing that inch would cost. Anticipation flickered through her in quick currents. Warmth brushed her chin, and for a moment she thought he might close the gap between them.

Her lashes dipped, bracing for it. *He's going to kiss me.*

She waited. Each second stretched, then slipped away.

He didn't.

Aniella's lashes lifted, uncertain.

He wasn't looking at her anymore, jaw tight, like he was holding a storm inside him. The kind of focus that looked like someone telling himself to calm down, to stay centered. The tension in him seemed to ache, as if it spoke. Aniella couldn't look away. There was precision to it. A man holding something volatile at bay. It fascinated her, how careful he was, like guarding fragility in his grip. Afraid of rejection? No. Whatever he was fighting ran deeper.

Aniella wavered back a step.

His eyes opened—certain, fierce, carrying the weight of a final decision. Suddenly, he was inside her stare. She sank back, past the invisible wall he'd always kept between them. Deeper than he'd ever let her go, and for once she didn't look away.

The space collapsed with the draw and resistance of a fight neither seemed willing to end, bound in the gravity of their own making.

He dragged his hand down his face, rough, as though he could wipe away the pull between them.

"Roman..." It was all she could manage to whisper.

He drew a ragged breath. "Aniella, I can't—"

"I know." She backed away, forcing a break neither of them wanted.

"No." He stepped forward, reclaiming the space she'd made. "I can't let you go this time."

She didn't know what to say. Every time she leaned toward him, he retreated; every time she tried to leave, he brought her back in. It spun her until she hardly knew which side she was on anymore.

He traced the curve of her lower lip, slow, almost reverent.

Another current moved through her, electric, and the words slipped out in a whisper. "The chemistry." Her hand tented her mouth, as if speaking it aloud had startled her.

His answer was a slight nod. No denial. No distance.

Their noses met in a closeness that held, and the back of his fingers brushed her cheek.

The kiss came quiet, so careful she almost wondered if she imagined it. The barest touch, as if he were testing her. Then another, a fraction longer, more deliberate. The third time their lips met, she kissed him back.

Their mouths found each other again, deeper. Quicker. A collision of restraint and surrender as their lips danced on contradiction.

Her purse strap slipped from her shoulder and hit the floor, unnoticed. He drew her by the waist, strong enough to leave her dizzy with the reminder of what he could do to her.

Aniella's palm met his chest, halting him. "We should stop."

But her palm stayed there, fingers curling against his shirt, the soft cotton conflicting with the strength beneath as she drew him closer instead of away. Her surrender brushed him unguarded, an invitation she couldn't take back.

Roman gathered her closer, what was left of his resistance unraveling. Every kiss built on the last, his touch firm along her back.

"Roman."

His name barely left her lips before he reclaimed her, hopeless and consuming. She looped her arms around his neck as he lifted her onto the entryway table. The lamp tipped, crashing against the floor as Aniella gasped—breaking their mouths apart. Roman steadied her, anchoring her, his body framed between her knees.

He pulled back just enough to hurt. "I need you."

Her answer was silent, only the look she gave him.

Enough.

Roman lifted her down from the table, palms cradling her face as he kissed her again, hungrier. His tongue teased past her lips, and she yielded, the heat between them rising like a pulse.

He pulled his shirt over his head, tossed aside, their movements clumsy as they trailed down the hall. She stumbled until his arms swept her off her feet. Her legs cinched around him, their mouths never breaking as he carried her into the bedroom.

The mattress caught her. He followed, his weight sinking close. His hands clasped her wrists, guiding them above her. Vulnerable, open.

"Aniella." He nuzzled against her ear. "I've been holding back for so long."

She caught his hair, thick and warm beneath her touch. "Don't hold back."

The sound of tearing fabric split the moment open. Layers that had separated them fell to the floor until there was nothing left to lose.

She pulled him closer by the neck, the tension between them taut and unrelenting. Her body resisted him, trembling between fear and longing.

A low groan met the sting of her nails tracing his back, her tremor breaking on his shoulder.

He held her, kissing a trail along her throat as he moved with her, every motion steeped in what neither could deny any longer.

# CHAPTER 13

## Doses of Self-Restraint

Silence thickened through the room as Roman's hand searched the mattress, dread curling with each inch. His fingers found lingering warmth, then the soft curve of Aniella's body. He pushed onto his elbows, watching the slow rise beneath the sheets. Confirmation. It was real. He had done it.

He tore the sheets away, the chill of consequence biting at his skin.

He turned on the faucet and splashed cold water over his face. The nightlight painted uneven shadows across his features. Water ran down his face as he stared into the mirror.

His jaw locked, grip pressing into the edges of the porcelain sink. *What the hell did I just do?*

He shoved back from the sink and paced. A bitter haze bore in as the magnitude of his mistake settled. He braced the sink again, head bowed. *How?*

\* \* \*

Sunlight slipped through the blinds and laid thin gold bands across the comforter.

The sheets still cupped the outline he'd left behind. Aniella stirred, aware of the stillness.

Down the hall, oil popped from a frying pan.

A plain T-shirt waited at the foot of the bed. *No pants?*

The gray tile met her bare feet, a cold snapping her fully awake. She showered fast, then caught her reflection. Damp hair, bare legs, his shirt already climbing her silhouette.

She rested her back to the door, its cool paint anchoring her. *This is crazy.* She had to face him.

The scent of cinnamon met her halfway down the hallway. She slowed at the kitchen's opening. He stood at the stove, back turned.

"French toast?"

Roman turned. The spatula slipped from his hand and hit the floor with a metallic clatter. He crouched to grab it but stopped short, attention caught by the hem of the shirt grazing her thighs—just shy of modest.

Heat moved up her throat. She stepped closer. "I'm sorry. I didn't mean to startle you."

He shook his head once, too quickly. "Pants," he said, already walking past her.

She heard him muttering down the hall, drawers opening, footsteps halting. When he came back, something about him felt different, tighter, as if he'd stumbled through a memory and hadn't left it behind.

"Here." He offered the sweatpants, a loose button resting on top. "Sorry. I can replace the blouse."

Her fingers brushed his knuckles as she took them. "It's okay."

The skillet crackled behind them, calling him back.

She pulled on the sweatpants, cotton still warm from his hands.

"Burnt the toast," he said, the charred bread landing in the trash. "Not much of a cook." He set two paper plates on the table. "Bacon made it out. Not alive, but..."

"Thank you, but I'm gonna get going."

He sprinkled pepper on his bacon. "Without breakfast?"

"I don't really like bacon."

"What'd bacon ever do to you?"

"Nothing. I just don't like the smell."

His brow lifted, a hint of a grin ghosting there. "Right." He bit into the bacon. "You like rustic and aquatic."

She flushed. "Did you say that to embarrass me?"

The grin fell away. "No."

She wanted to step back but didn't. "I went from not knowing where you live to waking up here. And you're acting like this is normal."

He squeezed the back of his neck. "It shouldn't have happened."

Her stomach twisted. *Then why did you let it?* He'd been the one pulling her closer last night, but now he was slamming the door shut.

"I didn't mean for it to happen, either." She turned toward the hallway, then faced him again. "You don't ever get lonely?"

"I'm busy."

"That's not what I asked."

He matched her tone evenly. "Work takes my time."

"You act like I'm asking something from you."

"Aren't you?"

The words hit. She turned away, but he moved in before she could gather a thought. The air between them felt charged again.

She hitched a nervous half-laugh she didn't finish.

Roman's hand lifted, careful, tracing the curve of her chin as if testing the edge of his self-control. Something flickered behind his expression—almost awe, as if he'd just realized how vulnerable she was.

"How do you do this to me?"

She didn't answer. Couldn't.

Their nearness tangled, hers unsteady, his subdued. She caught his collar on a quiet plea.

His mouth found hers, not fought, not rushed, just the inevitable reunion waiting for its time. When he paused, his fingertips lingered, guarding the moment in containment.

Then his hand slid lower, a question more than a motion.

She flinched. "Roman…" Her voice almost reduced to nothing. "I'm sore."

He paused, his expression darkening and softening at once. "Then we slow down."

She nodded, tightening her grip on his collar. He gathered her in, arms circling like a barricade against the world, and kissed her once more as if making sure she wanted it. They were in such a rush to have each other they didn't make it to the bedroom. He lifted her onto the kitchen table and slid off the sweatpants he'd just given her.

* * *

It was over. Their bodies trembled, the rush from what they'd unleashed still pulsing in their ears.

His hand drifted through her hair, pausing at the nape as if steadiness might be found there. She loosened her grip on his shoulders and let her touch trail the solid contour of his arm.

She eased off the table, her feet finding the cool floor. When he straightened his shirt back into place, a jagged scar above his hip flashed.

The moment felt too fragile to survive the question, and before she could ask, he stepped in until her back met the wall.

He trapped her lower lip between his teeth, then trailed along her neck in a slow descent that stole her balance.

He braced his hands against the wall beside her. "You're the hardest thing to say no to."

The hush swelled, his words hanging there like an admission she'd already guessed.

134

His tone, almost tender. "Aniella…"

She faced the ceiling, searching for something to hold on to. She blinked hard, as if that would contain the tears, but they slipped down her cheeks in warm lines anyway.

Her reply came quiet. "I know."

\* \* \*

Eli placed the narrow plastic strip between the bunks, his new toy race car rolling beneath his sneaker every turn.

"Why won't you adopt me so I can stay here with you?"

Roman crouched, watching the wheels click against plastic. "I don't have the kind of life that would be good for you. You need a home that's steady."

Eli raced the car forward. "But I don't want to go to someone else's home. I want to go to yours."

A cough sounded from down the hall, muffled by the partition wall.

"I know you do. But it's just me, and I'm barely home."

The toy skidded ahead, clipping the cot leg with a hollow ping.

Eli darted after it. "Can you stay the rest of the day?"

Roman's phone buzzed in his pocket. "I can't, buddy. I've got work."

Eli rolled the car once more, then let it coast to a stop.

\* \* \*

Simone passed Roman with a half-eaten bagel. "Viento, your mother rang. Said you'd know what it's about."

Roman did know. He just didn't want to answer.

The bullpen door clicked open.

"There you are." Loretta's tone teetered between relief and reprimand. "I've been looking for you for months."

That pitch was the height of a memory. *You should just shoot yourself since you want to pull the trigger so bad!*

The echo cut clean through him. "Hi."

"Hi?" She closed in, fluorescent lights catching the frost in her hair. "That's all I get? I called your old precinct. They said you transferred back ages ago. Then I hear you were suspended?"

"Three days."

"You didn't even tell me?"

He flipped a page he hadn't read. "Been busy."

"Too busy to tell your own mother you moved?" She planted herself in front of his desk. "Too busy to let me know you weren't shot dead somewhere?"

Roman didn't answer. The paper under his hand stayed blank.

Loretta inhaled too fast, the sound practiced. "I thought you forgave me."

He raised a hand, firm. "Enough."

She froze, then, just as suddenly, her tone lightened, singsong. "You're always welcome for dinner."

He studied her for a beat. "Yeah, I know."

"We finished remodeling the kitchen."

Roman slid the folder into the cabinet. "Bet it looks nice."

"Come see for yourself." Her sigh impatiently met his silence. "It's been too long, Roman. When are you coming for dinner?"

"Soon."

She swung her arms, mocking his restraint. "You always say that. 'Soon, soon.'" Her shoulders dropped as if exhausted. "I won't be around forever." She smoothed her top, as if nothing happened. "Just come for dinner, is all."

\* \* \*

The scent of fresh herbs and citrus drifted through the market, coasting between crates of produce and stacked jars of honey.

Customers shuffled past, baskets scraping the wood edges of narrow aisles.

Loretta paused at a stack of shallots, weighing one in her palm. "What about these?"

Roman turned one over, unfocused. "Looks good."

"What's been going on with you lately?"

"Not much."

She dropped the shallots into her basket. "Anyone in your life?"

Roman added one more. "What are you making with those?"

Beyond the citrus bins, Aniella lifted a carton of blueberries, tilting it toward the light. Roman stopped short, the image flashing through him. She lowered the carton, and for a moment their stillness held, longer than it should have.

Loretta followed his line of sight. "That must be her," she said. "We should invite her to dinner."

"No."

Loretta was already walking.

Roman rushed to intercept her. "Mom, don't."

She sidestepped him. "No, you don't."

Loretta approached Aniella and the older woman beside her. "I'm Loretta, Roman's mother."

A few blueberries rolled loose from her container, bumping against his shoe before settling between them.

Her grandma steadied on her walker. "If I'm not mistaken, you're the gentleman who helped me cross a street a while ago."

Roman lifted a corner of his mouth. "Nice to see you again."

"That's not how strangers act," her grandmother said, resting a hand on Aniella's arm. "You two know each other?"

"Yes, Grandma. We work together."

"You should join us for dinner," Loretta said, smile too wide.

Aniella set the blueberries where they didn't belong. "Oh, I already have plans."

"Nonsense," her grandmother said. "You told me Fern cancelled on you. Isn't that why we came here?"

Caught.

Loretta handed the basket to Roman. "Roman, you can pick her up later, can't you?"

Roman shifted the basket in his grip, the plastic biting into his skin.

"Well then," her grandmother said, turning her walker. "She'll be ready."

Aniella offered a faint smile to Loretta, then to Roman. "Thank you," she said, guiding her grandmother toward the street without the blueberries.

Loretta spun. "Don't you need her address?"

Roman's voice carried back as he walked toward the register. "Already have it. Let's go."

Inside, the conveyor belt clicked forward as he unloaded the basket.

Loretta's hand paused on the counter. "So you've already been to her place?"

Roman handed his card to the cashier. "Dropped her off after work a few times."

"And have you been inside?" she asked, tracing a large circle in the air.

Roman lifted the grocery bag. "You're nosy."

"Observant," she said, skipping out with him. "Like my detective son."

Roman said nothing.

"This is great for you, Roman."

Roman pressed the key fob, then loaded the groceries into the trunk. "Not really. We shouldn't see each other outside of work."

Loretta halted mid-step. "Don't make me feel bad for inviting her. Sounds like you've already broken the rules a few times." She smiled, pleased with her logic. "What's one more?"

\* \* \*

The porch bulb threw a tired glow across the siding, its light pooling over the step and the warped trim. Roman pressed the doorbell. A low hum answered from inside, followed by the shuffle of locks.

"I'm so sorry."

The door cracked open, the light outlining her in pieces.

"I tried to get out of it," she said.

He scuffed a chipped board with his shoe, buying himself a second. "It's fine."

The night carried the smell of cut grass and the low roll of distant traffic.

"I don't have to come," she said. "You can tell your mom I wasn't feeling well."

He shook his head. "We don't have to do that."

She clutched the knob. "Are you sure?"

His voice came steadier than he felt. "It's just dinner."

The drive lasted ten minutes, long enough for his thoughts to circle what waited at the house.

He parked, engine ticking as it cooled. "Just a heads-up," he said, the dash light fading. "My mother can be eccentric."

"That's okay, no worries," she said, applying a layer of lip balm. 'I won't judge."

He wasn't ready to play the son again.

*Hope she's having one of her good days.*

\* \* \*

Inside, warmth from the ovens met Aniella first.

Loretta swept toward her as if she'd been waiting for the signal. "I'm so glad you came!"

Aniella laughed, light and easy. "Of course! Thank you for the invite."

Loretta waved her toward the table. "Come on in. Peter will be here soon."

"Who's Peter?" Aniella asked.

"Stepdad."

The glasses made a faint knock as Peter arranged them on the cleared table. He poured for everyone, pausing at Roman. "Still skipping alcohol? There's Sprite if you'd rather."

"Yeah, I'll have a Sprite, thanks."

Peter cracked open the can and tipped it into Roman's glass.

Loretta turned the wineglass stem between her fingers. "Aniella, tell me a little more about yourself."

"I don't think she feels like being interviewed," Roman said.

"I'm not interviewing her," Loretta said. "Don't be so uptight."

Aniella laughed. "Yeah, Roman. Don't be uptight."

Roman took a sip from his glass.

"Well fine," Loretta said, lifting her glass. "Aniella, ask me a question instead."

Aniella brightened. A perfect opening. Too good to waste. "I'd love to, actually." She leaned forward, her tone light. "When did you move here from Italy?"

Roman sputtered mid-sip and set his glass down with a dull clink.

"Are you okay?" Aniella and Peter asked at once.

Roman coughed into his sleeve. "I'm fine. Went down the wrong way."

Loretta dabbed a clear droplet from the tablecloth. "Thank God that isn't wine. You would've stained it." She turned to Aniella. "What about Italy?"

"Unbelievable. I forgot dessert." Roman pushed away from the table. "The one time I actually…" He broke off, quieter now. "Sorry, Mom."

Loretta shifted, the chair legs creaking. "Is it that serious?" She waved toward the kitchen. "Peter brought sweets. They're in the fridge."

Roman nodded toward the kitchen. "Aniella, you wanna help me grab the desserts?"

Aniella followed him into the kitchen, watching as he opened the fridge and took the first thing within reach.

Aniella leaned against the counter. "Was it out of line asking about your mom moving from Italy?"

He held the fridge door a moment longer than needed. "It's a sensitive subject."

Aniella angled her head. "Sensitive? Or a lie?"

He smiled, as if forgiving her for misunderstanding. "She was sick when she was there. She's better now." He shut the fridge and handed her a tray of desserts.

"I just try to avoid upsetting her."

A pulse of self-consciousness ran through her. She loosened her stance. Had she crossed a family line, or did he want her second-guessing?

* * *

Headlights streaked across the garage door of Aniella's house. He cut the engine, the cabin settling into stillness.

"Sorry she cornered you at the market," Roman said at last.

Aniella's keys chimed faintly. "I had a nice time. I didn't mind."

He nodded once. "Good."

A pause stretched.

"How come you don't visit her often?" she asked. "It seemed like it had been a while since you'd been there."

"We're not that close."

He didn't know why he'd given her that piece of truth. Maybe because she was the only calm in his life. No noise, no sharp edges. She spoke like someone who'd never had to shout to be heard. In that gentleness, he'd found a version of peace that didn't exist anywhere else. She was safety. She was steady faith in human form. And he'd never known either.

Then he caught himself. His thumb had been tapping against the wheel. Steady, betraying. He froze it mid-beat.

"I'm sorry to hear that," she said. "She seemed happy to have us over. Enthusiastic, even."

He watched the faint smear of light on the windshield. "Enthusiasm's more about overcompensation."

"Overcompensation for what?"

The question cracked his history.

*No one's as worthless as you—I never loved you—you should just shoot yourself since you want to pull the trigger so bad!*

The gunshot rang inside his head, ricocheting through his memory until the aftermath weighed louder.

Roman removed his hand from the steering wheel. "We're just estranged. Like a lot of families."

He caught the subtle scrape of her keys against the armrest.

He hadn't expected her silence. Her curiosity usually filled every pause, but she stayed quiet. No more questions, no reach. Just the sound of the engine cooling between them. She couldn't know what he'd just seen, but somehow she matched it. The stillness from her seat wasn't absence—it was presence, like she was holding it with him.

For the first time in a long time, he didn't feel cornered. Just still. Seen, maybe.

"You've never shared anything with me before," she said, appreciation grounding her tone.

The words landed softly but reached deeper than she knew. Something inside him moved, undeniable. The mood turned, slow as a tide. The quick widening of her pupils gave her away.

He knew exactly where her mind had gone.

Aniella's grip found the door handle. "I should go."

"You should."

"I should."

The latch clicked, metal on metal.

He leaned in, his sleeve brushing her wrist. "Aniella."

Her name in his mouth was enough. He didn't think, just closed the distance. He slid the keys from her grasp and placed them on the dashboard. His lips settled on hers, slow at first, then deeper.

He broke the kiss, the current refusing to fade.

"Tell me to stop."

# CHAPTER 14

## Aftermath

Heaviness moved through Roman like molasses, a slow regret. He couldn't move. The sheets wrinkled under him, carrying the weight of what he'd done. The scent of clean linen lingered, warm vanilla, a sting that refused to fade.

Aniella dropped onto the mattress, the motion jolting him. A tray clattered across his lap.

"Good morning!" Her voice came joyful, oblivious. "I thought I'd make breakfast for you this time."

Roman pushed upright. The sheet slid to his waist, the chill catching on his bare skin.

French toast, lemon-peppered eggs, a grilled corn muffin. The smell should have stirred hunger, but unease sat heavier.

"I can't—"

Her hand raised. "I just thought I'd return the favor." She nudged the tray further up his lap. "It's just breakfast." She held out a fork. "Eat before it gets cold."

He took it from her, then set it down. "I can't eat right now."

Her excitement dimmed. "Oh…"

He scanned the room.

"Can't get out of here fast enough, can you?" she asked.

Roman met her stare, steady. "It's not that."

"I'm sorry," she said, tucking a strand of hair back. "That was uncalled for."

Control slipped, just enough for the truth to claw its way up before he could stop it. "I don't want to hurt you."

Her fingers brushed his forearm. "Then don't."

Whatever this was, whatever *she* was, it reached places he'd spent a lifetime barricading. Every kiss had been easier than this. Her words and tone were the threat. He thought of the night before, the way she'd dissolved his guard, the way he'd told her too much.

She was getting in.

No—she was already inside.

Too late to stop it.

Heat stung behind his eyes. He dragged his thumb across the bridge of his nose, a stalled attempt at composure. "Stop."

"Stop what?" She bunched the sheets on his side. "Are you okay?"

*That* tone, the gentle one, cut clean through him.

"I said stop."

She reached out anyway, palm hovering near his cheek. "Did I say something that upset you?"

He steadied, that fleeting vulnerability erased. "No. I'm allergic to pepper." He gestured to the tray. "You put pepper on something."

She paused before she straightened, her arms folding tightly. "Do you ever feel like a jerk?"

He lowered his hand, the move restrained. "For what?"

"For lying. Allergic to pepper? You doused your bacon in pepper."

He pushed the tray aside and stood. "Would you rather I admit you're right— that I can't wait to get out of here?"

Aniella rose too. "You're out of touch, Roman. You should really try to find someone."

"Someone like who?" His stance demanded an answer. "Let me guess. Someone like you?"

She squared her shoulders. "Do you have a hard time with relationships because of your job, or because you're just a jackass?"

Roman laughed once, no humor in it. "That's one hell of a question." He sought the floor for his clothes. "I'll have to think about that one."

"I'm just trying to understand you."

He stepped into his jeans. "You sure? Because it sounds like you're just trying to get jabs in."

"Why can't you admit what we both felt last night?"

He picked up his shirt from the floor. "Last night was another mistake."

Downstairs, china clinked, her grandmother's tea ritual starting.

"We can't keep doing this." He pulled his shirt down over his head. "This—whatever this is, is done."

\* \* \*

The conference room droned on within its recycled routine.

Aniella crossed the threshold with too much momentum, her folder clapping the table as she sat. The clap earned a few glances, then faded.

Her pencil tipped off and hit the floor, spiraling before resting against Roman's shoe.

He retrieved it and set it beside her notes.

The captain's briefing brought the room back to order. Pages shifted, pens marked. Attention drifted toward the front, except his.

"Viento." Ethan's voice cut across the aisle. "You got an answer or are we guessing today?"

Roman faced him. "To what?"

"Guess some of that training wore off." Ethan forwarded to the next slide. "Let's move on."

The meeting rolled on. Across the table, Tyler lingered on Aniella too long before redirecting to his notes. Roman let it pass. He adjusted his posture, a pointless motion, and waited for the meeting to drag to its end.

\* \* \*

A drawer rasped open, and a manila folder slipped up from the lip, before Iver shoved it closed again. "You'd be surprised how fast a name falls out of a file."

The vents carried a dry hum through the room, air thinning as if the building were listening.

"What are you saying?" Roman asked.

Iver handed him the folder. "Watch yours."

"What is it?"

Iver dusted his hands, tone dry. "Those guys from the basketball court tried to go through with an assault complaint. Had your name half-spelled before the system flagged it sealed."

"Thanks." Roman eased as he handed the folder back. "Appreciate it, Chief."

"I got other news." Iver hesitated. "It's not good."

A paperweight edged near the lip of the desk. Roman tracked its tilt.

"What is it?"

"Watch your back. More than ever."

The paperweight tipped a slow pendulum on the brink.

"Chief. Just say it."

\* \* \*

The revolving doors released them into a lobby full of light and marble glare. Roman steered for the counter, luggage trailing behind him.

146

"Two rooms. Adjoining."

The clerk typed. Keycards slid across.

Behind him, Aniella's reflection skimmed the polished floor. "Won't we get in trouble if we get separate rooms? Captain would never go for this."

His focus stayed on the registration pad. "I've dealt with him for years."

He took the cards and walked for the elevators.

The carpet muted their pace down the long, numbered corridor.

As they stopped outside their room, she spoke again. "Why are you breaking rules?" Her voice soft, but carried venom. "Are you afraid you can't control yourself?"

For a second, everything held, only the whir of the ice machine at the end of the hall.

Roman turned. Not fast.

Controlled.

He met her head-on, daring her to finish. "Excuse me?"

She didn't retreat. "You heard me."

Calm on the surface, but beneath it, something smoldered.

"I can't control myself?"

She plucked the keycard from his hand and tapped it to the lock. The light blinked green.

Inside, she crossed the room and dropped the card onto the nightstand. "I'm not getting written up because you can't take orders."

He parked the luggage beside the wall vent as it cycled a gust of cold.

Aniella grabbed the room-service menu and tossed it onto the comforter. "I said I'm not getting written up."

He didn't answer right away, just picked up the hotel pen and clicked it once, twice. The casing cracked under his grip. "That'd ruin everything for you, wouldn't it?"

She unclasped her earrings and placed them beside the phone. "He won't check receipts? How did he find out last time?"

Roman tugged once at his collar, loosening the tie. "He's not going to find out." He unfastened a button. Then another.

She slipped out of her heels, taking inches off her height. "If I don't report that you went against orders—"

His voice stayed level, but the restraint inside it felt combustible. "I didn't take you for a snitch, Fasquelle."

"Really? My last name?" She let her arms fall. "So we're strangers again. Third time's the charm, right?"

He said nothing.

She lifted her chin. "Since this is such a formal arrangement, and I've got a title to earn, I'm not risking getting caught." The next line seared with defiance. "I have a reputation to maintain."

"Nothing will ruin your reputation faster than that."

Whatever else he wanted to say stayed locked behind his jaw. He turned for the adjoining door.

Aniella followed, stride sharp enough to echo. "I don't understand why we can't just avoid getting in trouble and share a room like we're supposed to."

"Because it's not a good idea."

He reached the handle, but she braced the slab with her palm, halting it mid-swing.

"You're really gonna shut the door in my face?" she asked.

The line between them felt like a fuse waiting to burn.

"Step aside."

She crossed into the connecting room instead. "Then I'll stay in here."

"Why are you so damn persistent?" His thumb marked time against his pocket—he stopped.

She noticed. He could tell by how the space between them sharpened.

"Why is it not a good idea?" she asked.

Roman caught her by the arms and drew her from the doorway. The wall met her back with a dull thud. He held her pinned, close but measured. Heat and warning strained in the narrow gap between them. She reached for his sleeve, but he intercepted, locking both wrists against the painted plaster—firm, deliberate control.

His voice rasped. "Is this what you want?"

A battle coiled behind his restraint, unreadable but impossible to miss. Whatever held him together was splintering, and the fury beneath it burned through the cracks.

His breath ghosted over her mouth one last time. "*That's* why it's not a good idea."

Roman released her, then tore himself back, every muscle drawn tight enough to snap. Without another word, the adjoining door shut with a heavy, final turn of the lock.

* * *

Roman took in the nightstand, a hotel survey card, a folded notepad, the plastic remote, the alarm clock. His hand closed over the clock first, the cord sliding between his fingers as he pulled. The plug held, wedged tight behind the table. A harder tug rocked the lamp, and the cardboard coaster flung as the survey card flipped. The cord snagged on the outlet lip.

It came down to angle and leverage. He dragged the clock across the table edge, the plastic shrieking, the bedside cup tipping in protest. The plug tore free with a hollow pop. The alarm skittered across the carpet and fell still, its red digits glitching mid-flash.

He stood there, the warning from Iver sitting at the edge of his tongue.

He'd walked himself straight into this mess. No one to blame, no clean way out. The scope of it hit harder now, and worse, it wasn't fixable.

A text chimed on his cellphone.

It was Craig. "U there yet?"

"Be there in 30."

"30? Ready 2 go now."

"30."

Roman wasn't ready for anyone. He rubbed his temple, trying to scrape together a thought that made sense.

The hotel phone trilled on the nightstand.

He called through the wall. "That's not gonna work. I'm not answering!"

"I'm not calling you. That's not me!"

Roman untangled the cord. "Yeah?"

Ethan's voice came through the receiver. "Another reckless financial decision from you, Viento. Follow orders, or you're be benched for good next time."

* * *

The connecting door flew open, slamming hard against its frame. "Okay, you little snitch." His voice hit the room like an impact. "You proved your point."

Aniella sat up fast, pressing the power button on the TV. "Stop calling me a snitch!"

He hauled his suitcase onto the bed's edge. "You expect me to believe you didn't rat me out to the captain just now about the connecting rooms?"

"I swear I didn't!" Something in his hand stole her attention. "How dare you keep calling me that."

He dragged the zippers open.

"Just admit it," she said, remolding the sheets around herself like armor.

Roman pulled a T-shirt over his head, the same routine he always slipped into before leaving.

"You're avoiding the connection between us," she said. "You're afraid of the—"

"I'm attracted to you, Fasquelle. That doesn't mean I have feelings for you." The words landed merciless. He folded his dress shirt without pause, like he hadn't just gutted her.

She dug her nails into her palms. "Don't talk to me."

She waited for him to take it back. To show even a flicker of regret.

Nothing came.

"Roman?" Small, careful. "Why are you being so cold?"

Roman stuffed his gun into the back of his belt. "You let me lead you on because you wanted it so badly." He grabbed his wallet and a keycard from the nightstand. "Thanks to you, I have go try to get the department's precious money back from the connecting room."

The chain lock swung violently as the door slammed.

The room sealed itself around her, unbearable. "I don't want you in here, anyway!" She threw the hotel notepad across the distance, then bitterly yanked at the covers, desperate to disappear.

* * *

Aniella shuffled awake. *How long have I been sleeping?*

She pulled the curtain aside. Rain hammered the glass, streaking down in warped ribbons.

The cruelty. He had no idea how many times she'd protected him. She'd spent months covering for his deflecting questions.

Spite surged as she scrolled to the captain's name in her phone. Normally she wouldn't.

But he dismantled her. Left her feeling erased.

She tapped the captain's name on the screen and waited for the line to pick up, forcing the pain out of it.

"Polinski."

"Hi, Captain. Roman said he was leaving to fix getting two rooms I told you about, but that was a while ago, and I have no idea where he is."

A pause.

"Did he say when he was coming back?"

Guilt pricked her, but it was too late. "He didn't communicate anything with me."

"Do you feel comfortable trying to find him?" Ethan's tone shifted, expectant now. "Find out where he went."

* * *

Aniella searched the lobby, then the bar. Roman was out there somewhere, and she was going to catch him in the act.

She snapped her umbrella open and pushed through the downpour. "Oh my God, there's no way I'm going to find him in this."

Rain pounded the pavement, soaking her ankles within seconds. This was stupid. It wasn't worth this.

His line rang. Then nothing. But of course he didn't answer. If she wasn't trying to get him in trouble, she wouldn't be calling. She circled the hotel lot.

The line rang again, then voicemail. "*Detective Viento. Leave a message.*"

She held the phone to her ear for a second, then ended the call. A thought tugged at her. Had there been another phone in his hand earlier? Maybe she'd imagined it.

"Ugh! This is so ridiculous." Her clothes clung, sopping wet. "One more try, then I'm done."

Aniella rounded the corner, the call still ringing when a sharp crack split through the night.

She jumped. *What was that?*

A figure bolted in the opposite direction through the rain's blur, and a faint glow pulsed from the ground ahead. Her own phone still rang in her hand. The light, was it his?

Aniella jogged toward it, shoes sloshing through the puddles, then slowed when she spotted another figure in the distance.

"Hello?" She approached cautiously, the rain distorting everything ahead.

The outline resolved. It was Roman.

"Your phone's on the ground, getting ruined!" She wiped wet strands from her face. "What are you doing?"

The rain hammered all around them.

"Roman!" She raised the umbrella higher. "Why won't you answer me?" She took a step closer. "Answer me."

Roman's palms flattened over his chest, gaze lowering to where red bloomed through his shirt.

Her focus followed—then froze.

Blood spread through his jacket, dark and steady, pooling over his palms. Roman stumbled backward. The dumpster shuttered as he hit it, metal clanging as his legs buckled. He slipped down the front of it, collapsing onto the wet pavement.

Roman wasn't getting back up.

"No—Roman!" Aniella's knees cracked against the pavement beside him. She fumbled for her phone, hands trembling so hard the screen blurred. "Somebody please, help!"

"911, what's your emergency?"

"Please help, he's shot! Please send help!" Her head whipped over her shoulder, fearing her shrieks would draw the attention of the shooter.

Static crackled over the line.

"Is he conscious?"

Roman struggled for air, each draw shallow and ragged.

"He can't breathe, oh my God, please help! He can't breathe!"

"Where was he shot?"

Rain mixed with blood on her hands as she searched, desperate to find where it was coming from. She traced over him, frantic. Everything was slick—his shirt saturated, hiding everything. "I can't tell—there's too much blood!"

"Try to apply pressure to the wound the best you can. An ambulance is on its way."

Aniella shoved her phone in her pocket. "Oh my God, Roman. I'm so sorry." She tore off her raincoat, balled it tight, and forced it hard against his stomach. "Please let this be the right spot. Please."

His focus blurred, loosening their anchor. Roman was slipping.

She pushed harder. "Hang on, Roman, please, hang on. They're coming!"

She could do nothing but watch. The rise beneath her hands grew shallow. His weight folded, tilting him sideways against the dumpster.

Aniella hauled him upright before easing him flat. "Oh God, please let this be right."

A rough sound tore from his throat as blood welled and spilled down, the rain carrying it away in dark streams, like the night itself was bleeding him out.

"Help's coming, Roman! Help's coming!"

He started to look at her, then wavered, the fight draining out of him.

"Stay awake, Roman!" She squeezed his hand. "Stay awake!"

Sirens broke through the storm, red and blue cutting across the lot.

Puddles burst as paramedics hit the pavement running.

An officer's shout cut through the downpour. "Over here!"

A senior paramedic tilted Roman's head, light flickering once across his pupils. "Can you talk to us? Can you hear me?"

No response.

He glanced at Aniella, concentrated. "What's his name?"

"Roman!"

"Roman, can you talk to me?" The light snapped off. The paramedic met his partner's look. "Altered."

The stretcher clattered over the pavement. As they lifted him, a broken gasp slipped free. They strapped him down quickly.

Aniella clenched her hands together so hard her knuckles cracked. "Is he going to be okay?"

"We're doing everything we can." A hand slammed against the ambulance window. "Code 3, let's go, let's go, let's go!"

In the ambulance, scissors ripped through fabric, exposing the damage beneath. His skin had gone ashen, lips and fingers turning blue.

A medic leaned over him. "Roman, can you hear me?"

A jolt passed through him, brief but there. His fingers curled slightly, twitching, his body clinging to awareness.

IV tubing looped around the stretcher while a medic fitted an oxygen mask over him.

The senior medic tore it away. "Not enough. Bag him."

The medic hesitated—a second too long.

The senior medic grabbed the bag-valve mask. "Move. I've got it." He squeezed, forcing oxygen back into him.

Roman barely lifted with the effort.

"Come on—breathe."

A sting—then the cold rush of saline through the line.

"BP's 78 over 45—he's crashing, get another line going."

Another medic ripped open an IV kit and drove a line into the opposite arm.

"Heart rate's at 178—not holding."

They rolled him slightly, checking his flank. "Through and through, exit in the back." A medic blotted away the pooling blood. "Nine millimeter, most likely."

A stethoscope touched his side. "No lung sound on the right—tension pneumo."

Roman braced as a tremor rolled through him, pain threading its way deeper.

"We're losing him—needle decompression, now!"

# CHAPTER 15

## Trail of Secrets

The hospital doors burst open, the stretcher's wheels streaking across scuffed tile.

A doctor met the gurney mid-corridor. "Catch me up. What are we working with?"

"Gunshot wound to the chest, collapsed lung, high-risk for shock, needs blood transfusion."

The doctor glanced once at him. "He's slipping into it now."

"Needle decompression was done, still needs a chest drain."

"Page cardiology—prep Trauma One." The doctor fell in with the team, pushing the stretcher faster. "Priority's the bleed. We relieve the pressure, or he arrests."

Shapes blurred beside Roman, ceiling lights striking blades of white.

The trauma room doors swung open.

"Rapid abdomen at bedside," the doctor said, calm but in a hurry. "Portable X-ray—check for fragments. CT if the scan misses."

"Portable X-ray's en route."

The doctor scanned the monitor. "Traumatic hemopneumothorax. Chest drain prepped?"

"Ready."

The tube slid between Roman's ribs. Air hissed out—a burst of relief that hit like pain.

"Feels good to breathe again, doesn't it?" The doctor didn't wait for an answer. "All right, let's move. We need to close him up."

Roman's head rolled to the side, lips shaping words too heavy to rise.

The doctor gave his shoulder a quick squeeze. "Save your energy for surgery."

"I remember him," a nurse said. "Stab wound a while back. He refused something."

"Allergies?"

"I don't remember, but I flagged it in his file for him."

"Check it fast." The doctor motioned to another nurse. "He'll need coverage when he wakes. Get his pain orders."

\* \* \*

Aniella stared at the white walls, dulled to yellow, until the doctor stepped into the waiting room.

She sprang to her feet. "Doctor, is he okay?"

"He made it through surgery. He'll be in intensive care for now."

Aniella laced her fingers tight, joints straining. "Is he going to be okay?"

His hands disappeared into his coat pocket. "It's a miracle none of his major organs were ruptured, but he's not in the clear yet."

"Can I see him?"

"I'd like to see if his vitals stay stable overnight. No visitors until morning." He studied her face, drained, pale. "Go home. Get some rest."

\* \* \*

Aniella shifted in the waiting-room chair until her spine cracked. Morning light seeped through the blinds. Her arm, used overnight as a pillow, had long gone numb. Laughter cut through the quiet as families hurried past.

She rose, kneading the stiffness from her neck, and crossed to the front desk. "Hi, good morning. May I see Roman Viento?"

The receptionist didn't look up. "Who?"

Aniella's brows pinched. "Roman Viento. He came in last night. I just wanted to see if he could have visitors now."

The woman flipped through papers on her clipboard. "We don't have anybody here by that name."

"Was he moved?"

"Nope." She checked the list again. "No Roman Viento admitted here."

"That's impossible. He was brought here last night. He had an emergency surgery—"

"Sorry." The receptionist set the clipboard down. "Maybe you have the wrong hospital."

The fax machine beeped behind the counter.

"No—I've been here all night."

The phone trilled, and the receptionist answered it without another look at her.

Names on the clipboard blurred. She turned away, the distortion at odds with reality. *What in the world is going on?*

\* \* \*

Iver entered the break room, locked on Ethan like a heat-seeking missile. "Whose unit is this?"

A cabinet thudded closed as Ethan turned to face him. "Ours—"

"This is *my* unit. *I'm* king here." The edge of the plastic tablecloth lifted in the draft, territorial, like drawing a line in the sand. "I pulled Fasquelle off Viento's case. Don't ever add someone to an assignment without my consent again."

Ethan froze, words tangling. "Fasquelle was assigned to shadow him. She's logging field hours for promotion to Intelligence Analyst—"

"The cases I've got him on aren't yours to question. And I don't give a damn if some little admin aide who should be answering phones wants field training for her pipe dream. Understood?" Iver's stare hit like a spotlight. "He's on a high-priority lead. Keep it radio silence."

Heat crept through the mug into Ethan's palm. "I looked over the file. The task seemed—"

"I don't care what it seemed like. You don't ever make a call without running it by me first."

* * *

Aniella dragged her steps through the bullpen, searching each office door. *Where's Captain?*

Her phone flowed with missed calls. The captain had tried last night and again this morning.

The Chief, though, had also called. Once in the dead of night, then again at dawn. She knew why Ethan kept trying, but Iver was a mystery.

She found Iver in his office, leafing through papers as if the world hadn't cracked open.

The rustle stopped. "Fasquelle. I've been trying to reach you since last night."

Her feet felt too heavy to carry her farther. "I meant to call, but—" The image came back hard. Roman slumped against the dumpster, rain streaked red down his shirt. "I've never seen something so horrible in my life."

Iver nodded knowingly. "It's unfortunate when things like this happen. But they do." He motioned to the chair in front of him. "Sit." When she did, his tone dropped. "Don't share this with anyone. That includes the captain."

She pulled a frayed thread on her pants seam. "Don't tell the captain?"

"Viento's on a private operation. As you know, those run on a need-to-know." He leaned forward. "I was the only one in the department on that list."

Aniella's stomach knotted.

He broadened his shoulders. "That means no one knows he was shot. No one knows he was in the hospital. If anyone asks questions, direct them to me."

A paper slipped from the stack, its landing thinning the pause that followed.

Iver watched her closely. "I trust I can count on you to follow that."

"…Yes."

The papers bunched under his hand. "Yes?"

The frayed thread fell to the floor. "Yes, of course." She turned for the door.

"Fasquelle."

Aniella paused, fingers tightening around the knob. "Yes?"

"Don't go to see him."

The floor swallowed her feet, every step harder to lift. Ethan waited by her desk, coffee in hand.

He set the mug down as she approached. "What'd you find when you followed him? Was he with anyone?"

"Um…" The haze of Iver's office still blanketed her. "No. Nothing."

Ethan grabbed the mug handle, but didn't lift it. "What happened? Where did you find him? What was he doing?"

She hesitated. "No, he…"

This time he picked up the mug. "Nothing to indicate he was—"

"Captain." Aniella covered her mouth, as if nauseous. "I was going to ask if I could go home. I don't think I'd accomplish much today."

He dropped the mug back down, coffee splashing near her keyboard. "You're holding something back. And considering how fast Hackett pulled you from shadowing, I'm guessing you were told to keep quiet."

"No—I—" The apology tumbled out, twisted in uncertainty. "I was just—"

Ethan waved her off. "Go home, Fasquelle."

*He knows I'm lying.*

# CHAPTER 16

## Not the Same

Victor sagged into the recliner, arms spilling over the sides, the pale ladder of track marks exposed. "Give me enough liquid for a few days."

"If you can pay, smoke or sniff it." The dealer hitched his pant leg. "Save your veins."

"Well, I *can't* pay!" Victor flicked a hand toward the floor. "Give me enough for him too."

A small boy crouched on the floor, playing with toy trucks.

"You gonna share that with the kid?"

Victor slurred. "You want your money or not?"

The boy crashed two plastic trucks together, lost in the world of voices he invented that carried across the carpet.

The dealer traced a lazy cross—forehead, chest, shoulder to shoulder—then fished a bag from his pocket.

The screen door shut behind him.

Victor turned toward the boy and whistled through his teeth. "Come here."

The clack of plastic stopped. Roman rose, one sneaker dragging the carpet as he inched closer to the recliner.

Victor lunged, seizing Roman's arm and hauling him close.

Roman twisted against the grip. "Please stop! You're hurting me!"

Victor's grip tightened. "Quit squirming, you little shit!"

* * *

Roman's lungs seared from the sudden pull of air.

A hand shook his shoulder. "Hey, you okay?"

The room sharpened back into view, the nurse's chart half-closed mid-page.

Roman braced against the thin blanket. The cough that followed tore through him dry, jagged, punishing.

"Your cord came unplugged," she said, re-seating it until the monitors flared alive again. "You've been yelling in your sleep."

Roman brushed the moisture from his brow. "Sorry about that."

"Was it about the shooting?"

Roman shook his head. He wasn't about to explain.

"It's been eight days." She folded the blanket down with practiced neatness. "Doctor says you're good to go home after your checkup." The bed railing clicked into place as she lowered it.

Roman edged one leg over the side of the bed. A bolt of pain lanced through his chest, freezing him. *Standing. It's just standing.*

"Your body's been through hell," she said. "Take your time."

He grabbed the railing, then the IV pole, knuckles turning white as the plastic tubing brushed his wrist. He'd barely moved, yet the effort fogged his skin with sweat.

"A week ago, you couldn't even sit up on your own. Now look at you."

He managed a weak thumbs-up. On his feet for the first time without assistance since admission, and the room was already spinning. A few steps in, and he was already winded.

The nurse grabbed the incentive spirometer off the counter. "Let's do an exercise you'll need for recovery."

"You trying to kill me?"

"Only hurt you a little." She handed him the spirometer. "Deep. Hold, then cough."

His lungs, weak and unwilling. Frustration simmered stronger now. The pity, the spirometer barely budging, the slam of doors in the hall.

"Ten times an hour. Call us if you cough up blood."

Roman set the spirometer on the foot of the bed. No chance.

"It'll sting, but skip it and you'll risk pneumonia." She took the spirometer and placed it in a bag. "It's gonna be a few hours before we process your paperwork for discharge. Need anything in the meantime?"

The tray table had been cleared.

"That jello crap you guys give out." He lowered himself onto the bed, motion tight.

"Have the Naproxen and Tylenol been working?" she asked. "Want something stronger?"

Roman eased back, palm flat over the gauze. "No."

"I know you see pain as the lesser evil, but pain control is part of the healing process. Too much pain can slow your recovery, and if the—"

"No." His voice cut through, firm. "Don't ask again."

She started toward the door, then paused at the frame. "You've got a visitor."

Loretta bounced in, each step light and deliberate, like she'd rehearsed the entrance.

Roman went still, instinct locking him before thought could intervene.

Her chin lifted, nose angled high. "I had to threaten your chief with the local news just to find you," she said, pleased. "He said nobody's supposed to know you're here." Her attention searched his hospital gown. "You get shot and don't even call your mother?"

Roman clamped both palms to his temples, trying to grind her voice out of his head. "You did what?"

"How could you not call your mother when you were on your deathbed?"

"I'm fine."

"It's always 'I'm fine' with you." Her tremor was pure theatre. "You said that even when I tried to help you before."

Roman clenched so hard he half-expected to feel enamel splinter. "I don't want to hear this right now."

"I remember that night I came home late after working a double shift and I cracked your bedroom door open and you were passed out on the—"

He bit down harder, patience worn to wire. "We're not doing this."

"No, I need to tell you what I went through."

Of course. What *she* went through.

Roman's hand found the IV line, not to pull it out, but to anchor himself before he said something he'd regret.

"You have no idea what it was like—seeing my only child on the floor, not knowing if you were alive or dead." She drifted closer, fingertips grazing her throat like the memory still burned. "I shook you. I called your name again and again. You were nine."

Roman twisted the sheet edge once around his fist. *Steady.*

"I vowed to be a better mother years ago." Her tone dropped into that same old practiced martyr's pitch. "But *you* never let me."

Roman exhaled once, slow and measured. It was impressive, really, how even now she could twist the blame back toward him.

She was whisper-quiet, as if a secret just fell from the ceiling. "Did they give you drugs?"

His focus snapped up, sharp.

"Did you tell them what your father did to you? How he gave you a life full of struggles?"

"Mom—"

"Just tell me if they drugged you so I can get you help. Set up an NA meeting. Call a—"

His tongue locked against a molar. "I'm on Tylenol."

Loretta leaned forward, another speech chambered but nowhere to aim it.

"Oh." She rocked back, recalibrating. "Well... that's non-habit forming."

The IV line coiled once more in his hand.

"By the way, why do they have you—"

"We're not doing this right now."

She blinked twice, innocence weaponized. "Doing what?"

A hollow knock on the doorframe, then heavy footsteps.

"You're finally up."

Iver stepped in. An indecipherable glance passed between them. Roman felt her stare next, searching. For what, he wasn't sure. But he didn't give her anything.

Loretta's lifted her chin. Not quite a nod, not quite defiance. Something in between. "I'll let you two catch up." She swept out, silence trailing like residue.

Iver watched her exit, then dragged a chair closer. "How you holding up?"

Roman released the tangled IV. "You just saved me from tying this around my neck."

Iver gave a dry chuckle. "She's a character." His tone shifted, elbows settling on his knees. "Craig called me."

"Craig?"

"Said he found you hit when he got there for your meet. Saw someone else, so he took off."

Roman studied him. "Anyone else with him?"

"Didn't say. You think it was a setup?"

"Julian's still bitter about his fingers." Roman nudged the call button out of reach. "Craig's loyal to whoever lines his pockets, and Julian's got the cash to sway him. Besides, Craig's held a grudge on me too."

"Did you get a description at all?"

"Left-handed. Shorter than me, five-ten, maybe. I looked down when it burned. Looked back up, he was gone."

Julian was around five-ten. Also left-handed.

"That's something. Good details." Iver shifted. "I had to put out a few fires."

"Polinski?"

"Handled it. Told him you were working a cover. Fasquelle knows you're hit, but I warned her to keep quiet. It'll be another problem if she starts asking questions."

Roman smoothed a crease from the blanket. "She won't be a problem."

"How do you know?"

"Because she won't be. She's a mouse. Tell her to keep quiet, she will." Roman traced the weave of the blanket. "She's nothing to worry about."

Iver nodded. "I had the hospital list you under your alias. In case Julian or anyone started sniffing around."

"Thanks."

"Yeah, well, if this was intentional, better to keep your real name off the books."

Roman eased deeper into the pillow's give. "Appreciate it."

"How you gonna handle Julian?"

"Without proof it was him?"

"And Craig?"

* * *

Roman held the ice pack to his chest, the chill setting deep into the wound. He peeled back the bandage. The pale, gummy flesh stitched together in a rough seam. It was the first time he'd faced it in the mirror. He followed the bullet's path with his fingertip, then drifted lower to the old scar above his pelvis. Past and present. Two exits he wasn't supposed to survive. *I should be dead.* He swallowed the thought, then reached for the tape.

He sealed the fresh bandage, then stepped into the shower. The spray hit his back, needling against skin that hadn't known pressure in days. He tried to lift his arm, but his body refused. Fire laced through his ribs. He misjudged himself. Everyday strength, taken for granted. Outside, the world kept moving, but inside, he was weak, healing, and useless.

Something heavier stole the air from him.

It was her.

She'd been lying.

Roman left the shower, reached for a towel, and caught the phone buzzing against the porcelain. "Hey, Captain."

"You feeling good enough to answer your damn phone, or do I need to call your emergency contact?"

Emergency contact? *Shit.* He tightened the towel around his hand until the cotton stretched.

"Were you just going to waltz into the district with a bullet hole like nothing happened?"

*I thought Iver handled this.* "No, I—"

"I had to hear it from a patrolman, who heard it from a nurse. Imagine that exchange—'How's your detective holding up?' and me standing there like an idiot."

The alias. That's what mattered. Hospitals ran on aliases all the time—nurses treated false names like gospel. The nurse wouldn't have leaked that. That much he trusted.

"Tell me, Viento. Why the hell is one of my detectives bleeding out in a hospital for eight days and I hear about it by accident?"

"I didn't think it was relevant."

"Not relevant? You're shot! Hackett was moving all this? That why Fasquelle was pulled?"

"It wasn't personal."

"Here's what *is* personal. You're not cleared to come back. Not by a long shot. I put you on limited. You'll need a psych eval before you can even touch the stapler on your desk."

Roman let the towel fall from his grip.

"You've got an appointment tomorrow morning. And if I find out any more shady business is going on, you'll have problems far worse than a psych eval."

\* \* \*

Sirens tangled with street noise outside the district. The ground quivered from construction underneath. Paint peeled from the building that had eaten years of his life. Nothing sharpened purpose like almost dying.

On the third floor, the bullpen's chaos hit him like a strange kind of homecoming—phones ringing, files stacking, Scott cramming a cookie in his mouth.

Then, her voice. Melodic, threading through the noise.

Across the bullpen, Aniella sat with her back to him, a phone pressed to her ear. The sunlight caught in her hair as she shifted papers from one hand to the other. He couldn't make out the words, just the cadence and the calm that had once grounded him.

Scott closed the lid to the container. "Ro! You're back." He wiped his shirt, freeing crumbs to the floor.

Tyler leaned back in his chair, taking Roman in. "Damn, Viento. You're a walking crime scene."

Roman stayed still. Numb. Fixed on Aniella.

"She's been buried in calls all morning," Scott said, as if reading Roman's thoughts.

Tyler leaned forward fast. "What's worse? Getting shot or stabbed?"

Roman's thumb ticked once inside his pocket. "I don't know, Grave. Both kinda sucked."

"You good, Rome?" Scott asked.

"I've got an eval."

Scott's gaze flicked between Aniella and Roman. "Uh… Can we go to the break room real quick?"

\* \* \*

Roman sat at the break room table, elbow sliding off the slick surface while Scott went to war with the hand sanitizer.

Pump. Rub. Another pump. "You feeling all right?" Scott scrubbed like a surgeon prepping for battle.

Roman tapped once on the table. "Glorious."

Scott grabbed a paper towel and wiped his hands. "How's the healing going?"

"As expected."

Pump. Pump. Pump. The sanitizer might as well have been acid by now.

Roman squinted. "I said healing. Not contagious."

Scott rubbed his palms raw, syncing with Roman's slow tap on the table. "You sure you're all right?"

Roman traced the condensation ring along a water bottle. "Everything's fine."

Scott tossed the empty sanitizer bottle in the trash. "Nothing's going on?"

Roman peeled at the corner of the break room's flimsy napkin dispenser. "No."

"Come on," Scott said, playful disbelief under his tone. "You never fidget like this."

"Oh yeah? You just used up an entire bottle of hand sanitizer. What's going on with you?"

Scott rubbed his hands some more. "It, uh… must be hard for you."

Roman flicked a stray coffee ground off the table. "What?"

Scott cleared his throat. "Knowing you'd… go after Aniella—if you could."

Roman's hand tightened on the chair's edge. "What are you talking about?"

Scott shrugged. "I saw the way you were looking at her."

Nothing but silence.

"Aren't you gonna argue that?" Scott asked.

Roman hesitated. "It's complicated."

"Whoa, man of many secrets. Didn't expect that response."

"I'd say more, but you drink too much."

"Nothing could ever get me drunk enough to repeat this. Tell me."

Maybe it was the near-death clarity, or just exhaustion, but the secret broke loose anyway.

"We've been seeing each other," Roman said.

"You've been what?" Scott yanked open the cabinet and grabbed another sanitizer bottle. "You ever watch someone about to make a mistake but you can't stop them?"

"I know."

"But you're doing more than knowing. You're participating. That's risky."

Roman didn't answer. He'd already considered the outcome.

"What if the captain found out before you're ready?"

"I don't know."

"You don't know?" Scott asked. "You know what else?"

Roman crushed the water bottle in his palm. "Say it."

"Do you feel something for her?"

"That's not what this is." Roman's voice thinned. He set the heel of his palm against his sternum, like trying to quiet something that wouldn't stay down. "I just—do you think I'm... like—"

"I've never heard you stutter, you're making me nervous."

Roman stood, then let the wall take his weight. "You ever have someone just... hold you after?"

Scott blinked. "Well, yeah, it's a cuddle session."

Roman frowned. "What the hell is that?"

"You've never had a cuddle session?"

"Stop saying it like that."

Scott pumped sanitizer in his hands. "You've never been held before?"

"It's like..." Roman searched for words that didn't exist. "She runs her fingers through my hair, keeps me still. It's like nothing else is there but us... I don't even know what to call it."

Scott's brows lifted. "Well that answers that question."

"What question?"

"You're in love."

Roman stiffened. "What? No. That's not it."

"You almost died, and now you're realizing what's important to you." Scott nodded in agreement with himself. "Cause and effect."

The pressure mounted until Roman's thoughts collided behind his stillness.

"I get it," Scott said. "She's sweet, and you grew up around chaos. Anyone would chase that kind of peace."

Scott said it like a diagnosis, and worse, it fit. The hum of the fridge, the AC, the world. All of it merged until nothing could be separated.

"Roman?"

Every thought clawed for an escape. An escape out of the room, out of the talk, out of his own damn head.

"You all right, Rome?"

Air. He needed it. Roman pushed off the wall. "I can't—" He stopped himself, control splintering between his steps.

"Do you need me to call a doctor?"

Roman backed for the door. "I'm fine."

He cut through the bullpen, each step narrowing his focus to survival alone.

Then Aniella again. At her desk, tending the pink roses she always kept close. Her back was still turned, brushing a petal with the same careful touch that once steadied him. But it meant nothing now. Not after what she'd done.

* * *

Tyler posted up at Aniella's workstation. "Viento was just here, you missed him. Not surprised this happened to him, though."

Aniella gathered a few reports, paperclip in hand. "What's that supposed to mean?"

He flicked the corner of a folder, casual. "Just saying. Roman's got a way of finding trouble. Or maybe it finds him."

Simone powered on the printer machine. "You don't know what you're talking about, Grave."

"Don't I?" Tyler's tone dropped, conspiratorial. "The guy's always got something going on. Disappears for eight days, shows up looking like he went twelve rounds with the Reaper? What kind of detective takes more undercover gigs than homicide cases?"

The pages under Aniella's hand went still. "I trust Roman," she said. "He always has my back. So why would I—"

"That's cute. Really. But you don't know the first thing about Roman."

"And you do?" she asked.

"I do, and I'm telling you to be careful."

"Sounds like gossip to me."

Simone pulled out the tray and filled it with more paper. "All right, Grave, go stir shit somewhere else."

Tyler raised both hands in mock surrender. "Just giving some friendly advice."

Simone dropped into his chair, the wheels squealing. "Ignore him. He thinks he's the department's personal watchdog. He's also always had a thing for Roman."

\* \* \*

Roman stalled in the doorway, Scott's words still echoing inside. The white walls ahead seemed brighter than he remembered. Harsher. Like they'd been waiting for him.

Judy looked up from the sleek home-decor spread. "Detective." The magazine folded closed with a hush. "Welcome."

Roman still hadn't entered.

"Detective?"

Roman smoothed a hand down his thigh and crossed the threshold.

She gestured to the worn chair across from her. "Make yourself comfortable."

Roman lowered into the chair slowly. "Captain put me on modified."

"I'm aware." She lifted a notebook onto her lap. "Knowing where to start is usually the hardest part. Let's begin small."

His hands clasped once, still. "No offense, but I'd rather cut the small talk."

"All right. Let's get right into the shooting, then."

"I said everything in my debrief."

"You covered the facts, not the impact," she said. "I gave you space, but space has limits. You've never given a glimpse of what's inside." Her pen hovered above the page. "Let's make this hour count, since you have to be here."

The leather sighed under him.

"This isn't your first near-death call. That kind of repetition leaves marks."

Roman studied the gouge in the armrest. "I'm sure it would for some."

Judy turned a page in his file. "I requested your hospital records. Says here you nearly drowned in your own blood after your lung collapsed."

Rain fractured his memory—gunfire slicing through it, the shock, the slide against wet metal. Blood clotting his throat. No air. Only the cold drag of gravity pulling him down.

"Detective?"

Roman's focus hollowed as he returned. "It's like going to hell and coming back. You don't think you're gonna make it, but then you do, and the world's spinning again."

"So you're saying everything's back to normal?"

"I'm alive. That's good enough for me."

"I'm glad you see it that way. But what does normal look like to you, Detective?"

"Same as everyone else's."

Judy adjusted her glasses. "You shut the door on your own emotions, Detective. That's not what everyone else does. And it's not healthy."

"What are you looking for?" His tone sharpened. "The right button?"

"Are these questions pushing your buttons?"

"It's not a problem to talk about it," he said, his tone leveling again. "I just don't know why I've got to do it now."

"I try to respect people's comfort levels, but with your history, I can't." She put her pen down. "If it's not hard, why haven't you talked?"

"Never needed to."

"Why haven't you needed to?"

"Because I've moved on."

Judy picked up the pen. "Or you've pushed it down far enough to make yourself believe you have."

Roman's gaze remained on the floor.

"I don't think you've been honest with yourself in *years*, Detective. I'd bet you don't even step inside your own head, do you?"

"That's a hell of an assumption."

"Not an assumption. A conclusion. Those experiences leave memories. Suppressing them isn't the same as moving on."

His hand flattened on the armrest. "I don't sit around reliving it. Isn't that moving on?"

"You dodge questions. And I want to get to the reason for that."

"I dodge your questions because I don't like being told I have to share private parts of my life just to keep my job."

"I'm here to make sure you return to your job safely. You want to work, I want to do mine. You help me, I'll help you."

Aniella's face sliced through his thoughts, uninvited. He pushed it out. "You can't force someone to talk about something they're not ready to."

"I thought you were over those events?"

"I am."

"Then how are you not ready?"

"I am... ready. I just don't need to discuss them."

"No—you've buried it deep enough to fool yourself. I don't buy that a man with your record goes home clean." She rested the folder on the side table. "Give me one brief insight from your perspective. As soon as you do that, you're free to go."

Roman brushed at a spec on the armrest, the motion too deliberate to mean nothing.

"I'm done playing cat and mouse, Detective. If you can't give me something real, I won't sign you fit for duty."

"You're really pulling this?"

"You have to let me do my job."

"And I have to do mine. You're using this as an opportunity to drag something out of me. You'd feel like you'd earned it too, wouldn't you?"

"I'm sorry that you feel that way—"

"Don't apologize for your wrong impression about how I feel." His tone cut clean. "I'm sorry you feel this is the moment you get a reward."

"I'm not going to back down, Detective," she said. "I won't be bending the rules anymore."

"All right." His voice went flat. "Then I guess you'll just have to refuse to sign it."

\* \* \*

Roman pushed into Iver's office, catching him mid-sip of coffee.

"Shit, Viento—what the hell?"

"That fucking Polinski." Roman jabbed a finger toward the desk. "If you don't put a collar on him, I swear—"

Iver pushed back his chair. "What the hell happened?"

"He forced a psych eval and she's refusing to sign my slip."

Iver wiped coffee from his chin. "That son of a bitch. I told him to back off you." He punched the phone keys, each click louder than the last until the ring tone swallowed the room.

Roman's weight tipped forward, his body itching to move, but pain froze him where he stood.

Finally, the line clicked alive.

"It's the Chief," Iver said, edged in command. "Unless Viento's shown any clear sign of endangering himself, his colleagues, or the public, you have no right to hold that signature. Sign his slip now."

A beat. Then the receiver hit the cradle, the sound ricocheting off the walls.

# CHAPTER 17

## Unveiled

Roman's footsteps echoed along the worn wood of the desolate church. Frankincense and myrrh hung thick in the air. Each reluctant step drew him toward the glaring Christ carved into the crucifix, a reminder that he didn't belong. Emotion mounted, and he hadn't even confessed yet.

Roman steadied himself, thumb tracing the seam of his jeans as he opened the confessional door. The booth seemed to close in, ready to suffocate. Nausea waved through him as he thought of voicing what he'd done. He wondered if coming here was already too far. The confessional door waited, slit of shadow half-open. His thumb dug into his palm, anchoring the choice—stay and speak, or leave and never say a word. He reminded himself that his identity in the booth would remain private. That he could finally lay down the weight without fearing the judgment of someone who knew him. He exhaled, using the maroon carpet to steady himself against the pull to bolt. He stepped inside. Guilt. Grief. Rage. Every buried emotion surged up, stealing what little air remained in the booth. His knees threatened to give. The seat creaked. The wood pressed cold against his back. He scuffed his shoes against the carpet, and he was really in now.

Shadows netted the priest's face through the lattice.

A vibration hit his thigh, but this time it wasn't his thumb striking. He glanced down toward the feeling—his hands were shaking.

"Bless me, Father... I have sinned." Words scraped past him, and his throat tightened as the confession forced its way forward. "It's been several years since my last confession."

The rosary beads rubbed against each other. "I hear your reluctance," the priest said warmly. "What's kept you from returning to God's grace?"

Roman sifted through the moments that led him here. "Bad decisions, Father."

"A good man sometimes makes bad decisions," the priest said. "But when a good man continues to make bad ones, he eventually becomes what he does."

Roman found the edge of the booth's frame, desperate to swallow the guilt, but it kept rising—choking him. "I understand, Father."

The priest folded his cassock across his lap. "By the grace of God you're here now. What burdens your soul?"

The booth seemed to tilt, and the edges of his vision blackened, as if a cloth were being drawn over his sight. It was no longer an idea but a reckoning with the secrets he'd guarded all these years. His hands, once shaking, were now trembling. He slipped his hands under his legs.

"Time's supposed to heal. But the older I get, the worse it gets." He lowered his head. "I can't bring myself..."

The priest's silence drew the truth out of him like gravity.

"Someone I know says—" Roman stopped. "She says—" The word caught somewhere he couldn't reach. Beneath his legs, his thumb struck once against the wood, a pulse he couldn't stop. "She says something a lot."

Shadows shifted over the priest's face as he adjusted. "It brings you back to somewhere painful."

The booth seemed to contract.

"I was shot recently, and... the gunpowder, the ringing. It all dragged me back."

"To where?"

"I begged." Roman's brows drew tight. "I pleaded. Over and over…" His voice broke as he finally allowed himself access to his most suppressed memory.

The untold story of his childhood…

\* \* \*

"No—please!" Roman screamed, lip tearing wider, his cries falling on deaf ears. "Please!"

Victor and Loretta shouted back and forth like the bitter enemies they'd become, their hate for each other suffocating the room. Roman told himself everything would be okay. That they fought like this all the time, and that they'd forgive each other like they always had. He knew his father had anger issues, but he would never—

"Burn in hell!"

"I oughta take you with me!"

Victor raised the gun, anger unbridled. Roman struggled for it—and this time, got it. Victor lunged, his grip inches away. The shouting ceased as the gunshot shattered the air. Roman slowly lowered his arms, the gun still warm in his hands as he watched his father's body collapse.

"Victor!" Loretta dropped beside him as blood pooled. She turned to Roman. "Call an ambulance!"

Roman dragged his feet into the dark restroom. He passed the mirror, then froze, the reflection spattered with his father's blood. He sat on the closed toilet lid, knowing there was no reason to call for help. His father was gone. "You'll never hurt us again," he whispered. He blinked at last, the salt from his tears burning the split in his lip.

\* \* \*

Silence broke when a tear dropped onto the leather of Roman's shoe.

The priest dabbed his nose with a handkerchief. "It's easy to take what others have done to you and blame yourself. To mistake their sins for yours. You were a child, protecting your mother and yourself." He lifted the rosary to his mouth, a private vow in the motion. "I hear the ache in your voice, but strength has carried you this far. Continue that strength." His grip tightened around the beads. "I want to help you, but only you can make peace with this."

Roman swiped his damp lashes. "How?"

The priest tucked the rosary back inside his cassock. "You came here seeking forgiveness, but it is you who needs to forgive yourself."

\* \* \*

By the time Ethan looked up from the case file, Aniella was already seated, hands folded, waiting for judgment.

"I don't want word spreading that we ever had this conversation," he said.

"That makes sense."

"What doesn't make sense is how promising this looked at first," he said. "The last lead you gave me was that out-of-town trip. Something about a briefcase. That was a long time ago. I've been making excuses for you to spend time with him, and you're telling me nothing else has come up?"

She recounted everything: the house in the field, the strange cover story about the truck, the deflection when Italy came up, changing his clothes every time he left the hotel, bleeding by the dumpsters. They had to connect somehow.

She realized too late she should have told Ethan the truth. Instead, she'd played along when Roman pretended not to know her, and her own career ambitions clouded her choices. Now, tangled in the fallout, she wasn't sure what to do.

"No. There's nothing else since then that I can think of."

"You expect me to believe that Roman just happens to get himself shot? Who was he meeting with?"

"I wish I could tell you, but I found him alone."

"IAB said I lacked cause for an investigation, so you were supposed to help build a case in exchange for a fast-tracked career. You seem to have forgotten that, and you've brought me next to nothing. It's making me look like a fool." His voice sharpened. "He's dirty. I know it, and so do you." Ethan sprang to his feet. "Find me proof, fast, or this arrangement's over—and so are your career opportunities."

\* \* \*

"You look like you got hit by a truck." Craig dropped a freight box against the wall of the warehouse, a puff of dust rising between them. "You ever figure out who shot you?"

Roman pressed a fake sticker onto the box, the sting of last night's confession still lodged just below the surface. "Why, you got a clue?"

Craig worked a crowbar under the lid of another box. "I'm sure it had something to do with revenge."

Roman prepped another label. "You saying it was Julian?"

"Whoa, whoa." Craig stilled the crowbar. "Wouldn't dare imply something so calculating." The lid creaked under pressure. "But you did break a few of his fingers, and people get shot over less."

*You son of a bitch.* Roman pictured that crowbar turning, fast, through Craig's smug grin.

Craig struck a match, smoke curling up as the tip glowed. "What's with the stare, Roman?" He let the smoke drift sideways. "You got something against cigarettes?"

\* \* \*

Confession had cracked something loose. Keeping the rest buried felt impossible now. The silence had its own unbearable weight.

180

Roman stepped into Judy's office. She was realigning a row of uneven books, order restoring order.

"Detective. What brings you here?"

"A priest told me to forgive myself." He kept his hands deep in his pockets. "I don't know how."

She lowered her glasses. "You'll talk to a priest, but not to me?"

"Like I said, I don't trust you."

She motioned toward the chair.

He sat at the edge, restlessness taut.

"The wall is down?" she asked, her tone testing.

"I do better when I'm not cornered."

"I see. Why have you been avoiding therapy until now?"

"It's like digging up bones with nowhere to bury them again. You're left holding what should've stayed underground."

"So you don't trust yourself, either."

The overhead light flickered once, its bulb cutting through the pause.

"I commend you for showing up." Her voice softened. "Where do you want to start?"

"My mother stirred every fire. Put me in situations a kid should never be in. I avoid anything that makes me feel…" He faltered. "But I met someone…" He shifted in the chair. "I don't know."

"It's okay, Detective." Her pen rolled off the table and struck the tile. "Connection scares you. It unhooks control, letting someone in means surrender." She retrieved the pen and set it back in place. "Does she know what she means to you?"

"It doesn't matter. She's not who I thought she was."

"You said you needed forgiveness. Is this what you meant?"

He stared at the wall clock, the second hand jerking forward as if time itself had slowed. "I wake up in a panic sometimes."

"Nightmares. What are they about?"

"They're about…" The clock hand ticked again, steady, merciless. Every image waited, crowding his mind.

"About what?" she asked.

"A mother screaming," he said. "A child crying."

"Why is the child crying? And the mother screaming?"

"A stabbing," he said. The bulb hummed louder. "And a shooting."

"Is this the undercover case? The one where you got stabbed?"

He gave a small nod.

"The deal went bad," she said. "He stabbed you, you fired back. I remember." She paused. "The boy in your dream. How does he fit into this?"

Memory pressed where the scar lived, as if it could open again from the thought alone.

"I hesitated because I wanted a different outcome for him." The rest came scattered. "The pop. His mother screaming. His cries. Then nothing but the ringing."

"It's okay. Take your time."

"I took his father away. Just like that. Made him just like me." His voice cracked. "What kind of person does that?"

"You're not a horrible person."

"I'm supposed to protect people, not destroy their lives." He stared at the cracked couch seams like they might spit him out. "What happens when he finds out I'm the one who took his dad from him?"

"You keep in touch with the boy?"

Roman nodded, faster now. "I didn't want to do to him what I did to myself."

"What do you mean? You didn't want to do to him what you did to yourself?"

"My father used to beat my mother." The words left him hollow. "He was always so angry. I used to hide his gun in the floor vents. But one night—he found it." His hand lifted halfway before pain ripped through his chest and dragged him forward. His arm trembled from the effort. His palms pressed to his knees, just trying to hold himself up. The office closed in around him. Each inhale scraped the wound, a reminder that he was still here when he shouldn't be.

She crossed the space between them. "The boy being fatherless isn't your fault. His father put you both there. You hesitated, and you were stabbed. Another second and you'd be dead."

He stayed there, hearing her but not yet believing her.

"With your own father, you were trying to protect her. The guilt was never yours."

The words didn't absolve him. They only loosened their hold—enough for air, not forgiveness.

\* \* \*

Red cups and half-empty bottles covered every counter in Scott's house. The music punched hard enough to start a neighborhood complaint.

Tyler tossed an orange ball in a smooth arc over the table. It dropped into one of Scott's last two cups. "Drink up, Hoffman."

Foam sloshed over the rim as Scott tipped the cup back, half missing his mouth. "Man, you're killing me."

Tyler lined up another shot. Scott's turn came, and the ball skimmed the rim before rolling under the couch.

The place was packed with the squad, voices overlapping and drinks lifted mid-story.

"Where're Viento and Fasquelle?" Tyler asked.

Scott lobbed a ball that veered too wide. "Maybe, hic, they're with each other."

Tyler picked up the fallen pong ball and wiped it slowly on the pocket of his shirt. "Why would you think they're together?"

"Dunno, makes you wonder, hic, if they're together."

Tyler lowered his hand and squinted. "Hey. Mr. Loose Lips." He tossed a pong ball at Scott. "You know something I don't?"

Scott clutched himself. "Gotta use the pisser."

Scott drifted toward the kitchen, shoes squeaking on the tile as he brushed past Aniella. Her purse stayed tucked against her side when she stepped into the living room.

Tyler moved in. "Look who decided to show."

Her answer lagged, a beat late. "Why wouldn't I?"

"Viento's not here."

"Oh." Her voice lifted too lightly. "He's not here?"

"Ah. And here I thought Hoffman was just being his usual self." He watched her scan the room. "Wanna know what he just told me?"

"It depends on how drunk he is." The laugh came thin and quick.

"I'm just gonna come out and ask," he said. "Are you and Viento a thing?"

Aniella fumbled with the strap of her bag. "What?"

Tyler crossed his arms. "You seem defensive."

"I seem defensive because you sound accusatory."

"It's a simple question. I thought I told you to watch out for him. Do you two have a thing going or not?"

"We most certainly do not." Aniella turned for the door. On her way through the kitchen, she grabbed a cup from the counter without slowing.

* * *

Shadows moved behind the thin curtain of Roman's house. He was home. Aniella stood on the walkway, every shared moment replaying through her mind like film spliced out of order. The looks, the words, the half-truths that had once sounded like something real. He had told her that wanting her never meant caring.

She wasn't sure what was real or not anymore. But none of it mattered now. She needed answers.

Aniella mussed her hair until it was just shy of chaotic. She untucked half her blouse, then scrunched it at the bottom. Last, she tipped a little liquor over her pant leg, took a sip, and swished it between her teeth.

After several knocks, the deadbolt turned.

"Aniella?" He took in her rumpled state. "Are you okay?"

"I'm fine." She edged forward, the floorboards giving a dry creak.

"You sure?"

"I should be asking you how you've been."

His voice carried regret she didn't want to hear. "I haven't had the chance to apologize for how I treated you at the hotel."

*Don't do this, Roman.* If she softened now, she'd lose her reason for coming. "Oh, you know. It is what it is."

He looked at her a moment longer. "How much have you had to drink?"

"I'm not drunk."

His glanced toward the street. "How'd you get here?"

"I walked." She kept her head low, letting the night speak for her.

He opened the door wider. "Why'd you stop by?"

"I can't stop by to say hi to a colleague?" She stumbled over her own two feet. "To someone who's been more than that?"

He let the door fall against the wall. "All right, let me take you home."

She raised the cup like a challenge. "I can walk back myself." She turned to leave.

The liquor rippled as his hand caught her wrist. "That's not safe."

"I made it here fine." She took a sip.

"Give me the cup."

"Take it." She tipped it forward, whiskey spilling across his shirt. She covered her mouth with a laugh. "I'm so sorry!"

He looked down, fabric sticking to him. "I'm taking you home. Come in."

In the kitchen, he poured her water and set the glass down on the counter. "Here. My bandage can't stay wet. I'll be back."

She trailed after him down the hall, squeezing her damp pant leg and wiping her lips to maintain the scent of alcohol.

At the doorway of the laundry room, Aniella stopped short. He stood by the washer, one hand braced on the machine for balance, the other fighting with the wet shirt that clung over the wound. He looked up, suspended between effort and embarrassment. The tension in the room turned brittle, like a wire pulled too tight.

For a second, neither moved. Then she crossed the last few steps, voice quieter than she meant. "Let me." She waited, pulse thrumming in the quiet.

The shirt had turned almost black where it touched his bandage. His hand hovered, then he lifted his arm just enough for her to take hold. She eased the hem upward, peeling inch by inch, careful not to drag across the gauze. Each fold released the faint trace of whiskey mixed with his cologne.

When the fabric cleared his shoulders, a flash of him surfaced, the line of the wound still pink from healing. She turned away and set the shirt across the washer.

He carefully peeled off the damp bandage covering the wound.

"I'm so sorry that happened to you," she said, tracing what violence had left behind.

He watched her fingertips explore the outside edges of his wound. "I wish you were sober."

"Why?"

"There's something I need to ask you." He gently moved her hand away. "But not like this."

"I can handle it."

He shook his head. "I wouldn't be here if you hadn't found me."

*Now you choose to open up?* The space between them felt too close, too intimate. "You would've done the same." She stepped backward, her balance uneven. "I'll let you change your bandage."

Aniella had an idea, and she had to execute it fast if she had a chance. She lay back on his bed, curled up to his pillow.

From the hall came the faint rhythm of his steps. First the kitchen, then the living room. A door opened, shut. He was looking for her.

The footsteps drew closer. She kept still, letting her hand fall slack beside her. The doorway filled with his shape.

"Aniella." His voice was quiet, almost unsure.

The mattress dipped with the weight of the blanket he spread over her. Then the light snapped off. The floor creaked once as he turned away.

She waited until the house went still again. Seconds stretched. Then pipes groaned, water starting somewhere down the hall. A shower.

*Perfect.*

She leaped off the bed and ran to his dresser. She glanced once toward the hall. *Am I really doing this?* She opened the top drawer and shuffled through his belongings, quickly working through all of them.

*There's got to be something.*

Aniella peeked under his mattress. Nothing. She rummaged in and around his nightstand. Empty. Her fear turned into confusion, then frustration. She ripped through his closet and in every place she thought could be a hiding spot. Still nothing. *Where does he hide all his secrets?* At a loss for her next move, she stood in front of his window and folded her arms.

Then the furnace kicked on. Warm air rushed through the vent, carrying a faint crackle, like plastic stirring. She froze. The sound came from beneath her.

She crouched beside the vent. The screws gave after a few turns. A black plastic bag sat on the narrow shelf inside. *Clever.* She pulled it free.

Inside, objects glimmered in the dim light. Her fingers brushed over them to make sure they were real.

She took her phone, snapped photos quickly, then replaced everything as it had been.

She took one last look at the vent, barely able to believe what she'd found. Aniella brushed the damp strands of hair stuck to her forehead. She had to leave—now. She swiped her purse from his bed, then headed toward the door. The motion caught mid-air. A shadow stretched across the floor, looming in a heavy, silent warning.

It was Roman.

# CHAPTER 18

## Who is Benedetti?

The purse strap slid off Aniella's shoulder as she jerked back. *How long has he been standing there?* "You scared me."

His shape filled the doorway, bending the light as he stepped in. "You're scared to see me? In my own home?"

She twisted the leather strap. "I thought you were in the shower."

The blanket sagged from the bed's edge, one corner nearly brushing the floor.

"And I thought you were sleeping," he said.

"Well, I—I shouldn't have come over, I just—"

He advanced a step. "You're nervous."

"I just remembered—" The purse rode tight against her side as if its weight could guard her. "I have to be somewhere."

Roman stood between her and the doorway. "This late at night?"

"Yes, I'm so sorry!" The purse swung hard at her side as she moved past him, her pace quickening toward the front door, praying he wouldn't follow.

\* \* \*

The ventilation looped roasted peanuts and paper through Iver's office. A torn pack slouched on a dented cabinet, coffee rings ghosting its surface. A page lifted, then settled, evidence someone else had entered.

"Grave told me Viento and Fasquelle might have more than a working relationship," Ethan said.

A peanut split, shell fragments scattering. "Technically against policy," Iver said. "But why would Grave give a shit?"

"Something's going on with Viento. Something bigger."

"Another wild-goose chase?" A paperclip drifted, snagging the file corner. "You've been on his ass since the day he got back."

"I'm not imagining this. And if the rumor's true—"

"Then what, write him up for improper workplace conduct?" He rolled another peanut until it cracked. "Come on, Polinski."

"I'm just saying. If something's going on, I'll find out."

The thought almost made Iver laugh. Viento and Fasquelle? That was a reach. No chance he'd go anywhere near her. The rumor itself was a perfect distraction. Let Ethan keep busy chasing his own tail.

"You go right ahead." Iver skimmed a line like it mattered. "Let me know if you come up with anything."

* * *

Aniella crouched in the dark interview room, lights cut, waiting.

*Maybe he has a reason.* She eased off her heels for flats. *But hiding what I found in his vent? What reason would he have for that?*

The bullpen's final light flicked off. It was go time.

She slipped out, trailing him from a distance. Down the elevator, out to the street. His stride was easy, until it wasn't. He moved faster. Aniella quickened to match.

*Where is he going?*

Roman turned down a narrow alley hemmed by rusted fire escapes and sour dumpsters. *Where did he go?* Vanished.

She edged forward into fog so dense her shoes disappeared. Fingers mapped the rough brick guiding her through. When the alley spilled onto another street, she scanned the emptiness, but he was still gone.

Steam jetted from a sewer grate beside her, the hiss startling her in its direction. Something yanked her back around, balance tipping from her.

The fog dissipated, revealing Roman's hold on her.

The grip pulsed, unsteady, knuckles faded white.

*He's trembling.*

Was it the chill of the night making his hand quiver? The clipped breeze stabbing through the cold? No. It was something else, something deeper. His anger was shaking him. Anger barely contained.

"Why are you following me?"

She pulled, but his hold locked her there. "Oh, thank God it's you! I thought you were in front of me, so when I felt someone grab me from behind, I thought—"

Roman's shadow leaned over the alley wall, stretching as if it meant to pin her there. "Try again."

She tried to draw back again, but he stayed firm. The brick scraped her sleeve. "I—I wasn't following you. I was just walking around."

"You said I was in front of you." His tone carried the depth of what she'd stepped into. "Try again."

"I just—happened to see you." She tugged again, voice shaking in the alley's darkness. "I wanted to wander a bit—I just—"

A streetlamp flared across his stare, glazing them the color of stormwater, darker than usual, more deliberate. "I gave you enough chances to be honest," he said, letting go. "You've been on me since I left the district."

"How—wha—well I—I'm sorry, I was just—I was worried about you, that's all." She coddled her arm close, the sleeve creasing under her palm. "Ever since you got shot." She straightened. "I just wanted to make sure you were okay."

190

The alley seemed to dim with him, the weak lamplight receding. She'd used his shooting as her excuse, and he knew it.

"You need to go. Now."

* * *

Roman had drifted out of focus since glancing back one last time before entering the building, confirming Aniella hadn't continued to follow him.

A scent of exhaustion pretending to be clean filled the space, all burnt coffee and cheap disinfectant.

He wrote his name with a black marker and smoothed the sticker flat on his chest. A few empty chairs waited, arranged in an uneven circle. He sat, hands clasped loosely between his knees, thoughts tangled in knots he couldn't untie. He had already walked this road before, stabbed, shot, buried under the weight of his own guilt. And now he was back, trapped in the same hopeless cycle. The shooting didn't just drag him back to that alley. It yanked him through time, through memories he'd buried so deep he thought they'd suffocated. But they were still there. Waiting. The shooting had been a turning point, but into what, he couldn't tell. It made him question everything, his choices and his future. Did he even have one, or was he just drifting toward the next inevitable disaster? And guilt. His father had been a monster, but Roman still carried the weight of taking his life. The irony was that his father had given him a life he never chose, and now here he was, back in an NA meeting, full circle. He sat surrounded by people he found it hard to listen to. A place full of people who had all lost control at some point. He didn't have the same story.

Because he stayed in control. Control was the only way he knew how to survive. Keeping everything sealed, tight or distant enough that nothing could reach him. He had learned early that losing control meant losing himself.

His father taught him that.

The first time heroin hit his veins, it wasn't his choice. His body's first betrayal hadn't been losing control—it was never having any to begin with. His father had stolen that from him.

His body had never belonged to him. No control as a child in a darkened room, his father sealing rubber around his arm, the sting of needle breaking skin. No control when the fever came, no control when the sickness burned, or when the withdrawals scraped him raw.

That was the first time control had been stolen from him.

The night he took his father's life was the moment he swore he'd never let it happen again.

Roman controlled everything now, his tone, his rhythm, his every move. He had to be. Because the moment he lost that grip, he wasn't Roman anymore. He was that scared kid in the basement, powerless to stop what was happening.

A dull ache threaded beneath his ribs where the wound was still knitting. It reminded him that even now, grown and guarded, he wasn't in control of everything.

He could feel his pulse in his ribs, the wound still healing, a dull, throbbing reminder that even now, even as a grown man, he still wasn't in control of everything.

"Roman? Would you like to share where that is?" The group leader's voice cut through the fog.

His head lifted slightly. "Where what is?"

"We're talking about triggers you can avoid or face when you're ready. Where's your trigger place?"

Scuff marks and drag lines dulled the floor in worn patterns.

*Where?*

It was his father's recliner, casually destroying his life like it was nothing. The undercover case, taking a boy's father from him. It was the alley. The hospital bed. It was everywhere.

The concrete held steady beneath him, unmoved by everything breaking inside.

"Inside my head."

* * *

Aniella rubbed the rim of her mug, the frothy swirl of whipped cream dissolving into the hot chocolate.

Across from her, Fern's cup landed with a clink that rippled through the small café.

"Did you take it?" Fern asked. "Do you have it?"

"The USB?" A bead of chocolate ran down her mug, tracing a slow curve to the saucer.

"Did you take it?"

"No, but I thought about it."

Fern's elbow hit the edge of the sugar caddy, sending a packet out onto the table. "I don't know whether to call that smart or stupid."

Steam feathered from Aniella's mug as she circled the spoon through the cream. "I'm supposed to meet with my captain next week."

"And?"

The spoon stilled as chocolate slid back into the mug. "Roman has secrets."

"You said he goes undercover. Maybe it's just a habit."

"He was livid when he caught me following him. I've never seen him that way." A chair creaked at the next table, loud against their hush. "It was scary."

"You sure you want to dig so deep into this guy?" Fern asked. "You don't know what you could be getting into. What would he do if he found out you were digging through his things?"

The espresso machine hissed from the counter, punctuating the thought. "I'm sure he already knows I don't trust him."

"Sleeping with someone you don't trust? And he knows it?" Fern's coffee splattered onto the saucer. "Dangerous game." She set her mug aside. "Just be careful. If he's dirty, there's no telling what he'll do when he finds out you have the power to take him down."

\* \* \*

Fists pounded on the front door.

Roman jolted awake, pulse slamming once before he went still, listening. Another hit. Then another. He crossed to the door and checked the peephole.

Aniella stood there, drenched, shivering, mascara streaked.

He yanked the door open. "Are you all right?"

Rain poured over her face, tracing her cheeks in thin, uneven trails.

"You're soaked. Come inside." He reached for her arm, but she flinched away. Her knees buckled.

Roman moved fast, arms locking around her waist before she hit the ground. Pain lanced through his wound, but he held on.

"You can't be out here like this." He lifted her. Every muscle screamed as he carried her into the living room and lowered her onto the couch.

"Talk to me." He draped a blanket along her shoulders and sat beside her. "What's going on?"

Aniella sank into the blanket as she wiped her face. "I know why you don't let people close to you."

"And why is that?"

"Because if someone got too close, they'd start asking questions. And you don't want people asking questions."

"What are you talking about?"

She balled a corner of the blanket. "Should I be scared of you?"

"Scared of me?" He rested his hand against her knee, gentle. "For what?"

She gathered enough steadiness to speak. "Is Viento your real last name?"

"Of course it is."

The clock ticked like a bomb now.

She shoved his hand off her knee. "That's a lie."

"It's not."

Aniella straightened. "Give me a reason to believe you."

"Why are you asking if my last name is real?"

The blanket tightened around her, then loosened again, as if deciding to answer or not. "Your vent. I saw what's in your vent."

Roman held steady. No caution. No tell. Nothing to read, not even for her.

"Why were you going through my things?"

"If Viento's your last name, then who's Benedetti?"

Roman's mind ran through the vent, cataloging what else she might have seen. The contents from the briefcase. The old ID. More information on Eli.

"I keep those as a reminder," he said. "That was an alias from an undercover case."

"You're too calm," she said, blanket getting tighter again. "Did you already know I went through your vent?"

"No. But I do want to know why you faked being drunk just to snoop around my things."

She flinched. "You knew?"

"Not until I saw you standing in my bedroom, desperate to get out."

She pushed to her feet, the blanket falling from her shoulders unto the carpet. "Don't turn this on me, I came here to get answers from you!"

Roman's patience thinned as she began pacing. "What answers?"

"The drive we went on. You drove two different cars that day, neither of them yours." Her words hit sharp and quick. "What was in the briefcase? And what was in that supposed packet you tried to pass off as meat?"

"I'm not going in circles all night."

"What about the night you got shot? Who did you go to meet?"

"You're trying to solve my shooting now?"

"You getting shot is being swept under the rug," she said, her words rushing out. "Are you going to tell me why no one seems to care a cop got hit?"

"No." His restraint snapped. "Because you don't want to believe a damn thing I tell you."

The clock, once silenced by her shuffling, now announced every passing second.

"Because you never tell the truth," she said.

Roman shot to his feet. He almost called her out for what he knew. "Go on—what else?"

"You tell me! You had so much anger when I cornered you in the alley, you looked like—" Her voice shrank. "Like you could've hurt me."

"Trust me, I would've never—"

"Trust you?" she laughed, sharp and humorless. "You're corrupt!"

She lunged for the front door. Roman moved after her, catching it before it swung wide. The frame shuddered as he shouldered the door shut. She fought the handle, but his palm held it there. She scanned the room once, then bolted for the kitchen.

Roman followed, pain sparking beneath every attempt to keep up.

At the end of the narrow kitchen, the counter boxed her in. She'd trapped herself.

She turned as he closed the gap. "Leave me alone!"

"I can't let you leave like this."

"Can't let me leave?" She grabbed the first thing within reach. A plate from the counter.

Roman's stance tightened, muscles bracing on instinct. "Aniella."

The plate flung through the air like a Frisbee.

He ducked—the plate burst against the wall in a scatter of white shards behind him. Glass from the impact flecked the floor.

Roman steadied upright, and slowly raised his hands in surrender. "I know you're upset," he said calmly. "But don't put us in this position."

She pulled a drawer open between them, cutlery rattling. "In what position?"

"If I were dirty," he said, stepping forward, "then think about what's at stake right now."

She edged backward, her hip brushing the cabinet.

"Think of how much I'd have to lose." He continued forward. "And how concerned I'd be that you're going to say the wrong things to someone."

She grabbed a fork from the drawer. "So you're threatening me."

"Not a threat."

The rain beat down against the windows, a crack of thunder ripping through it. She bolted again.

Roman reached her in the hallway. She thrashed, wild and fast, but his hold stayed unyielding. Control, reflex more than choice.

The fight left her, motion ebbing until everything went still.

Roman released her carefully, his back finding the wall. The anger never came, only the drag of exhaustion. He cinched the bandage's edge, pain circling back through him. He'd been chasing, restraining, holding on when he should've let go.

He coughed, ragged. "First of all, I'm incredibly disappointed you went through my things." He drew in, palm still anchored where the bandage lay. "Second, if you think I'm dirty, why haven't you gone to your captain?" He pushed off the wall, steadying himself. "You have secrets too, Aniella."

A small sound left her before she spoke. "Sometimes omitting information is as bad as lying."

He nodded once. "I understand that. But I'm still struggling with trusting you."

"Trusting *me*?"

"You've got some nerve pretending innocence." Fragments from the broken plate tracked into the hallway, glinting from the kitchen light. "You staged that night just to go through my things. All that effort just to dig." He bent slightly, resting a palm against the wall for balance. "And you used being concerned about me getting shot as your excuse to follow me."

There was more, but that was enough for one night. He wasn't sure yet how he wanted to handle the rest of what he knew.

His voice went quieter. "You talk about trust like I'm the only one breaking it."

\* \* \*

Tyler muttered about the microwave's incompetence while peeling the wrapper from a half-cooked Hot Pocket. Scorched cheese burned as Roman switched on the coffeemaker.

Tyler bit into the Hot Pocket with theatrical patience.

Roman cleared his throat. "Something you want to say?"

"Looks like you had a rough night."

Roman tore a sugar packet, then tipped it into a cup. "Yeah?"

Tyler swallowed, words coated in smug satisfaction. "There've been questions going around about you and Fasquelle."

Roman opened the fridge and grabbed the milk carton. "That so?"

"People seem to think you two should be the topic of conversation."

Roman poured milk over the sugar. "What's that supposed to mean?"

Tyler took a corner bite of the pocket. "I guess Mr. Loose Lips can't keep his mouth shut. But don't worry, your secret's safe." His grin climbed. "We've all had a bet going to see who could have her first. How is she?"

Roman gripped the top of the cup, fingers digging into the ceramic. "That a sick joke?"

"How long has that been going on? Right under everyone's noses, how'd you pull that off?"

"I got a question." Roman lifted and set the cup down hard—milk jumping the rim. "Why the hell are you so concerned with my private life?"

Tyler squared himself, jaw setting for a fight he'd never win. "Fasquelle's got a right to know who she's dealing with."

Roman left the cup where it sat. "There's nothing between us. Whatever story you're selling, drop it."

Tyler stepped back. "Seems like I hit a nerve, and if the captain got wind of this—"

"Sounds like you've already run your mouth."

Tyler's smirk soured. "Don't raise your voice to me, Viento. I'm not having it today."

Roman advanced. "You start rumors, drag a good woman through it, and think you're the victim?" Another step. "Back off."

"Is that a threat?"

Roman's fingers curled at his sides. "Find out, Grave."

Ethan slowed at the break room threshold. Roman and Tyler stood toe to toe, words sharp enough to cut through the hum of the vending machine. "What the hell's going on in here?"

\* \* \*

Roman stood behind the chair, its frame cool beneath his grip. Iver paced, dried leaves scraping against the window, carried by the wind's restless pull.

Iver stopped. "I can't protect you if you keep screwing up. Polinski's already on your ass, and you've managed to make it worse. That argument with Grave? Technically qualifies as abusive conduct, and now I've got to pull strings to keep his damn trap shut. That's not even the real problem." The blinds shifted in the draft. "He's digging into you. Deeper."

The blind cords tapped the sill in uneven rhythm.

"Anything I should know about?" Iver asked.

Wind dragged another scrape across the window.

Roman didn't break eye contact. "Nothing to worry about."

\* \* \*

Ethan entered Iver's office, a laptop tucked under his arm. "Chief, you need to see this." He slid the laptop across the desk and pressed play.

The screen's glow rippled across the office walls. At first, nothing. Just another recording. Then Iver's stomach twisted. He found the armrest but kept still. Whatever played on that screen shouldn't exist. Across the desk, the glow slid over Ethan too.

"I told you," Ethan said. "I've always had my suspicions about Viento. When he got transferred back, I reached out to IAB."

The hum of the vent filled the pause before Iver spoke. He set his glasses down with practiced calm. "IAB? You should've looped me in immediately."

"Right. And you'd have done what, exactly? You've got a soft spot for him, you'd never see it. And if you did, you'd protect him."

"Protect him from what?" The monitor's light pulsed. "This doesn't look like an issue for IAB."

"They told me I didn't have enough to justify a formal investigation."

Iver scoffed. "You don't."

"When I interviewed Fasquelle for Administrative Aid, I noticed she carried herself with an unassuming manner, highly observant, striking memory. She aspired to be an intelligence analyst. It was the perfect excuse to give her field training, and keep track of Viento."

The radiator clicked once, heat rising too slow for the cold crawling through him.

"I had her partnered with him, made sure she spent time on his assignments," Ethan said. "She's in the bullpen. Ears on everything. If there was something suspicious, I wanted her to find it. And when she came to me about the briefcase—"

The briefcase. The one Wes and Julian had given Roman.

Iver kept his tone mild. "What briefcase?"

The laptop screen dimmed.

"She managed to get into his car during one of his unauthorized excursions. He drove her to a house far from here, made her wait by the car, but there was a briefcase when they started. And when they left, there wasn't."

Paper edges lifted in the vent's draft.

"That wasn't enough for IAB?" Iver asked.

"She told me he said they switched cars," Ethan said. "So the briefcase must've gone with it. No way to track what was inside."

The wind outside shoved a branch against the glass, its scrape running long before breaking off.

"None of this bothers you?" Ethan asked.

Iver exhaled, the blinds swaying with it. "Sounds like a couple of passionate kids sneaking behind our backs. Nothing for IAB to be concerned about."

"She said she'd get me more on him."

"If she's been having an affair with him, her word won't stand. She loses all credibility."

The cursor on the pause blinked once, waiting. The realization settled between them, heavy as the hum of the laptop fan.

"So you can see why this would be a problem," Ethan said. "This would risk the entire IAB investigation."

Yes, Iver saw, just not for the same reason. He didn't allow himself a sigh of relief. Instead, he sighed sharply, mirroring Ethan's frustration. "How do you propose we go about this?"

# CHAPTER 19

## The Wrath of a King and a Liar

Roman pulled a slice of stale pizza from a grease-stained box in the break room fridge.

Heels clacked down the hall, measured, certain. Aniella. This time, no cheerful greeting as she entered.

He chewed slowly. The last time he'd seen her, she'd been hurling dishes and accusations. The bite turned to paste before he could swallow. *How's this gonna go?*

"I know the other night was a lot," she said, easing past to the fridge. "And I wanted to say I'm sorry."

He swallowed, waited a beat. "What was a lot? The yelling or the flying dishes?"

Her nails curved around the fridge handle. He saw it, the smallest giveaway, and that steadied him more than it should have. He stayed casual, unbothered, because anger would give her proof. She was apologizing to the man she'd called corrupt. He let the irony sit between them.

"Mostly for throwing the plate at you," she said. "Thanks for the grace."

The words felt strange, forced with warmth.

He took another bite. "It's all right."

"Now that we have that out of the way…" She grabbed the mustard bottle.

No bread. "Tell me what you're hiding."

Roman dropped the crust in the bin. "This isn't round two, is it?" He leaned against the counter. "Cause the budget's short on mugs, and I didn't get much sleep last night." He crossed his ankles. "Won't be able to duck as fast."

She reached for a slice of cheese, tore it straight from the wrapper, and dropped it on the counter beside the mustard. "You left a lot unanswered."

He pushed off the counter, quick. "If you really think I'm dirty, go to the captain. Go to the Chief." His thumb found the pocket seam, a brief stall before stilling. "Hell, take it to IAB."

She squeezed the mustard bottle without shaking it, mostly water coming out, rolling off the cheese and mixing with coffee grounds. "I just want to trust you."

Roman took the mustard bottle from her. "Did Grave earn your trust? Because you sure as hell took his word over mine."

She grabbed the bottle back, mustard droplets splattering on the fridge handle. "You're the one with all the secrets, not Tyler."

The lie waited on his tongue. He could've said anything, kept the act clean. But some part of him wanted to ease that look on her face, to make her stop looking at him like that, like he was an enemy.

His hands found their way into his pockets. "We've been on a rollercoaster since we met. If you care about me at all, don't twist something innocent into something that'll ruin both of us."

She held the mustard so tight it oozed down the side. "This isn't right."

*Do it.*

"Listen to yourself." He stepped in, closing the space until the hum of the fridge filled what neither said. "I've tried to pull you back from this, but you're obsessed with theories. You're so convinced there's something to find, you can't see all the damage you'll cause." He caught the flicker of doubt, and sealed it with finality. "Think about what that'll do to me. What that'll do to you."

The truth wouldn't set either of them free. It would only change who held the chains.

\* \* \*

The bullpen carried the tremor of Iver's steps before his voice hit. "Viento!"

Roman paused mid-wipe across the whiteboard, the eraser dragging a dull streak before stalling.

Iver appeared in the doorway. Whatever followed him in wasn't patience.

Roman set the eraser on the tray, leaving the half-erased smudge behind him.

Inside the office, a laptop glowed on the desk, Ethan beside it, posture taut as a drawn line.

Roman nodded. "Chief. Captain."

The air carried an uncomfortable pause, like it hadn't decided which way to move.

"What's this about?" Roman asked.

"Sit down," Iver said.

Roman sat opposite of the laptop, gaze tracking between them.

Ethan slid the laptop forward and hit play.

Footage from last fall filled the screen. Roman's desk, an empty bullpen, that faint lamplight staking out his corner of the night. He waited, unsure what trap was being set.

And then. Aniella entered the frame.

Now he knew—the chipped paint, the fallen stapler, how close they'd come before reason pulled him back.

The screen froze, their outlines locked in frame.

"Explain this scandal," Ethan said, the remote's red light flashing against his cuff.

"Scandal?" The word landed flat, almost bored. "Captain, you've been itching to hang something on me since I got back. There's nothing in that video that crosses a line." He gave them a beat. "Did you even let it play through? Because nothing happened."

"Does Fasquelle know about your discrepancies?" Ethan asked.

Roman tilted his head. "My what?"

"Does she help cover them up for you?"

Roman let out a short, flat laugh. "That's absurd. How would she cover something that isn't there?"

"That's a lie!" Ethan's shadow crossed the monitor's glow. "How many things has she covered for you?"

"That's enough," Iver said, hard enough to break the tension.

"We should suspend him!" Ethan said, the remote skidding across the table.

"On what grounds?" Roman asked.

"Pending an investigation. You—"

"Investigation?" Roman stood, the chair legs rasping the tile.

Ethan shoved at the chair's back. "Sit back down!"

"Polinski!" Iver's words cracked through the room. "I said enough!"

Ethan's sleeve bit the desk's edge. "I'm done watching you walk away from everything."

Iver struck the desk so hard the laptop jumped. "I reign king here, and I said that's enough!" The echo settled. "Let me handle the rest."

Ethan reset his jacket, the tug pulling a trace of dandruff from the fabric.

The door's slam rattled the blinds.

Roman adjusted in the chair. "Wasn't expecting to walk into *this* shit."

Iver rounded on him. "You're six feet under in this with me, and you're screwing the one person planted to sniff us out!"

"I'm not."

"I warned you." Iver stabbed a finger toward the frozen frame on the monitor. "Right before your last side job, I said someone was here to snitch."

That call into Iver's office, the warning to watch his back. It explained her persistence, the night by the wall when control cracked. The person meant to spy on him was the same person, the only person he had ever let his guard down with. Then came the shooting, and the pieces shifted again. He hadn't known what to do about all of it, so he hadn't done anything. Until now. Now Iver knew.

"You really think I'd be that reckless?" Roman asked.

Iver crossed the room in short, uneven passes. "I'm nervous, Roman. Really nervous."

"You have nothing to be nervous about."

"What's going to come up when he keeps digging?"

"He can dig all he wants. There's nothing."

"What's Fasquelle going to say?"

"Nothing."

Iver stopped mid-turn. "Polinski needs to think he's getting somewhere." He poked at the screen as though strategy lived inside the pixels. "If they believe she's been with you, her words turn into garbage. Tell them you were. It'll destroy her credibility. She know anything?"

"Absolutely not," Roman's calm held. "Everything's sealed tight."

"That's sealed tight?" Iver jabbed the play key with one knuckle, the frame glaring back. Aniella inches from him, dusty blue paint-chips on her skirt, his hands slack at his sides. "What happened after?"

"I drove her home. That was it."

The monitor light fixed both men in place. Silence thinned until Iver's short laugh snapped it. "You're a damn good liar, Roman."

"I'm not lying." Roman leaned a fraction forward. "After everything this year, you don't trust I would know better?"

"That's the problem. I can't tell when you're lying." The laptop clicked shut, killing the light between them. "So prove it."

"How?"

"Ethan thinks she'll help him bring you down, which circles back to me. We need to move before he does." Iver dropped it plain and cold. "Take a polygraph."

"You want me to fail on purpose? Lie and say we've been fooling around."

"You take the test. You fail it. She's done. They both look stupid." Iver dragged the blinds half open and sunlight knifed across the desk. "You'll have no problem manipulating the score, right?"

It was a brilliant move. Strategic, bulletproof. Ethan had next to nothing, which meant she had kept quiet. Mostly. But it would wreck her career, her dream, her credibility. He could torch it down. All he had to do was fail one test to take it away from her.

\* \* \*

Roman's shoe concealed the tack as he followed the hallway past the lockers. He descended the back stairwell, keeping the weight of his toe light so the point didn't catch. The air cooled and the noise from upstairs vanished. The room ahead was stripped bare, a metal table at the center, a cluster of machines and wire. The technician waited behind the equipment, expression flat.

Roman had done this before, early in his undercover training. Learning how to steer his own rhythm, flatten heart rate, trick the spikes into thinking control meant truth. It could never tell the difference. Not unless he let it.

*Make it look like you and Fasquelle were involved. They'll never use her words against yours.*

Roman lowered himself into the chair. The technician fastened straps and electrodes in quiet sequence, the cuffs, the cords, the adhesive patches. Sensors blinked to life across the console.

The edge of the tack waited under his toe as the blood-pressure cuff constricted. He could end this easily. Too easily.

Roman focused on the back wall as questions began.

"Is your name Roman Paul Viento?"

"Yes."

"Do you live in Chicago?"

"Yes."

"Have you ever accessed evidence logs without authorization?"

Roman pictured the ocean. Waves rolling in, pulling out. Steady. Unbothered. "No."

"Have you ever shared classified information about your cases with anyone?"

"No."

"Have you ever lied to someone who trusted you?"

"Yes."

"Do you plan on lying during this polygraph?"

"No."

"Do you work with Aniella Fasquelle?"

"Yes."

"Have you had intimate encounters with Aniella Fasquelle, physical or otherwise?"

The pause that followed was deliberate. He could keep the rhythm of his pulse, keep every reflex in check, and she'd walk away unscathed. But that would risk Iver's trust, and his own cover. The second Iver thought he was shielding her, he'd dig until there was nothing left to find. And shielding her only meant his own demise.

Roman drove the tack deeper, the point splitting skin inside his shoe. "No."

The technician made a small mark on his pad, focus never leaving the chart. "That's all for now."

Roman ripped the wires free, one after another. The machine rocked against the table from the force. A line of ink spiked across the chart, the only trace of his fury.

\* \* \*

Roman dropped into his chair as he reached for his shoe. He found the tack, pressing it into his palm before pulling it free. He held it for a beat, a pinhead of metal that decided more than it should have. He flicked it into the trash, the clink echoing against the bin.

Scott hid a bakery box under a folder when it happened. "Roman, are you okay?"

"I gotta go." Roman tugged his jacket from the chair's back.

"Go where?" Scott asked, crumbs already dusting his tie.

Roman crossed the bullpen, footsteps dull on the way out.

"Guess I'll hold down the fort." Scott reached for another cookie just as Iver thundered in from the hallway.

Iver appeared at Scott's desk. "Where is he?"

Scott sifted the folder over the bakery box again. "Who?"

"Don't be a smartass. Roman."

"Oh. Uh… out."

"No shit. Where?"

"Couldn't say, Chief." Scott uncovered the box and lifted it toward him. "Can I interest you in a cookie?"

\* \* \*

Roman turned into the alley and waited. Delivery trucks idled at the curb, exhaust spewing into the evening. A takeout bag skidded across the asphalt, bumping a drain. As the digits on his phone rolled over, she rounded the corner.

He gripped her sleeve and pulled her between the brick walls, her scream ricocheting off the guttering overhead.

"It's me," he said, voice cutting fast. "It's me."

Recognition hit.

"You scared the crap out of me. I have to make it back from lunch—"

"Listen to me." The command clipped the alley still. "You probably don't want to do me any favors right now, but this hits you, too."

"What are you talking about?"

"They know," he said. "About us."

The torn flyer wrestled loose from the fence and spun down the alley.

"How—how do they know?"

"They pulled footage from the bullpen that night."

"But we didn't—we just almost. You could've told them it never turned into anything. They would've believed you."

"It doesn't matter. They suspect it, and that's enough." He straightened, tension loading the pause. "Whatever happens when you go in, whatever they ask, don't let them push you into admitting anything."

"The captain knows?" The words slipped out, half-swallowed by the wind.

"What is it?" He stayed level, precise. "You've got something on your mind." The pause carried its own pressure. "Something you want to say."

A test. A chance for her to come clean.

"No, I'm just..." She turned toward the brick.

A gust swept through, lifting grit along the brick.

"Whatever the fallout, don't confirm we were ever together," he said. "Can I trust you to do that?"

* * *

The bullpen lingered in quiet order, phones waiting to ring. She aligned her pencils, all facing down, busying herself with motions that didn't need doing.

Was she worried over nothing? Had Roman been paranoid?

The intercom crackled to life.

"Fasquelle." It was the captain. "Meet me in my office."

Aniella entered, forcing brightness in her step. "How's your day going so far?"

Ethan opened a holder but didn't look at her. "I wanted to share something that came through today."

*Please not about Roman. Please not about us.* Her posture straightened. "Oh, nice! What is it?"

"Your position as Administrative Assistant is no longer required." Ethan slipped a document from the folder across the desk. "Effective immediately, your contract is terminated."

Her throat rasped raw. "I'm—sorry. Terminated?" The paper shook in her hands. "Does this have to do with not giving you—"

"It has nothing to do with that." Ethan watched, as if expectant. "Came from HR. They rarely include details."

"Captain, if this is because—"

He gestured toward the door. "You can collect your things and leave immediately."

# CHAPTER 20

## Disconnections

Roman dipped under a wild hook, sweat spinning from the glove's edge. The burn through his shoulder was sharp, scar tissue pulling where the bullet had torn, but the pain steadied him. He needed the fight more than the win.

"Take it easy," his partner said. "You're still healing."

Roman slipped past another jab, swinging. Ribs, jaw, silence. The hits cracked clean.

"How could you!"

Roman turned. Aniella cut through the gym, the shuffle of ropes and thud of gloves pausing in her wake. Her voice cleaved through the clang of plates.

He ducked under the rope, sneakers thudding the mat.

"How dare you!" Her steps broke the rhythm that ruled the room.

Roman pulled his mouthguard free. "How dare I what?"

"You got me fired!"

He tore the strap loose at his wrist. "You got fired?" The words barely cleared before she closed in.

"Don't act surprised—you did this."

Roman ripped the second glove free, Velcro rasping. "I had nothing to do with it."

"I'll bet you'll deny taking that polygraph, too." Her arm brushed the jump rope post, setting it into a slow swing. "No talk, no explanation, nothing. Just gone. Funny how it took Tyler to tell me what you left out."

Roman dropped his gloves to the mat. "I left out the test because it didn't matter, they already knew."

"You could've passed that test!" Her voice hit flat steel. "You failed on purpose—you wanted me gone!"

Gloves hit heavy bags down the row, the only rhythm left as faces turned their way.

He lowered his voice. "I'd have a hell of a time explaining that, wouldn't I?"

She closed the space by a single mat square. "You've got plenty of reasons to want me gone. Why should I believe you now?"

"Because I had nothing to do with it."

A timer clicked over the wall, red digits blinking like a warning.

"I wish I never gave you any part of me," she said.

Roman's mouthguard sank in his palm. Whether to argue or let her go, he couldn't tell.

But she didn't wait. Her footsteps faded past the lockers. The sting she left behind outlasted every hit he had taken that day.

* * *

"Great job, you failed your test." Iver rolled the brass paperweight until it struck the keyboard. "Ethan's flipping his shit. We move now. Cut loose ends before he digs up anything else."

"What's the play?" Roman asked.

"We sever ties with Julian's line." Iver flipped a matchbook open, the sulfur scent spiking the air. "Tell the department you kept working the New York case

212

unauthorized after it closed. You couldn't let it go after putting in six months. Building evidence for a big move." The printer jammed somewhere in the bullpen. "They grew suspicious of you, guns came out. You had no choice, you shot in self-defense."

"You want me to draw on three men and expect to survive it?" The line on the phone blinked, waiting. "The second I reach for a weapon they reaching back. Easy math."

Iver tapped the matchbook laid flat. "Flawed. But fixable."

"How about a route that doesn't put me in a shootout I can't win."

"If anything slips, they'll rat us out before the ink dries on their plea deal. They'll use me as a bargain."

"We could let Craig be the face of it."

"Too many moving parts."

The wall clock stepped over a minute. Then—

"We use Hoffman."

"Hoffman?"

"They'll react big when they see Scott after how he acted last time. His paranoia will make them reach first. You defend. The rest follows."

"No." Roman's voice was final.

"Bring Hoffman. Tell him you need backup. He'll run with you without question. You were operating off-book. Who do you call when the heat gets real? Your old partner."

"We're not dragging Hoffman into this."

"Then find another route. Fast. And after that, deal with Fasquelle."

"She's out. IAB wrote her off. She's not even—"

"I said handle her."

*  *  *

The night's chill seeped through Roman's sleeves as he stood at the door. The porch light buzzed, haloed by gnats. He knocked once, waited, then again.

The second knock lingered, absorbed by the quiet house. Floorboards murmured on the other side before hinges loosened a slow groan. Aniella's grandmother filled the frame, cardigan mismatched, warmth radiating from the doorway.

"It's you!" she said, delighted, giving a playful shake of both hands. "Aniella, dear, it's that nice young man from work!"

Her cheer landed heavier than guilt.

She stepped aside, clearing a path. "Don't mind me, names come and go these days, but come in."

Lemon polish and folded linen hung in the air, too clean for what was about to take place.

"I'd offer you supper," she said, "but the kitchen's asleep for the night."

He crossed the welcome mat. "I'm fine, thank you."

"You've got company, dear!" She called toward the stairwell. "I can't holler like I used to. Go on up, she's in her room."

He stopped at the base of the stairs. Her door waited above, pale under the hallway lamp. Each board gave a weary creak, adjusting to his climb.

At her door, he checked his jacket pocket, weight still there.

The floor below kept living, kettle settling on the stove, the old house pretending not to listen.

He steadied once, then knocked.

Music cut mid-chorus. The door cracked open, trapping them between past and present.

"Before you slam the—"

The strike landed fast, snapping across his jaw sharp enough to turn his head and echo down the hallway. The light above her dresser flickered, as if unwilling to witness.

"How dare you come here."

The sting spread like needles across his cheek. He faced her again, voice even. "I know you're upset—"

"I lost my job. I help support my grandmother, and you got me *fired*."

"Can we talk inside?"

"No."

"You want your grandmother catching pieces of this?"

"She can't hear anything from down there."

Aniella started to close the door, but the hinge snagged instead.

"I'm not leaving."

A moment passed. Then she turned away, leaving the door open.

She anchored near the wall while he entered, the air still charged from the hit.

Roman kept his pace even. "You're not the only one who's been hurt in this."

Her laugh came thin. "I'm supposed to care that *you're* hurting?"

"You sold yourself well. I wondered if any of it was real."

The ribbon on her lamp trembled from the draft as she switched footing.

He circled to her dresser, necklaces lined like suspects. "Forcing your way into my car. Tagging along on my cases. Building a file behind my back. All in the name of pure curiosity or field training." He stopped where the mirror framed his reflection beside hers. "And yet..." He faced her. "I'm the liar?"

The kettle downstairs let out a long scream.

"Did Polinski plant you at the shelter too?" he asked, lifting a hand between them, testing space.

"What? No. No, he didn't. Not that it would matter."

He advanced until the wardrobe shadow swallowed both of theirs. "He tell you to get close? Make me trust you?" He stood close enough for her perfume to mix with the faint night air still clinging to his jacket. "Tell you to be everything I'd never suspect so I'd drop my guard?"

"Wait, no... None of that was..."

He stepped back, carpet denting underneath his boots. "Anything that threatens me gets cut loose. That includes you."

The mirror blurred their figures.

"What are you saying?" she asked, her bracelet nearly slipping from her wrist.

"You wedged yourself into things that could get you killed."

The floorboard between them creaked like it might break.

"You'd rather see me disappear than risk your name," she said. "That's who you are."

He reached into his inner jacket pocket.

The radiator clicked once. He saw her focus lock on his hand as he drew the motion slow, deliberate, the way someone moved after already deciding. A faint rattle came from her wardrobe door. He drew a packet wrapped in paper from inside his jacket. Roman offered it forward.

She unfolded it, the paper crinkling as contents revealed themselves. A passport slid out, her own photo looking back. "Is this real?"

"Don't tell anyone where you go." His voice stayed even. "Not me. Not your grandmother. No one."

She held the passport as if it might scorch. "I can't just leave my grandmother." The words fractured. "I moved here to be with her. I can't just vanish and leave her alone."

Roman let the silence answer.

"You have no idea what you've done." She moved toward him, the space between them shrinking to memory. "You *ruined* my career. My life. Now you're hurting her." The passport struck his shoulder. "You ruin everything you touch."

Roman glanced once at the passport's bent cover, then away.

Aniella flattened the passport against a book on the nightstand, as if locking it there. "I'll leave," she said, hoarse as stone. "But I'll *never* forgive you for this."

# CHAPTER 21

## The Loss

Scott eased the mug closer, coffee threading with fresh ink and newsprint. "Newspaper, check. Coffee, check." He raised a warm chocolate-chip cookie, the heat and sugar blooming like an invitation. "And the best part."

The cookie halted midair when a firm hand snatched it away.

Iver loomed above, chewing. "Damn, that's a good cookie."

"That was mine, uh, Chief."

"Yeah, well, you've got bigger things to chew on." Iver flicked it into the bin. "Viento needs backup on a warehouse call. Routine, but after the shooting, better to have coverage."

"He said he needed backup?"

"Aren't you his best friend and old partner? Wouldn't you want him covered?"

"I mean, of course—"

"Then it's settled."

\* \* \*

Roman slid his jacket onto the coat rack. An open container of Scott's cookies sat beside a cooling mug.

*He must've stepped out for a minute.*

Roman rapped the doorframe. "Hey, Chief."

The office felt close.

"Did you handle her?" Iver asked.

"It's done."

Iver fetched a napkin from the drawer. "That still leaves the problem at the warehouse."

"Your plan's a death sentence. Give me a day or two and I'll figure something out."

"I messaged Wes and the others." Iver patted the napkin over the dampness. "I told them to meet you at the warehouse. It's already in play."

"If you think I'm going into that warehouse to pull my gun on three to one, you're wrong."

"You don't seem to understand the urgency in this," Iver said, mask slipping just long enough for truth to show. "I fed him scraps to keep my own table standing. This comes down to survival." He crumpled the napkin. "Hoffman's already on the way there. I wouldn't want to find out how they'll respond to seeing him again, with his badge this time."

The radio on the desk clicked once, then started to whine, feedback trapped in its circuit.

"What did you do?"

"I need my ties cut now. Unless you want Hoffman walking into that warehouse alone, you'd better move."

* * *

Roman nearly lost his grip on the phone as he bolted from the district. *Pick up, pick up.* It rang again and again. "Come on, pick up, Scott."

The ringing cut out and a playful voice slipped through the speaker: "You've reached Detective Hoffman, vaguely known as several nicknames I'd rather not disclose—"

Roman hung up, reality funneling toward the buzz of the disconnected line.

*　*　*

Scott crept low along the warehouse wall. He inched toward the window, lifting until the grime-streaked pane flashed with a blur of movement inside.

No Roman. Three men instead, familiar faces from New York.

*What is going on?*

He dropped beneath the sill, gripping the phone hard enough to smudge the screen. He typed fast, the message stacking. HELP!! ROMAN IN TROUBLE 5th & 29th DECKER STREET BRING BACKUP NOW!!

*　*　*

Simone licked ketchup from his fingers as Brett peeled foil from a hot dog. Tyler parked his drink on the trash-can rim outside the stand.

Their phones chirped in unison.

Tyler's screen lit, then he stuffed the phone into his pocket. "Hoffman."

Simone fought with the spill. "You not gonna read it?"

"You read it." Tyler slurped. "It's to all of us."

Simone lifted his phone, sauce still on his fingers, then held the screen out. "Whoa. Read this."

They leaned closer to see the screen.

Tyler shook the ice in his drink. "Could be a prank."

"I'm not willing to chance that." Simone tucked the phone back into his pocket. "Let's call it in and go."

Simone's phone buzzed. "Ro just texted." He read the message aloud. "SOS warehouse off 5th & 29th Decker St. Don't notify Chief or Captain."

The three shared the same flat pause, steam from the grill curling between them.

"That's the same address Hoffman sent."

"So Hoffman's calling for backup, but Roman wants it quiet?"

"That's what it looks like."

"So who do we listen to?"

Simone folded the foil into a tight square. "If we bring backup, Captain gets involved. If Roman doesn't want that, there's a reason."

The grill hissed, filling the pause.

"Brett and I will check it out." Simone hailed a taxi. "Tyler, hang back. If we text you the go-ahead, you call it in."

Tyler crushed his wrapper. "If this goes south, Captain's gonna have our nuts in a jar."

\* \* \*

Kirk shoved Scott through the warehouse door, the muzzle digging between Scott's shoulder blades.

The place stretched wide and bare, concrete stained in oil. Pallets sat in stacks. A work light carved a hard circle across the floor.

Wes stood inside the light's circle, counting bills at a flimsy table. He stopped mid-count. "We open a zoo?"

"Found him snooping." Kirk gave Scott one last push, sending him into the light.

Scott hesitated under the glare. He managed a crooked smile.

"Gotta be a good reason you're here," Wes said. "Well?"

Scott laughed, thin. "No, no good one."

"Peeking through windows for no good one."

"Uh, heard Roman was here."

"You heard wrong."

That hit like a drop through ice.

"Why you shaking like that?" Wes stepped in, suspicion flattening his tone. "I've seen you before. The anxious guy. Didn't we see you in New York?"

"He's visiting," Roman said from the far end.

Wes turned halfway. "Visiting who?"

"Me." Roman moved out from the doorway, staying outside the edge of the light. "I told him to meet me here before I could explain."

"What's he doing here?" Wes asked, irritation replacing interest.

"I'm just—"

"He's a connect." Roman cut in. "You know this."

Wes lowered the roll of bills. "I knew he was yours, not mine. You bring him, he brings trouble. Remember last time?"

Scott tugged his ear. "Last time Chief—"

"Scott!" Roman's voice sliced through the warehouse, hard and exact.

A side door slung open, the echo breaking across the space.

A voice carried from the doorway. "Let him finish."

Julian's pace hit the concrete like a countdown. His grin found Scott before the rest of him. "I just got some very interesting information."

Dust shimmered under the lamp, lazy and damning.

"What's that?" Wes asked.

Julian stepped into the light. "Benedetti's undercover."

Kirk shifted at the edge of the light, his weapon resting against his thigh. "Like... a cop?"

"Who's Benedetti?" Scott held both earlobes down.

Everything stilled, except the hanging work light, swaying slightly, spinning shadow like a clock hand.

"Hackett must want to get rid of us all," Roman said. "Don't take his word for it."

Julian's head turned back to Roman, his grin gone. "I never trusted you."

Roman's focus narrowed to the triangle of men. To the geometry Hackett had trapped him in.

Exactly the way Iver planned it.

Everybody in, nobody out.

"That makes two of us." Roman drew his gun, quick and measured.

A gunshot cracked, not from Roman. The light blew out, glass showering the floor. Muzzles flashed in the dark. Everyone scattered to hide behind crates. Cash lifted from the table, thrusting through the air like dirty feathers.

"Roman!" Julian's voice cut through the echo.

"What, Julian?"

"Drop it."

"You first."

"Rather aim it at you."

A second flash. A crate splintered near Roman as a round ripped past. He fired back. To the left, Kirk yelled, then a thud followed, dust bursting upward.

Roman checked for a second magazine, ears ringing. "Scott, status!"

"Yeah!" Scott said, shaky but alive. "You?"

"Stay low."

Footsteps crunched. The smell of oil thickened as it mixed with gunpowder, stray rounds striking crates and piping.

Roman slammed the magazine home, the click landing like punctuation. He lifted, fired twice. One round shattered a light cage, raining sparks. Another found nothing but echo.

Somewhere, a boot shifted through broken glass.

"I've done everything you've asked," Roman said. "If I were a cop, how'd you explain all that?" He stepped out from behind the crate, barrel trained on the dark. "You want proof?"

No answer. Then, the scrape of steel.

The next shot cracked, splitting the dark clean in two.

* * *

Tyler cut into Ethan's briefing, panic sharp enough to still the room. "Captain, something's off. The boys and I got an SOS text from Hoffman and Viento, then nothing."

The projector stuttered, its beam jittering over the charts.

"Where?"

\* \* \*

Gunfire ricocheted through the warehouse, shell casings skittering across concrete.

Julian kicked through the rear door, Wes cowering right behind.

Roman turned sharply, aiming. Click. The trigger gave nothing back.

"Roman, your gun's empty?"

"Not now, Loose Lips!"

"Take mine!"

Scott shoved the gun across the floor. The metal screeched through dust and oil, slowing to a halt short of Roman's crate. Scott pushed from cover, crouched low, and rose halfway as he reached for the gun, the move born more of instinct than sense.

"Scott, get back!"

Scott lunged the final step. A shot tore through the air, sharp as a thunderclap.

The bullet hit—jerking Scott violently. A weak sound clogged in his throat, his arms faltering at his sides. He folded under his own weight and collapsed against the stack of crates. He landed hard, a weak, broken sound leaving him. One hand clamped to his stomach, blood spreading fast beneath it.

Kirk stood near the shattered light, barrel smoking.

The room tunneled—rage breaking clean through restraint. Roman seized Scott's gun and fired, rounds punching through Kirk before reflex could catch up.

One.

Two.

Three.

Four.

Each shot fueled by what grief couldn't hold.

Wes crashed into the folding table, blood streaking the cash before both fell over.

Roman fired until the slide locked empty.

The spent gun fell as he dropped beside Scott, pulling him into his arms. "Look at me, Scott."

Scott's pulse came shallow, uneven. His gaze fixed somewhere past the ceiling.

"Scott, look at me." Roman eased Scott's hand from the wound. The hole gaped below his ribs, flooding underneath him.

"I don't feel too good, Rome."

"You're okay, you hear me?" Roman held him tighter. "Stay with me."

Scott's hand found his wrist. "… Rome." The sound was almost gone.

Roman bent close. "I'm here, Scott. Right here."

Scott drew a thin laugh. "I wonder… who's gonna… get the last, cookie from my desk."

Roman exhaled, half laugh, half disbelief. "You'll get that cookie," he said. "It's yours."

"You've always… like a brother…"

The rest never made it out.

"No, no, no, you're okay." Roman bore down on the wound, blood seeping through his fingers faster than he could stop it. "Talk to me."

Scott's fingers loosened. His hold slackened and his color drained.

Roman seized his hand, but it slipped free in the blood. "No, no, don't do that." He held Scott closer, rocking him against his chest. "Scott, talk to me. Come on, say something."

The world slowed. Scott didn't move. Didn't blink. Didn't breathe.

"Scottie—don't do this. Don't go." Roman reached for his hand again, but it slipped free once more. "No, no no…" His words faintly whispered against his friend's forehead. "Scottie, no… Scottie…"

The room gave nothing back but echo.

* * *

The rag ran red. Roman wiped it over his hands, then threw it at the mop bucket. It landed on the rim, streaking pink into the gray water.

Tyler ripped his badge from around his neck and flung it into the locker, metal clanging. "This is why you never handle things alone."

Roman turned on him. "Don't fucking talk to me about what went wrong!" A stool clattered aside. "I told you to meet me there. All three of you."

Simone dropped his duffel onto the bench. "We came as soon as we got it."

"Soon as you got it?" Roman wrung another rag. "Scott was already gone by the time you did!"

Brett sat on the end of the bench, hands clasped. "We didn't know it was that bad."

Tyler slammed his locker door. "We can't just roll out without clearance—"

"Did Scott wait?" Roman asked. "You think he'd let any one of us go in alone?" Pain sparked under his ribs as he stepped forward. "Even panicked, he'd never leave you behind."

Tyler's locker door rebounded. "So this is all on us? If you hadn't been there, he wouldn't have been either!"

Roman shoved him into the lockers. The motion tore through his stitches, pain shooting up his side. "He would've never left you hanging, you piece of shit!"

"Roman, stop!" Simone caught his arm. "You'll mess yourself up."

Tyler shoved him back. "You think this is all on us?"

The lockers rattled as Ethan stepped in from the hall. "That's enough," he said. "Everybody out. Now."

No one moved.

Ethan's gaze fixed on Roman. "You're already hanging by a thread. Don't make me cut it."

Roman's breath came shallow, the mop bucket sloshing beside him. The rag floated, water bleeding pale pink across the tile.

"I don't care," Roman said, shoving past them.

But he did. God help him, he did.

* * *

Roman locked himself in the restroom stall for hours. Rain battered the frosted window, hammering at the pane like it might break in. Pipes groaned behind the wall, their noise granting him the mercy of being unheard.

Eventually he unlatched the door and stepped out. The porcelain sink chilled his palms as he gripped the edge. He twisted the faucet and splashed his face. The water ran red, then cleared. He stayed until the warmth gave out, then dragged a towel across his skin, scrubbing as if he could erase the hours behind him.

*Get it together.*

But grief had already hollowed him.

The floor tilted. He fell beside the sink, arms locking around the porcelain post. His cheek met the cold curve as the pipes shuddered from the impact. The faucet kept running, splashing water over the basin and striking the tile. He held on, shaking, then broke apart.

When he finally pushed out, the bullpen waited. Dim, stripped of life. Desks sat abandoned, chairs angled away. Scott's cookies were still there on his desk, the plastic lid half-open. Roman crossed the room and secured the cover until it sealed. He left it there. He couldn't bring himself to sit at that desk.

He went to his own. The chipped blue paint flaked under his fingertips. Scott had fought to save it when the district remodeled, swearing Roman would need it when he returned.

A napkin lay beside the keyboard, a cookie balanced on top. A smiley face drawn in black marker stared up at him.

A sound tore through him before he could stop it. "I can't do this anymore."

* * *

Ethan pulled his coat tighter as he trudged the city's slick sidewalk, a laptop thudding against his hip. The dim, flickering streetlights illuminated his path in short bursts. He descended the cement steps into the park, letting the light sweep over the benches. A figure detached from one of them. Roman.

Ethan closed the distance with measured steps. "What's this about?"

Roman squared his shoulders. "Take off your coat."

Ethan paused at the top button, fingers lingering.

Roman inclined his head once. "If we're going to do this, it has to be my way."

Ethan unbuttoned the coat, shrugging it free from his shoulders. "What's next? Lift my shirt?"

Roman's face stayed flat. "Yes."

"This is ridiculous." Ethan fumbled the hem up, then let the fabric fall back into place. "Now talk."

Roman held out a USB drive. "Evidence." He handed the drive over.

Ethan took the drive, then turned it once in his hand. "On who?"

Roman sat back on the bench, muscles tight. "Hackett."

Cold prickled the back of Ethan's neck. He sat beside Roman and opened the laptop. "This better not be bullshit." He slid the drive into the port.

The screen populated with images, call logs, bank transactions. He scrolled, his cursor pausing as folders unfurled. "My God. Roman, this is dangerous."

Roman's gaze anchored on the park's dark line of trees.

Ethan pivoted on the bench. "I don't know what to say." He held Roman's face in the lamp light, taking in the furrow at his mouth and the lines etched across his forehead. "Why didn't you trust me? We could have done this together."

Roman's shoulders tightened for a fraction, then eased. "Like you said. It's dangerous."

Ethan stalled over a folder labeled Fasquelle. "He... he asked you to..."

Roman's nod was subtle under the streetlamp.

"Does Iver suspect you?"

"No. Just considered a loose end."

"You risked everything for this."

Ethan shut the laptop and tucked the USB drive in his pocket. "Lie low until I sort this. I'll call my on-call DA. He won't get away with this, not after Hoffman."

Roman rose from the bench. "I gave you what you need. Now take him down."

# CHAPTER 22

## A Long Way to Go

His badge rested by the sink, a ring marking its long stay. Water surged into the tub, steam coiling upward.

*Scott.*

The running water shattered his reflection into nothing.

*You took advice from me, a man who never minded dying, when I should have listened to you, a man who found no greater joy in living.*

Roman slipped under. The heat sealed around him, fierce but useless, unable to burn away the guilt. The weight dragged him lower, the surface folding closed. He let the dark take him, the light blurring out as bubbles rose and vanished.

*Bang, bang, bang.* The door rattled against its frame. *Bang, bang, bang.*

"Viento! You in there?" Simone's voice slammed against the door, every shout timed to his pounding fist.

Water climbed higher as Roman slid lower, bubbles scattering the edge of the tub.

"Viento!" The sound warped through the door, muffled by steam and distance. "Don't make me break it down!"

Roman shot up from the water, sending ripples that slapped the tile.

Steam thickened over the mirror, clouding the light until the room seemed to fold in on itself. He turned from the mirror, blotting out the warped reflection that wouldn't stop watching him.

The pounding kept hammering through his place, shaking the latch in its socket.

Water trailed in uneven streams as he dragged himself toward the door, each step tugging the faucet's hiss along.

At the door, he paused. The handle turned slowly, resisting as if it understood why.

Simone filled the doorway. "No one's heard from you. I had to come by." He scanned the soaked clothes and raw edges that made Roman look half drowned in his own life. "Come on. I'm taking you to your court hearing."

* * *

The television stuttered through half-heard headlines, the anchor's voice firing facts like warnings.

"The detective faces multiple charges. The Department of Justice says if convicted, he could—"

Travis Lawson, Roman's defense counsel, clicked the remote. The screen went black, the echo of the reporter's tone still hanging. The remote clattered onto the glass table.

"It'll pass," Ethan said, squeezing Roman's shoulder. "The judge will see reason."

Travis sorted through his notes, pages worn at the corners from overuse. "They denied our request for a bench trial. The court wants a jury." He licked his finger and turned another page. "You'll hear some ugly things in there. Just try to stay quiet, no matter what gets thrown around."

"He can handle that," Ethan said.

Travis stacked the papers. "The DOJ wants someone to answer for Scott's death. You followed a lead, but on record, it wasn't authorized. Fair or not, that decision put him in that warehouse."

The black screen on the television still stared back at Roman. *Forgive yourself,* the priest had said. Forgiveness was nowhere in reach.

Travis closed his briefcase. "They're also reopening the Kirk shooting. Claiming you used excessive force."

The case barely left the table before Ethan's hand found the handle. "Excessive—"

"They're saying he took more shots than necessary." Travis read from the report. "And I quote, 'an unreasonable number of bullets.'"

"That was months ago," Ethan said. "They can't tack that on now."

"They do it all the time," Travis said. "Add charges last minute so we don't have time to counter them. Doesn't look like self-defense on paper."

"A defense?" Ethan snapped. "He was under fire from a felon. A felon shooting at two of my detectives? There's your defense."

Travis lifted the briefcase from the table. "They're painting him reckless. Out of control. It's an uphill climb."

\* \* \*

The judge entered the courtroom. "All rise."

Roman stood with the others, fixed on the seal above the bench.

"Plaintiff, state your representation," the judge said.

"We stand today for the Undercover Operations Review Board, your Honor."

The judge turned to Roman. "State your title and division."

"Detective Viento, Undercover and Sensitive Operations Division, your Honor."

"I was under the impression the defendant served with Homicide at the Twenty-Ninth District."

"He did, sir," the prosecutor said. "However, the charges concern actions that began while he was assigned to an undercover unit."

The judge nodded once. "Is the Department of Justice present?"

"Yes, your Honor," Travis said from the defense table.

"Proceed."

The prosecutor straightened his lapel. "There's no authorization for the defendant's operation at the warehouse where Detective Scott Hoffman was found dead. Nor any sanctioned contact between Detective Viento and Kirk Winsher, also deceased."

"I'm still not clear on this," the judge said. "Which department has jurisdiction? Homicide or Undercover Operations?"

"Detective Viento was detailed from Homicide to the Undercover Division but remained housed at his district," the prosecutor said.

"That's unusual," the judge said. "I'll want more details on that, but continue."

"By the department's own guidelines, his conduct violated protocol." The prosecutor gestured toward Roman. "This is a case of unchecked power crossing lines. A detective who entered a warehouse without identification, no badge, no authorization. The only reason to hide an ID is if you're not truly undercover but pursuing your own agenda."

"Objection," Travis said. "Speculation, your Honor. There's no proof my client deliberately left his identification behind. He could have forgotten it."

The judge nudged the gavel aside. "There's a lot we don't know yet."

Travis stood. "Your Honor, my client acted in good faith. He neither ordered nor encouraged anyone to enter that building. The defense renews its motion for a nonjury trial."

The judge lifted a hand. "Mr. Lawson, that request has already been denied. I will not entertain it again. If you're so certain your client is innocent, then let jury a settle it."

\* \* \*

Outside the courthouse, reporters swarmed for a statement. Roman kept walking, Simone and Ethan in stride. He didn't look back at the camera's or the van idling at the curb, the one marked Department Transport. Hackett would be in it, cuffed, surrounded by men he used to command. Roman didn't need to see it. Knowing was enough.

# CHAPTER 23

## Between Verdicts

The trial closed the following winter. Headlines ran for months, then faded, like they always do.

Iver took the stand, his own lies catching light for once. Roman stayed quiet through most of it and let the evidence tell its story. Enough of it pointed his way to stain his name, but not enough to convict. The system he'd served had nearly devoured him, and walking free didn't feel like winning.

Therapy came next, court ordered at first, until he chose to keep going with Judy. She already knew his story, and it was hell enough without starting from scratch with someone new.

Eli had been back in the adoption cycle, waiting for a home. Roman had retired from the district, no longer a detective. He worked out of a small community center as a youth mentor for kids marked by trauma and addiction. He met with kids on probation, kids who'd seen too much, kids who reminded him of himself. Most afternoons, he stayed late, walking them through how to stay clean and out of trouble. The therapy helped too and convinced him he might finally have a shot. Enough to give Eli a safe home.

A caseworker traced the living room with her clipboard, the pen cap clicking. Roman kept still and let the house speak. The grocery list on the fridge. The magnet poetry on the stove spelled out: sky, train, lion. A new deadbolt waited on what might become Eli's door.

"School will need a plan," she said. "Attendance. Counselor."

"I'll coordinate."

She read his face too long, then wrote something down. "You were there when his father died."

"The boy was there when his father died."

"You said you're in therapy?"

"Three days a week."

She clicked the pen shut. "From what I've seen, we can proceed with temporary placement."

Roman followed her to the door. Outside, Eli waited on the step, a backpack bigger than his shoulders.

"You mean I get to stay here now? With you? For real?"

"For now," she said. "If all goes well, maybe longer."

When the car pulled away, Roman sat on the step beside him.

Eli leaned close and gripped his leg. "So we're really staying together? You're not going away again, right?"

"That's the plan, buddy."

"Are you going to be my new daddy?"

Words wouldn't come.

Eli pulled out his toy race car from his backpack pocket and rolled it up Roman's pant leg. "I'm glad you finally chose me."

Roman steadied his elbow. "I've always chosen you. But before we make this official, you have to choose me too."

"What do you mean?"

"There's something I have to tell you. And if you still want to choose me after that, you'll be staying here for good. No pressure, bud."

The wheels slowed in Eli's hand. "Okay… What is it?"

Roman turned toward the setting sun. Light flickered through the trees and caught the toy car still parked at his knee.

"I'll tell you inside."

# CHAPTER 24

## Wilted Rose

Two years later.

Midnight wind tangled through Aniella's hair as she leaned on the bridge rail. The river churned beneath her, water breaking against the rocks. She let the dark come, her mind leaning forward, measuring her fall. The pull of the wind, the cold promise of the drop.

No one she knew was in Holland, Pennsylvania, and she preferred it that way. From time to time, she still snuck back to Chicago to visit her grandmother, always by train. Never too long. Never enough to pull her back into the life she left.

Her fingers ached when she let go of the rail. It was finally time to move. She started down the pebbled walk.

A car raced through the wet street, tires spitting puddles her way. Its headlight felt like an intrusion, cutting the dark she wanted to keep.

She kicked a stone across the road. A puddle caught her step. Her fingers brushed a damp fold in her pocket. What she'd meant to throw from the bridge.

She knelt and unfolded the paper, rain freckles spotting the ink. The eviction notice had smudged under the rain.

Aniella ripped the paper into uneven pieces and let them fall.

* * *

Dishes clattered and silverware chimed, the restaurant moving in its endless rhythm to keep the demanding fed.

Aniella stood in front of the bread machine, watching the conveyor drag each slice through the toaster, inch by inch.

Last night she'd cut off most of her hair. She'd swept the strands into the trash, telling herself it was only hair. Only change. But the mirror didn't lie. It wasn't just hair, it was proof of loss.

She'd sworn she wouldn't let herself slide back into this place. She'd promised she'd smile more, try harder. Fake it till you make it. But who was left to fake it for?

The toaster dinged.

The bread was ready. She barely found the will to lift the toast onto the plate. She reminded herself there'd been a reason to move, to start over, to answer to a new name.

"Rose!"

She hesitated before turning, responding to the name that still felt foreign. "What?"

"A six-top just sat in your section."

She placed another round of bread into the toaster. "A table of six?"

"Put on a smile! Let's make some tips tonight!"

She took the plate of bread and headed toward the table, but a hand closed around her arm. "You okay? You look like you're running on fumes."

She shook her head. "Just tired."

A palm opened in front of her, two pale yellow pills resting in it. "This will get you through the night."

"I told you I don't want them," Aniella said.

"In case you change your mind." They slipped them into her apron pocket.

\* \* \*

"All the silverware's rolled," Aniella said, leaning into the supervisor's doorway. "Anything else?"

The supervisor hunched over the counter, sifting through a stack of bills without looking up. "Nope. You're good to go."

Caged freedom met her skin as she left the restaurant. Another shift over. Another day survived. It was also another day of dodging advances born of her co-workers' habits. Aniella would pass the trash bin before her car. She reached into her apron, fingers wading through the crumpled mess.

A voice broke the quiet. "Hey."

She scanned the empty lot. "We're closed."

A tall figure stepped into the streetlamp's gleam. The light flickered—muted green, tempered with silver—cutting through the dark like it remembered her too. He closed the distance that had kept the world wrong.

"You picked a quaint little town to hide in."

\* \* \*

Aniella pushed the front door and brushed the switch. "Welcome to my place."

She tossed her purse into the corner. Roman stepped in and stopped, taking in the room. Only two rusted garden chairs and a tilted clothing rack, nothing else.

"I planned on getting real furniture, but…" A shrug followed. "Anyway. Hungry?"

"I'm all right. Thanks."

Silence filled the room, resentment heavy in it.

"It's been two years, Roman."

He could have told her the trial dragged on. He could have said the therapy

239

was endless, that the system took what was left of him. But crossing all this distance to hide behind a lie would've been pointless.

"I wanted to," he said, finally. "But I needed to find a reason for you to forgive me. I never found one."

She crossed her arms, as if doing so held her together. "But you found me, Detective."

Roman studied her in the low light, memorizing what two years had changed.

"I changed my name," she said, letting her arms swing back to their sides. "How'd you do it?"

He almost smiled. "You always kept roses on your desk. I figured you'd pick something that still felt like you."

Her brows lifted.

"It wasn't one of my first few guesses," he said. "You were still hell to find."

Aniella blinked, maybe surprised by how far he'd gone to reach her.

"I followed your trial. It was…"

"Terrible."

Silence again, thick with all they hadn't said.

Roman dragged a hand through his hair. "It's late. I've got a hotel nearby."

"Please stay."

Her whisper stopped him cold. He hesitated, then closed the distance, drawing her in. She didn't resist. She pressed into him, drawn by the familiar scent, the warmth, the memory of safety. His hold tightened, warmth grazing her skin as he leaned in. His lips hovered, close enough for memory to mistake for touch.

Then her hand met his chest, a quiet wall between them.

The stillness of her touch said everything. His chest rose against her palm, then held there. He waited for her hand to fall away. It didn't.

The distance stayed, unyielding. She'd changed, cooler now, shadowed where she used to shine.

Roman leaned in just enough for her hand to feel the weight of him, every heartbeat of distance between them a question. "Don't push me away," he whispered, more plea than warning.

\* \* \*

Aniella's alarm rattled against the nightstand. When she reached to shut it off, a few things shifted from her apron.

Roman stirred. "Do you have to go in now?"

"Not yet," she said, rolling over to him.

He let his hand drift through her shorter hair, learning the new feel of it. Soft, uneven, too brief.

"Do you like it?" she asked.

"Yeah, I do." He managed to smile, even if it was fleeting.

She hesitated, tracing a path down his chest until her fingers met the scar, the texture raised. "You've been through so much. Are you okay?"

He didn't answer. The pause stretched until silence started to say it for him.

"I hope you've been okay," she said.

"I can finally eat. Sleep. It's not the same, but… it's better now."

The bedsheets settled over them, a soft veil of ease.

"Hackett's locked up now," he said. "It'd be safe if you wanted to come back to Chicago with me."

She closed her eyes while his fingers moved through her hair. For a moment, he could almost believe the world had gone quiet again.

Roman shifted, catching a glimpse of something on the nightstand behind her. His muscles locked and his hand stopped mid-motion.

She turned as he reached past her, plucking it off the nightstand.

"What are you doing with these?" he asked, a pill pinched between his fingers.

Her mouth widened. "Give me that!" She lunged, but he closed his fist and pulled away.

Aniella tried again, prying at his tight knuckles. "Give it back!"

241

The air soured with chaos, the kind he'd spent a lifetime keeping out.

"How long have you been doing this?" he asked.

"So it's fine for you go through my things, but not the other way around?" She spun off the bed, sheets tangling around her ankle and tripping her to the floor. She fought the sheets free, then threw them over him and stormed out of the bedroom.

Roman threw back the bedsheets and followed her. "These were in plain sight on your nightstand!"

Aniella spun around in the hallway. "I've never taken them! What does it matter to you?"

Roman's voice snapped out. "What does it matter to me?" He stepped in, the air bending under his height, control tipping over her as she braced hard beneath it. "You have any idea what I've done to keep you safe? You had a clean slate—an entire new life—and you're gambling it for this?

She didn't back off. Her chin lifted just enough to hold the space he'd claimed. "You call this a new life? I had a home, a career, my grandmother! And you burned it all down!"

Her words hit dead center. Scott. Eli's father. His own. Every name he carried was proof he destroyed what he touched. His throat cinched. The hallway seemed to close in around him. He turned sideways and brushed past, heading for the door.

"I didn't mean that," she said, following down the hallway after him. "You don't understand—"

"I do." He grabbed his shirt from the garden chair. "I shouldn't have gotten you caught up in everything." He dragged the shirt over his shoulders, the fabric tightening as the seams held. The motion steadied him. Controlled him.

He bent for his shoes.

"Roman." Her voice cracked, but he kept lacing. "I've never used, and I meant to throw them away."

"If you haven't been then why'd you try to get them back?"

"Roman." Louder now.

"Why'd you even have them?"

The cabinet doors rattled behind her, glass shifting inside. "Roman!"

He froze halfway upright, the sound cutting through whatever trance he'd sunk into. The silence between them held the question neither would answer.

The air trembled, charged, waiting. For once, he didn't know whether walking away was strength or cowardice. He straightened slowly, muscle drawn, jaw locked.

* * *

Craig burst in, lungs burning from the sprint. Julian held the glass at his lip, rolled the liquor in an idle arc, then let it fall back into the bowl.

"You're not gonna believe this." Craig leaned over, hands on kneecaps.

Julian took a long sip, then set the glass down with a single clink. "You say that and it's nothing."

"You told me to track Roman. I didn't find old friends or blood. He adopted a kid."

"You got the wrong guy," Julian said at first.

"No, I'm telling you." Craig straightened. "He's had the boy since after he got cleared from the trial. Full-time. That's his kid now."

Julian's fingers tightened at the rim.

"Funny, ain't it?" Craig said. "Taking in an orphan like he's trying to atone for something he did."

"We'll make him regret it." Julian pushed the blinds aside with two slow fingers, careful now the way Roman had been ever since those fingers healed wrong. The room funneled to the slice of street beyond. "He wants to play house? Thinks he can enjoy a fresh life while we're hiding out?" His tone went flat. "We'll see how long that lasts."

243

# CHAPTER 25

## Protection

Chicago.

The cart wheels whirred over polished flooring as Aniella guided it forward, Eli skipping beside her.

"Thank you for always being the best helper, Eli."

"Does this get me any dessert I want?"

"Oh, is that what this is about?"

"Chocolate pudding!"

Aniella smiled. "I don't think they have that here."

"They do, I saw it at the entrance. I'll go get it!"

He bolted down the aisle.

"Eli." She turned the cart, searching the front lanes. "How is this boy so much like me when he's not even mine?"

Near the checkout displays, Eli waited beside a scruffy man holding chocolate pudding.

"See, Aniella! I told you they had it here. He helped me find it."

"That's fine," she said, steering closer.

"I'm Eli." He set the pudding into the cart.

"Ah," the man said. "How old?"

"If I told you he was almost thirteen, would you believe me?"

A beat. "Honestly? No."

"That's because he's nine. But going on thirteen."

"Now that age, I can believe." He rolled a piece of fruit across his palm, its waxy skin catching glare. "Are you from around here?"

"I grew up in Connecticut, but I lived here once before. Moved away, then came back a few months ago."

"So you've started to put down roots," he said. "I came a few weeks ago for a construction job. Haven't made any friends yet, though. Don't even know where to go around here."

"We can show you around!" Eli said.

"That's generous," the man said. "I wouldn't want to intrude."

"We can be your tour guides!" Eli turned to Aniella. "Can we, Aniella? Please?"

She lingered by the cart handle. "We could show you around to a few places."

"Then it's settled," the man said. "I'll owe you one."

* * *

The mower engine rumbled across the front lawn, flinging grass flecks against Roman's boots. He killed the throttle, stripping the blade's sweat off his forearm with the back of his wrist. A sedan eased to the curb.

"Aniella. The potential's here."

He unhooked the catcher bag, dumping the clippings against the compost bin as the visitor crossed the path.

Down by the garden bed, Aniella pressed the last tulip bulb into the soil, tamping the dirt firm. A warm breeze teased the strays of her braid. "Please don't refer to her as 'potential' in front of her."

Roman hauled the mower toward the garage, its frame scoring trails through the yard. "Noted."

The woman approached, red curls frizzed from humidity and too many necklaces crowding a single neckline.

"I'm a little early," she said, with much effort. "I hope that's okay."

* * *

The woman perched on the couch, claiming the throw Aniella always kept draped there.

"This is a beautiful home," she said, smoothing the corner she'd disturbed.

Aniella unwound the wind chime's knotted cords hanging near the window. "Thank you. We like the privacy here."

Roman lingered near the bookshelf, posture loose by design. Each motion logged itself—the handbag she kept readjusting, the band around her finger, a mark too recent to be memory. "You've worked with children before?"

"Three families," she said too quickly. "Twins once. The others, just after-school."

"Why leave?"

"The hours changed. One of the families moved." She smoothed the throw again, though it longer needed it.

Roman let the quiet spool out.

Aniella passed behind him, the diffuser's mist trailing along. "We're hoping to find someone to babysit him once in a while," she said, the kind of buffer line that softened most rooms. "Nothing too demanding. We'd just like to go out together once in a while, just the two of us."

The woman's smile stretched. "I'm reliable, really."

Roman tracked the theme. Stretch, hold, release. All rehearsal. "You're local?"

"I rent a studio not even thirty minutes from here."

He angled nearer, just enough to read her pulse through the air. "References?"

246

"Of course." She fished through her tote until a crumpled paper rustled out. "Here."

The first number, handwritten, smudged, last digit darker than the rest. "You won't mind if I call tonight."

"Tonight?" A thin laugh escaped. "Sure. No problem."

A thread of scent drifted toward the couch as Aniella switched off the diffuser. "Roman, maybe give her until morning?"

He placed the paper on the bookshelf. "Morning's fine."

The woman's tote strap caught on the throw again as she got up to leave. "Thank you both."

Roman opened the entryway, letting a draft slip through. "We'll be in touch."

When it clicked shut, Aniella exhaled tension through her shoulders. "You realize she was two seconds away from sprinting to her car?"

"She twitched on every lie."

"She twitched because you treated her like a suspect."

"Dinner's ready!" Eli called from the kitchen, brightness breaking the room's strain.

"You cooked?" she asked.

"Mostly," Eli said, stepping in with a spoon streaked in sauce. "I didn't even spill this time!"

Roman brushed his shoulder against hers, allowing the moment to soften the edge in him. "We should probably check what 'mostly' means."

Aniella slid the green beans across the kitchen table. "Share the ravioli, too."

"How'd the lady do?" Eli asked. "Will she be my babysitter?"

"I don't know yet," she said. "He turned the interview into an interrogation."

"It wasn't that bad," Roman said, tearing a roll. "Had to be sure Eli's safe."

He brushed the crumbs from Eli's cheek, the kind of small care that had become habit. He'd told Eli everything that mattered. The rest stayed buried where it belonged.

"You should give her a background check!" Eli said.

"That's a great idea," Roman said, the corner of his mouth hinting at mischief.

"Are we going to have the man from the market over next?" Eli asked.

Roman's fork clinked against his plate. "What man?"

"There was a man at the market," Eli said through half-chewed words. "Aniella said we could show him around! He's new in town and doesn't know anyone."

Roman's attention fixed on Aniella. "She did?"

"Just a lonely someone who moved into town and doesn't know his way around," she said.

"… He found his way to the market."

Eli laughed at the edge in Roman's tone.

"I felt obligated to offer," she said.

Roman dragged his roll through the butter on his plate. "We're not introducing strangers into our lives."

"We were just trying to be good neighbors," she said. "I think you're being overly cautious."

"Too cautious?" he asked, calm threading into challenge. "Who's the one always called too naive?"

She stood from the table, clearing her plate. "Roman, don't."

\* \* \*

The latch to the bedroom door snapped into place, sharp, final.

"When were you planning on telling me?" Roman asked.

Aniella eased beneath the comforter. "It never even crossed my mind."

"You thought about taking him around to the same places we eat and visit with Eli?"

"I get you think there's a lack of safety in that, but Eli volunteered us before I could stop him." She twisted the cap of her cream. "Maybe try to be more open." She smoothed the lotion into her palms. "We can't live under a rock. Some people are just kind."

"You offered before I could even vet the guy."

Aniella fluffed the center of her pillow. "Eli offered."

"What was his name?" Roman asked. "Description?"

"Sam."

"His number?"

"Yes." The screen glowed as she scrolled to the contact. "Are we supposed to spend the rest of our lives assuming everyone's a threat?" She handed him her phone. "That's not good for Eli. He needs friends. Community."

* * *

She lingered in the doorway, smoothing the strap of her dress.

The lamplight caught along her collarbone, then dropped to the curve of her waist. The silk shaped her, cinched where his hand once fit.

Roman set the gun on the dresser, beside his wallet and keys. He came up from behind her and rested his chin on her shoulder. He kissed the nape of her neck.

"You look less dangerous in a shirt," she said.

He let the corner of his mouth lift. "Don't get used to it."

Her gaze slipped to the weapon. "If I asked you to leave that at home tonight... would you?"

For a second, he almost told her no. But she'd already done enough for him— sat through therapy sessions she didn't owe, trusted him again when she had every reason not to, opened her heart to Eli like he was hers.

If she was asking for one night without the gun, he could give her that much.

He looked up, slow. "You using my attraction against me?"

She laughed. "Maybe."

"If I still carried my badge, I'd arrest you for attempting to bribe an officer."

She faced him, their breaths meeting one another's.

"You'd have to catch me first," she said, a whisper.

He studied her, tracing the line of her dress down to the slit that stopped mid-thigh. "Then I'll leave it here," he said. "For evidence."

"Of what, Officer?"

"Premeditation."

* * *

The restaurant's sign lettering caught the glare as they stepped in from the street.

*Please Wait to Be Seated.*

The word hit like a warning. His thumb ticked against his thigh.

Not here. Not tonight.

A plea for a normalcy. He'd listened.

Now, crossing past the polished sign, he wasn't sure he should have.

At the table, the low hum of other conversations crowded near. Glassware chimed, laughter brushing the table's corner as Aniella's fingers stilled against her napkin.

"Everything's fine," she said. "Let's just enjoy this."

The wineglass shimmered near her wrist, reflecting the ease she was trying to gift him.

He let his shoulders loosen. "I'm here," he said. "With you."

Her smile landed soft, grateful. For a moment, the room almost felt safe.

Laughter followed them out, too light for the weight that never left Roman's chest. Aniella slipped her arm through his, the scent of wine still clinging to her. When he stopped, the shift in his body stilled her voice. The lot stretched wide and dim, lines of cars catching the dull reflections.

*Something's off.*

"Are you okay?" Aniella asked, searching his face.

He unlinked their arms and gently turned toward her. "I left my wallet inside. Can you grab it while I bring the car up?"

As she disappeared through the glass doors, Roman sought the lot with more intention, replaying the night in fragments, hunting for the detail that had set him on edge.

He ran through the faces at dinner. Servers, diners, shadows beyond the kitchen. The same unease nudged him toward the back of the building, where a figure stood in the spill of a security light. The man froze, then slipped out of sight. Roman sprinted to the rear entrance. Empty. He held still, straining for movement, but there was nothing.

Aniella was waiting outside the entrance as Roman rushed toward her.

"Your wallet wasn't in there."

He caught her arm. "We need to go, now."

"You look upset, what happened? Do you have your wallet?"

Roman gunned the engine and tore out of the lot. "The sitter's not picking up." He ended the call and dropped the phone onto the console.

"What's going on?" Aniella asked. "Talk to me!"

"Don't know yet." He gripped the wheel, forcing his voice steady. "The man from the market, what did he look like? Describe him to me."

"He was… I don't know. He said he worked in construction and he looked it."

"Tattoos? Scars? Crooked teeth? Anything distinctive?"

"I'm sorry, Roman. Nothing stood out. He was shorter than you, average build. Brown hair." She reached for him. "Why? What's going on?"

Roman cut through traffic. "We're not staying home. Try to call the sitter again and have her help pack a bag for Eli."

\* \* \*

Roman shoved through the front door, Aniella right behind him.

He swept the living room. "Where's the sitter?"

The kitchen next. Empty.

"Eli!"

Roman bolted down the hall to Eli's room. "Eli?"

He snapped the light on. Nothing.

"Eli!"

"They're not here?" Aniella asked, catching up. "Should I call 911?"

Roman brushed past her, then felt her stop short behind him. He turned. "What?"

Aniella's hand flew to her mouth, her gaze fixed past him. "It's—it's the man from the market."

# CHAPTER 26

## Closure Can't Come with Open Caskets

Footsteps cut through the hall, a gun catching stray light as it tracked Roman.

Roman lifted his hands, slow, open, enough to keep the aim where it belonged. "Craig." The name landed like a strike. The gun, the intrusion, the hollow echo of his own house. "Where's Eli?"

"Make it easy." Craig said. "If you want to see the kid, come with me."

"That's not how this works." Roman closed the gap a fraction, testing the muzzle's tolerance.

Craig flicked the barrel. "Back."

Aniella's cry broke the standoff.

Roman stepped back a hair, using the sound to reset the distance. "Easy, Craig."

Craig lowered the gun an inch, then snapped it back up. "Don't test me."

"What'd you do with Eli?" Roman asked, edged. "What's this about?"

The gun clicked under his finger. "I'm offering you a deal," Craig said. "But if you don't *want* one…" He smiled like a wound. "Sound familiar?"

The words struck dirty, no room to flinch. Roman used them once to corner

253

him when he didn't stand a chance, and now they came back loaded.

"You turned me into a snitch." Craig's voice scraped raw. "Didn't even keep my name out of your trial. I'm burned. Hiding till I'm dead, and you stand there asking why." The gun tapped metal to metal.

"You would've killed me by now if you wanted to," Roman said, watching the gun's micro-movements. "So what do you want?"

"You think you can make this a negotiation?" Craig aimed past Roman, angling down the hall. "Maybe I make it a lesson, instead."

Roman stepped across the barrel's line and planted himself between Aniella and the muzzle. "Stop. I'll go with you."

Aniella lunged, nails clutching Roman's sleeve as she reached for him. "Roman, no!"

Craig dumped zip-ties onto the floor. "Tie her to the chair. Tight."

Roman crouched for the plastic ties.

The chair jittered against the tile as Roman angled it, using the back to funnel her down.

"I'm sorry—I told you not to bring it," she said, resisting the seat. "If you had it—" Her voice broke. "I'm so sorry."

"You did nothing." He bent close, kept his voice low. "Call dispatch. Get it from the safe."

"Please don't go, Roman." Her voice cracked. "What if he doesn't let you back?"

"What else can we do?" He fastened the first strap around her wrist. "Leave Eli with him?" He tightened the next strap. "Imagine how scared he is."

Tears cut tracks down her face as the plastic cinched with a harsh snap.

Roman watched Craig's stance in the window's reflection. "Don't worry. The second I get a chance, I take it."

"No conspiracies," Craig said. "Stop whispering."

Roman secured the last strap around her ankle, then stood. He turned to Craig.

"Your turn." Craig jabbed the barrel at him. "Hands behind your back."

"You're not zip-tying me."

"You want to see the kid? Then put your hands behind your back. No tricks, or the kid pays for it."

Roman's resolve wavered, then locked.

Crickets droned around them as they moved down the drive.

Craig circled to the trunk, the hinge groaning as it lifted. "Get in."

Roman hesitated, then climbed in, folding himself into the dark metal space.

Craig lingered above the open trunk. "Julian would've come himself, but thanks to you, he's lying low."

Roman fought the cuffs, pressure building in his wrists where they bit in. "I—"

The trunk slammed, swallowing him in the dark.

\* \* \*

Craig yanked Roman through the warehouse door, dragging him over the concrete floor slick with oil and dust. The place was still shut down, caution tape slumped from beams and freight boxes smeared with dried blood. A radio on the floor creaked with police chatter buried in static. Julian adjusted the volume, the flicker of transmission slicing through the space. The oil patch glimmered where Scott's body had once been, the echo of a gunshot still living in the walls.

Craig shoved him forward.

Roman hit the concrete hard, knees cracking, crimson spotting the floor before he could steady his weight. Bound hands strained behind him as he lifted his head.

"I see you already had some fun with him," Julian said.

Roman's sight narrowed against the harsh warehouse lights. "Where's Eli?"

Julian circled once. "Roman Benedetti. You two-timing son of a bitch." He seized a fistful of hair and jerked his head back. "Or should I call you Detective Viento?"

Pain ripped through his scalp. "I love when you talk dirty."

Julian's grip faltered, a strange quiet riding the pause. He let go.

"Where's Eli?"

Craig clapped once, sharp. "We paid your babysitter to dose him. He's still at your house, dumbass. Locked in your own bathroom. Never left."

The words hit like the building had shifted on its foundation. A warped board slipped through the rafters, kicking dust loose in the corner.

"We had to lure you here somehow," Craig said. "But that's how you get what you want, though, remember? I learned that from you! Force a man to make his choices through fear. Like threatening to tell everyone on the street I was a rat— even if I wasn't one."

Roman kept the room in pieces he could hold. The oil stain. The radio static. The chalk mark on the floor where the evidence team had once measured Scott's body.

"I never asked you to become this," he said.

Craig's mouth twisted. "You asked me to be useful."

"I'm sorry, Craig," Roman said. "I was trying to keep you clean."

Julian wandered a slow circle and let Craig run.

"Yeah?" Craig stepped closer, words breaking through years of swallowed rage. "Then how'd my name came up on the stand like I was a spare tire? You said I'd stay out of prison if I worked for you!"

"I did keep you out of prison," Roman said. "Until Iver stepped in."

Craig laughed under his breath. "Bullshit. You never registered me as a CI. And you promised me I'd be good. I was out there breaking the same laws you were supposed to stop. You broke some of them with me!"

The words landed harder than any hit Julian could blow. Roman didn't argue. There was no defense left that didn't taste like guilt.

Julian paced, a knife tapping against his leg with every turn. Then he stopped. "Cut him free."

Craig stooped, drew a knife from his sneaker, the same pair Roman bought him years ago, and sawed through the ties.

Roman flexed his wrists, the skin throbbing where the plastic had chewed through.

A trigger clicked behind him.

"Stand," Julian said.

Roman pushed from the floor, hand braced against his knee.

"Let's see if these busted fingers still know how to hurt." Julian drove his fist into Roman's chest.

Roman folded, a sound cutting short in his throat.

Julian shook out his hand. "Forgot you're still carrying a few souvenirs from when I put a hole there."

Blood slicked Roman's teeth as he levered himself up on an elbow, forcing focus through the haze. The memory hit like recoil. It had been Julian.

Julian kicked him flat. "Didn't think I'd ever get to see your face when you found out it was me."

Roman dragged air through grit and heaved himself upright, every muscle rebelling against him.

Before he could balance, Julian's fist cracked his jaw sideways. He waited, then struck another into the same spot. Red specked the concrete, and Craig watched like it was sport.

Roman sagged forward, coughing as his forehead grazed the floor, metallic taste spreading through him.

"Stand up, you back-stabber." Julian hauled him by the collar, then dropped him again.

Hits kept coming until his face blurred under ruin. The room swayed, gravity pulling him down. He rolled onto his back.

Julian set his boot on Roman's ribs. "Wonder how much pressure it takes before something gives." The floor braced beneath the weight as bone met concrete.

A rough sound tore out of Roman—half involuntary, half refusal.

Julian lifted his boot. "Eye for an eye?" He dropped it again, this time on

Roman's hand, heel crushing bone beneath. "Or should I say fingers?" Julian twisted his heel.

Roman's arm jerked, but he couldn't get his hand away.

"You know what I'm going to enjoy?" Julian asked, static slicing across the radio. "Watching you lose everything, and then going back to make Aniella and Eli lose too." He crouched close, searching for the break.

The pulse in Roman's throat beat visibly.

Julian's grin spread slow. "Ahh... not so steady anymore, are you?"

Roman tipped his weight, trembling from effort. "Don't touch them."

Julian cupped a hand to his ear. "What was that?" His grin widened. "Can't hear you."

Roman stifled a cough. "Don't hurt them."

Julian turned back to the radio, fiddling with the dial as Craig leaned on a crate, blade idly tracing the grime under his nails. The space filled with static.

Roman pushed from the floor, forcing air through his lungs until the blur steadied. "Don't do this."

"Stay down," Craig warned.

"Let him stand," Julian said, drawing the gun from his belt. "Makes for a cleaner shot."

"Fine," Craig said, stepping close, voice jeering. "You made me do your dirty work so I'd take the fall when it blew back."

Roman's voice thinned. "Hackett. Not me."

"You did nothing to stop it!" Craig kicked out, blade raised, but Roman caught his ankle and yanked. The crack of skull on concrete split the air.

The knife skittered across the floor. Roman crawled for it, fingers burning as he closed around the blade. He drove it under Craig's jaw.

Craig clawed for Roman's wrists, blood pulsing between their grips. Terror flared—shock then realization. A wet gurgle bubbled as Roman pressed harder, blade driving deeper until the fight left him. A final twitch, then stillness. Roman twisted the steel free.

He levered up, then sagged sideways against the bitter concrete.

Julian kicked the knife away. "Done?"

The blade spun out of reach. Roman didn't move.

"Playtime's over." Julian cocked the gun. "Beg for your life, Detective. Maybe I'll make it painless."

Roman's voice rasped. "Let's be honest." He let the silence stretch, feeding Julian's need to gloat. Every second he talked was another second Aniella might get free. "You were never going to make this painless."

Julian glanced down at Craig's body. "Any last words?"

Roman let the world narrow, pulse betraying what his body refused to show. In the dark behind that stillness, there was only Aniella and Eli.

"This is it. The end." Julian seized his collar, jerking him upright. "On your knees."

Roman braced a hand to the floor and rose halfway, unsteady.

"Beg."

Roman stayed silent, every movement measured. *Get out, Aniella. Get Eli.*

Julian wanted power. Needed it. "Don't be stoic—beg me!"

Roman tunneled harder to Aniella and Eli, but the past broke through.

His father's gun. The echo of his own plea.

Begging hadn't saved him then.

It wouldn't now.

Roman exhaled. "Wait."

The radio's static climbed, as if feeding on Julian's amusement. "Go ahead."

Roman raised his head, vision burning from blood and light. "I have something to tell you."

"Say it."

Roman spat red onto his boots. "Go to hell."

Julian fired a shot beside him, then leveled the barrel again. "I said beg!"

Roman bowed his head, silence holding.

*Father,* he prayed. *I've failed more than I can count. Forgive me. Forgive me for never forgiving myself. Please watch after Aniella and Eli. Keep them safe.*

Julian stepped back, gun steady at his forehead, finger tightening on the trigger. "Then die on your fucking knees."

And somewhere beyond the noise, a mercy greater than his pain reached back for him.

# Reader Discussion Guide and More

Want to know what happened to Roman? Two additional chapters will be released via my newsletter in the coming months. Visit HeatherMarsala.com to subscribe. Emails are never shared, and you may unsubscribe at any time.

In the meantime, my Reader Discussion Guide is available on my website, and spoiler highlights are available on my Instagram @HeatherMarsala. You're also welcome to DM me for all things *Desire & Protection* related, or to share your experience. I'd love to hear it. If you enjoyed *Desire & Protection*, reviews on Amazon, Goodreads, and Barnes & Noble are a great way to help readers discover new authors.

If your group captures any photos, videos, or favorite discussion moments, feel free to tag me @HeatherMarsala. I'd love to be in on the fun (or heartbreak) on my socials!

# Thank you to my readers

I'd love to hear what touched you most.

There are so many layers that did not surface fully on the page. If you'd like to explore more behind the story, connect with me on Instagram @heathermarsala or visit my website at www.HeatherMarsala.com

My next book: *The Rise and The Fall*
A story of family, loyalty, moral collapse, and the moment that breaks everything.

# Acknowledgements

My deepest gratitude to my editor, Christopher Cervelloni, for his sharp insight and unshakable dedication to craft. Thank you for all the thoughtful lessons along the way.

To the paramedics, nurses, and officers who shared their experiences and closed-door lingo with me, your candor helped make this story feel more authentic.

To my friends and family who believed in me through every draft and deadline, your encouragement kept me going.

"The last shall be first." Thank you God, for Your wisdom in every step, and thank you, Jesus, for Your love that never fails.

# About the Author

Based just outside of Boston, Heather Marsala built a successful career in luxury management, where nuance was a way of life. She found that shifting from that high-energy world to the quieter rhythm of writing was an adjustment—but one she's grown to appreciate. Her characters, she likes to joke, keep her company.

Beyond writing, Heather has a heart for bringing people together. She has a passion for service, cooking, and hosting lively gatherings at her home. Equal parts homemaker and city girl, she finds joy in new adventures, late-night laughter, and the beauty tucked within everyday details.

www.ingramcontent.com/pod-product-compliance
Lightning Source LLC
Chambersburg PA
CBHW020125120726
47903CB00007B/2108